DUCHESS
By DECEPTION

Books by Marie Force

The Gilded Series
Duchess by Deception

The Gansett Island Series
Gansett Island Boxed Set, Books 1–3
Gansett Island Boxed Set, Books 4–6
Gansett Island Boxed Set, Books 7–9
Gansett Island Boxed Set, Books 1–10.5
Book 1: Maid for Love
(*Maddie & Mac*)
Book 2: Fool for Love
(*Joe & Janey*)
Book 3: Ready for Love
(*Luke & Sydney*)
Book 4: Falling for Love
(*Grant & Stephanie*)
Book 5: Hoping for Love
(*Evan & Grace*)
Book 6: Season for Love
(*Owen & Laura*)
Book 7: Longing for Love
(*Blaine & Tiffany*)
Book 8: Waiting for Love
(*Adam & Abby*)
Book 9: Time for Love
(*David & Daisy*)
Book 10: Meant for Love
(*Jenny & Alex*)
Book 10.5: Chance for Love, A Gansett Island Novella
(*Jared & Lizzie*)
Book 11: Gansett After Dark
(*Owen & Laura*)
Book 12: Kisses After Dark
(*Shane & Katie*)
Book 13: Love After Dark
(*Paul & Hope*)
Book 14: Celebration After Dark
(*Big Mac & Linda*)
Book 15: Desire After Dark
(*Slim & Erin*)
Book 16: Light After Dark
(*Mallory & Quinn*)
Book 17: Episode 1: Victoria & Shannon
Book 18: Episode 2: Kevin & Chelsea

DUCHESS *By* DECEPTION

MARIE FORCE

ZEBRA BOOKS
KENSINGTON PUBLISHING CORP.
www.kensingtonbooks.com

ZEBRA BOOKS are published by

Kensington Publishing Corp.
119 West 40th Street
New York, NY 10018

All Kensington titles, imprints, and distributed lines are available at special quantity discounts for bulk purchases for sales promotion, premiums, fund-raising, educational, or institutional use.

Special book excerpts or customized printings can also be created to fit specific needs. For details, write or phone the office of the Kensington Sales Manager: Attn.: Sales Department. Kensington Publishing Corp., 119 West 40th Street, New York, NY 10018. Phone: 1-800-221-2647.

Zebra and the Z logo Reg. U.S. Pat. & TM Off.

First Printing: February 2019
ISBN-13: 978-1-4201-4785-8
ISBN-10: 1-4201-4785-4

ISBN-13: 978-1-4201-4786-5 (eBook)
ISBN-10: 1-4201-4786-2 (eBook)

10 9 8 7 6 5 4 3 2 1

Printed in the United States of America

Chapter One

"I cannot bear another minute of this charade," Derek Eagan, the seventh Duke of Westwood, declared to his cohorts as they watched a simpering group of debutantes work the gilded ballroom. He tugged impatiently at his starched attachable collar and wished he could remove it and the tie that choked him without sending yet another tedious scandal rippling through the *ton*.

"What charade?" asked Lord Justin Enderly, his smile dripping with the charm that had endeared him to many a mother. "Watching nubile young things flit about with love and marriage on their minds?" As the second son of an earl, Enderly was much less desirable to the simpering debs than Derek, once again considered the Season's top prize— and Enderly knew it, of course.

"All of it." Derek gestured to the glittering scene before them in the Earl of Chadwick's enormous ballroom. Surely half the aristocracy was in attendance at one of the Season's most anticipated balls. Women in frothy gowns made of the finest silks and satins, dripping in exquisite gems. Men in their most dashing evening wear. "The balls, the gowns, the dance cards, the ludicrous conversations, the desperate mothers. I've grown so weary of it, I could spit."

Aubrey Nelson, the American-born industrialist who'd humored his English-born mother with a second Season, nodded in agreement. "The pomp, the ceremony, the *rules*." He shook his head. "I'll be back in New York—or banished from polite society—long before I master them all."

Unlike Nelson, Derek had been raised for the charade, but many of the rules escaped him, as well. "Utter drivel," Derek murmured. "I've half a mind to compromise a willing young maiden and be done with the whole nightmare."

"What's stopping you?" Enderly asked, crooking a wicked eyebrow.

"I'd have to attempt to converse with her for the rest of my days," Derek grumbled. His friends and the hangers-on surrounding them howled with laughter. "I've talked to every one of them and haven't found one who interests me enough to pursue anything further."

"Same as last year," Enderly said.

"And the year before, and the year before that," Derek said, the despair creeping in once again. It wasn't that he didn't *want* to find a wife. He would love nothing more than to have one person in the world who belonged only to him and vice versa. Not to mention he *needed* a wife, albeit for altogether different reasons. Yet he wasn't willing to settle.

Each year he approached the Season with a new sense of hope, and each year, as the young women got younger and he got older, the disappointment afterward became more intense and longer lasting. This year, however, the bloody *deadline* loomed large, coloring his view of the Season's limited options.

"This year's group seems particularly *young*," Enderly noted.

"Or perhaps we're just getting particularly old," Derek said morosely.

"No doubt," Enderly said. As a second son he was under much less pressure to marry than Derek and enjoyed his bachelor life far too much to give it up before he absolutely had to. For that matter, *everyone* was under less pressure to marry than Derek, thanks to the damned deadline.

"Is there one among them who cares about something other than her hair or her gown or her slippers?" Derek asked. Was there one among them, he wanted to ask, who looked at him and saw anything other than his title, his rank, his wealth *or* the looming deadline that had filled the betting books all over town?

"They *all* care about their dance cards," Nelson said dryly.

"Too true," Derek concurred. "Speaking only for myself, I've had enough. I'm returning to Westwood Hall in the morning."

"But the Season still has weeks left to go," Enderly said in obvious distress. "You can't go yet, Your Grace. What of your deadline? What will Lord Anthony say?"

"He would hardly care. He's practically salivating, *hoping* I fail to marry in time."

"Whatever could your ancestor have been thinking, putting such an utterly daft provision in his will?" Nelson asked. "Enter into a 'suitable state of matrimony'—whatever that is—by thirty or abdicate your title? I've never heard of such a thing."

Of course, he hadn't, Derek mused. The colonists had left such barbaric practices behind in England. "I suppose he was out to ensure the bloodline. Instead, he placed a matrimonial pox upon each succeeding generation."

"What happens if you don't marry in time?" Nelson asked.

"The title and all accompanying holdings transfer to my uncle and then later to Simon, who, as the heir, would also be required to marry *post haste*. *That* would truly be a travesty." If anyone was less suited to a life of marriage, responsibility and duty, it was Derek's happy-go-lucky first cousin and dear friend.

"Have any of your ancestors missed the deadline?" Nelson asked, seeming genuinely intrigued by the drama of it all whereas Derek was just weary—from thinking about it, dreading it and from imagining being married to a nameless, faceless woman just to preserve his title. He shuddered at the thought of shackles and chains.

"Not so far, and I have no desire to be the first. However, I refuse to pick just anyone in order to keep my title." His ancestor's efforts to ensure the dukedom had put Derek in a serious quandary. His thirtieth birthday was now mere days away without a female prospect in sight who sparked anything in him other than utter apathy, not to mention *despair* at the idea of having to actually talk to her for the rest of his life.

Naturally, the entire *haute ton* was captivated by Derek's plight, but not a one of them gave a fig about his happiness or well-being. He would almost prefer to surrender the title than be shackled for life to a "suitable" woman who did nothing else for him but ensure his place in the aristocracy.

Almost.

With his deadline the talk of the Season, every available young maiden had been marched before him—more than once. Judging his prospects by what he'd seen of the Season's available crop, he was in no danger of imminent betrothal. "What's the point of hanging around when I already know that none of them suit me?"

"They don't have to suit you, Your Grace," Enderly reminded him. "You only need one with the proper equipment to provide an heir—and a spare if you're feeling particularly randy."

"And you need her to say, 'I do,' by the sixteenth of May," Nelson added with a wry grin.

"Don't remind me," Derek grumbled. Was it just him, or was it exceedingly warm tonight? Or was it the reminder of his coming birthday that had him sweating? Perhaps it was the rampant wagering that had him on edge. He'd lost track of whom among his so-called peers and "friends" was betting for or against the likelihood of his securing a suitable marriage before his birthday.

Derek never would've chosen the title he'd inherited at the tender age of six when his parents were killed in a carriage accident. Over the years since his majority, however, he'd grown into his role as one of the most powerful and influential men in England. He didn't relish the idea of turning over his title and holdings to an arrogant, greedy, overly ambitious uncle who would care far more about how he was judged in polite society than he ever would about ensuring that their tenants had adequate roofs over their heads. Nor did Derek wish to see his cousin constrained by a life he had no interest in. Too many people depended on the dukedom to see it end up in the hands of someone who couldn't care less about it.

A vexing debate for sure, especially since Derek often dreamed of shedding his responsibilities and taking off to see the world as he'd always wanted to do. But then he thought, as he often did, of his late parents. Since their deaths, he'd aimed to live his life in a manner and fashion that would've made them proud. Losing his title, especially to an uncle his father had despised, would not make them proud, so Derek would do what was expected of him because that was what he'd always done—no matter what it might've cost him.

"What of all your meetings?" Enderly asked.

"I had the last of them today with the Newcastle upon Tyne Electric Supply Company to pump some capital into their Neptune Bank Power Station. They're doing some intriguing work with three-phase electrical power distribution." The blank looks on the faces of his friends tampered his enthusiasm. Where he would absorb such information with obsessive attention to detail, he'd come to realize that others were less interested in the *how* of electrical lighting and other innovations. They were, however, more than content to fully luxuriate in modern conveniences without bothering themselves with the details. Electricity was making its way into wealthy homes and public buildings in town, but it would be a while yet before it reached the country.

"Wasn't there another one?" Justin asked. "Something with brothers?"

Derek nodded. "I'll be providing emergency financing to the brothers from America who believe they've found the secret to manned flight."

"You can't be serious," Nelson said. "The Wright brothers?"

Derek nodded, used to his peers finding his investment decisions questionable at best. They couldn't, however, argue with his results.

"Has everyone in America finally said no to them?" Nelson asked.

"I didn't ask that. I simply wish to be a part of what they're doing. I believe they will attain success, perhaps before the end of the decade."

Nelson rolled his eyes. "It's your money to throw away."

"What's next?" Enderly asked, his tone tinged with sarcasm. "Motorcars?"

"As a matter of fact, due to my involvement in Wolseley Tool and Motor Car Company, I was asked to back a venture with Lord Austin and his brother that will bring production of motorcars to England in the foreseeable future."

"Why am I not surprised?" Enderly asked with a smile.

One of the most annoying of that year's debutantes, Lady Charlotte something or other, flashed Derek a suggestive smile full of invitation. As he'd learned early in his first Season, he didn't make eye contact unless he wished to encourage attention, which he most assuredly did not.

"All you'd have to do is snap your fingers, and Lady Charlotte would say 'I do,'" Enderly said.

Derek could have been mistaken, but it seemed as if his friend was enjoying baiting him. "If I'm going to shackle myself to a woman for life, she's got to have more than the proper plumbing." Derek tugged again on the collar that poked at his neck and the strangling tie. His valet Gregory had been rather rigid in his knot tying that night, as if he too were out to constrain Derek to his husbandly fate.

"What is it exactly that you seek, Your Grace?" Nelson asked with a kind smile.

"Damned if I know. I just hope I'll recognize it when I see it, and I hope I'll see it soon." She was out there somewhere. He had no doubt of that. If only he knew where to look.

"You're holding out for a love match then?" Enderly asked.

"I don't necessarily yearn for the mess that accompanies a love match, but is it too much to hope for some intelligent conversation with my after-dinner port?" The utter despair of his situation came crashing down as he viewed the gay scene before him. "What in the world would I *talk* about to any of them?"

Apparently, neither of his friends could supply a satisfactory answer.

Enderly shifted with discomfort from one foot to the other. "What are your plans, Westy?" he asked softly, reverting to Derek's nickname from their years together at Eton.

"I need to spend some time riding Hercules and thinking. I can't think here. Just a few days, and then I'll come back and bite the proverbial bullet." He'd have no other option but to choose one of the young women flitting before him unless he wanted everything he had to slip through his fingers to an uncle who didn't deserve it. But the thought of being stuck with a wife who didn't suit him made him ill.

"You'll be the talk of the *ton*," Enderly declared, scandalized.

"Let them talk. I won't hear it in Essex."

"But it won't be any fun without you, Your Grace," Nelson said mournfully.

Enderly nodded in agreement. "Nor will the ladies flock about us with quite the same . . ."

"*Desperation?*" Derek asked with a grin. His friends laughed. As usual, they had kept this dreadful experience from being a total loss.

"Lady Patience will wish to visit," Enderly said with an evil grin. "She's apt to follow you to the country."

"She won't gain an audience with me even if she does give chase," Derek said of the Duke of Devonshire's daughter, who had pursued him with relentless determination. "She holds even less appeal than the others."

"Why is that?" Nelson asked.

"She brays like a donkey when she laughs."

"Ouch," Enderly said, chuckling.

"I quite fear that no woman will meet the discriminating requirements of our dear, distinguished friend," Nelson said to Enderly.

"That's just fine with me," Derek said, happier than he'd been in weeks now that a decision had been made. "I'd rather be a lonely commoner than be shackled for life to a 'suitable' braying donkey."

Lord Anthony Eagan, son of a duke, brother of a duke and uncle to the current duke, reclined on a red velvet chaise and took a sip from his glass of port. Always on the outside looking in, just barely on the fringes of tremendous wealth and power. Thankfully, all three dukes had provided handsomely for him, allowing him the freedom to pursue his own interests.

But what interested Anthony, what *seduced* him more than anything else ever could, was the *power* of the title. When the Duke of Westwood entered a room, people noticed. Society noticed. No one paid much heed, on the other hand, to the duke's second son, his brother, or his uncle. In the fifteen years he'd served as his nephew's guardian, he had sampled a generous helping of power. Having to cede it to a boy just barely out of leading strings had been demoralizing, to say the least. The subsequent years had reduced Anthony once again to the fringes. He didn't much care for the fringes, and he never had.

While Derek had stepped nobly and with infuriating independence into the position he'd been born to, Anthony had been relegated to watching and seething and planning. Now, on the eve of Derek's thirtieth birthday, came opportunity. If Derek failed to marry by the sixteenth of May, the title would revert to Anthony, and he would finally be the Duke of Westwood. The way it always should have been.

And while he had come to grudgingly respect his nephew's acumen with finance and his bearing among the *haute ton*, he disdained the boy's inner softness. That softness, Anthony mused, would be his downfall, just as it had been his father's. Perhaps it was because Derek had lost his parents at such a tender age or maybe it was the guilt that came from being the twin who'd survived the journey into this world. Regardless of the cause, Derek lacked the inner fortitude that Anthony possessed in spades.

Anthony wasn't afraid to use that fortitude to gain what should've been his all along. Derek was supposed to have been in that carriage the night his parents had been killed. They had planned to dine as a family at a neighboring estate. No one had bothered to tell Anthony that the boy had been left behind in the nursery when he showed signs of fever.

No one had told him until it was far too late, until he'd been saddled with an orphaned young nephew and vast holdings to "oversee" until that nephew gained his majority.

The holdings were supposed to have been *his*. Instead, he became the steward rather than the duke. Instead, it was left to him to nurse his grief-stricken nephew through those dreadful months after "the accident." Since another "accident" so soon after the first would've raised suspicions, he had nursed when he'd wanted to strangle. He'd mentored when he wanted to stab. If only the boy had been where he was supposed to be, Anthony would've had what was rightfully his for all this time.

Soon, Anthony mused. That softness within Derek wouldn't permit him to marry for the sake of his title. Like the fool he was, Derek wanted *more*. The softness would be his downfall. Anthony was betting on it and breathing a bit easier after realizing that none of the Season's debutantes had caught his discerning nephew's eye.

Lucy Dexter, one of London's most accomplished courtesans, crawled from the foot of the chaise to envelop him in soft curves and sweet scent. Silky dark hair cascaded invitingly over his chest.

"What troubles you tonight, my lord?"

"Nothing of any consequence."

"You ponder the fate of your nephew and the duchy you covet."

Anthony raised an imperious brow. "It is rather impertinent for you to speak so boldly of things that are none of your concern."

Lucy's husky laugh caught the attention of his recently satisfied libido. "How can you say such things are none of my concern when you've made them my concern by *unburdening* yourself to me quite regularly?"

The double entendre wasn't lost on Anthony. Through the silk dressing gown he had given her, he cupped a bountiful breast and pinched the nipple roughly between his fingers, drawing a surprised gasp from her bow-shaped mouth. "If you speak of my concerns with anyone else, madam, you will quickly discover my less-than-amiable side, which I usually prefer to keep hidden from the fairer sex."

Her blue eyes hardened with displeasure. "I believe I have proven my allegiance time and again over these many years, my lord. There is no need for threats nor less-than-subtle attempts at intimidation."

She could quite ruin him. She knew it. He knew it. *Power*. He had given her far too much, he realized, and that was something he might, at some point, need to contend with. But certainly not right now, not when she was pushing his

Marie Force

dressing gown aside to drop soft, openmouthed kisses on his chest.

Anthony sighed with satisfaction, placed the empty glass on a table and buried his fingers in silky tresses. When she took his cock into the velvety warmth of her mouth, he closed his eyes and let his head fall back in surrender.

Power—the only commodity that truly counted. As she sucked and licked him to explosive fulfillment, it hardly mattered that he had ceded some of his to her for the time being. Before long, he'd have more than he knew what to do with. It was only a matter of time.

Chapter Two

The next morning, Derek rode his black stallion Hercules out of London, heading for his country estate in Essex. He'd left without a word to the London household staff. They'd discover soon enough that he'd taken his leave and would send word to Anthony before the day was out. After taking their orders from Anthony during Derek's adolescence, some of them were more loyal to his uncle than they were to him.

Following weeks of being cooped up in the city, Hercules seemed as anxious as Derek to return home, so Derek gave the big horse his head, and they made good time. They stopped only once for food and water, and Derek was grateful not to be recognized at the roadside inn. Otherwise, he might've been detained while the innkeeper tried to impress him. That was why he'd worn simple leather breeches, a white linen shirt and riding boots. After weeks on parade before the *beau monde*, it was a welcome relief to blend in with the unwashed masses.

Within a few hours, Derek and Hercules reached the southeastern corner of Derek's vast estate and headed north. During the long journey, Derek had tried to put aside his disappointment over another failed Season and focus on the many tasks that awaited him at home. Here he knew who he was and what was expected of him. In polite society, all the lines became fuzzy, and he was forced to become someone he barely recognized.

If the pattern of years past was repeated, he could expect a dark mood to set in soon after he arrived home and settled back into the monotony of daily life, alone as always. That he had to go back, choose one of the simpering debs, apply for a special license and speak his vows sometime in the next ten days made him shudder. The thoughts were enough to get the dark mood started early.

It wasn't that he didn't *like* women. Oh no, he *loved* women. He loved their soft skin, their endlessly alluring scents, their long hair and lush curves. Other than his horses, he loved nothing more than losing himself in a willing woman. Sadly, in his corner of the country, suitable women were few and far between.

During the second of his many Seasons, Derek had befriended a courtesan named Kitty who saw to his more basic needs during his semi-regular visits to the city. While he liked and admired her, it wasn't lost on him that were it not for the easy familiarity he shared with Kitty, he might've settled into a marriage long before now.

He'd never expected to reach the age of nine and twenty still unattached with no prospects on the horizon, not to mention any hope of producing an heir he could shape and mold into the future Duke of Westwood. The idea of constraining his own son to the life of a duke pained him, but Derek planned to live to a ripe old age, giving his son the chance Derek never had to experience life before being shackled with endless responsibilities and obligations. Perhaps he'd even take drastic steps to change the barbaric marriage rule in the family tenet, so his son would never feel the pressure that now threatened to suffocate Derek.

He chuckled softly. *Getting a bit ahead of yourself, old sod. You can't even find a wife, and you're already making plans for the son you'll never have at this rate.*

He thought about how thrilled his uncle Anthony would be to push Derek aside and take on the title he'd coveted all his life, even while pretending to have Derek's best interests at heart. With these thoughts weighing heavily on his mind he almost missed it. A man was digging feverishly in a glade set back from the road. Derek reined in Hercules. "Whoa, boy."

The horse snorted in protest.

"Easy." Derek patted the horse's neck while he watched for a minute before urging Hercules toward the digger. As he approached, he noticed the man wasn't very tall. His ill-fitting clothes were caked with dirt, his boots scuffed and his breathing labored as he went about his work with single-minded determination, oblivious to the fact that he was being watched.

"You there!" Derek called out.

Startled by Derek's sudden appearance, the man dropped the shovel and fell back on his rear.

Suppressing the urge to laugh at the shocked expression on the man's dirty face, Derek dismounted and approached, offering a hand to help him up. From what Derek could see under the brim of the cap the man wore, his features were delicate, almost effeminate, and his filthy hands seemed too small to wield such a heavy shovel.

Ignoring Derek's offered hand, the young man scrambled to his feet, rubbing his hands on his pants in a nervous gesture.

"Don't even think about running," Derek said. Dark eyes filled with fear stared back at him. "What do you think you're doing digging here? This is private property. Anything you uncover belongs to the Duke of Westwood."

The young man's face twisted with scorn, but still he didn't speak.

Derek noticed the other man's hands were trembling. "I won't harm you. I just want to know what you're doing." When that got him nowhere, he bent to retrieve the shovel. "If you won't answer my questions, I'll have to confiscate this."

Uttering an animalistic growl, the man lunged for the shovel. As he and Derek crashed together, his threadbare cap flew off his head, and long, curly blond hair spilled down his—or rather *her*—back.

Deep navy-blue eyes stared up at him as she quaked in terror.

Shocked to realize his trespasser was a woman who was deathly afraid of him, Derek reached out to steady her. "Easy now. I won't hurt you."

She released a gasp as her legs seemed to collapse beneath her.

Derek caught her just before she hit the ground in a dead faint. By holding her over his shoulder, Derek managed to struggle the featherweight woman and her small valise onto Hercules. Once astride, he arranged her so she rested against him. Right away Derek could feel the heat of her fever through his shirt. Her hair was matted with grime, and she smelled, well, less than fresh. Derek wondered how long she'd been battling the elements on her own and when she'd last eaten.

Tightening his hold on his passenger, Derek urged Hercules into a canter. They arrived at Westwood Hall less than an hour later. Derek's cousin Simon, butler Rutledge and several footmen met them.

"Your Grace!" Rutledge cried. "We had no idea you'd be home so soon!" He curled up his regal nose at the sight of the ruffian with Derek. "And who have you brought?"

"I encountered her out on the south quarter. She's burning up with fever." Derek signaled one of the footmen, who approached to relieve him of his passenger. "Take her to the blue guest room." Derek dismounted and handed the reins to a second footman. "And send for the doctor right away."

"Yes, Your Grace," Rutledge said, gesturing to the second footman as he, Derek and Simon followed the man carrying the sick woman into the house.

"Who is she?" Simon asked.

"I have no idea. She was digging in the glade when I came across her."

"Digging for what?"

"She passed out before I could ask her," Derek said as he rushed inside with Simon on his heels.

Mrs. Langingham, the housekeeper, met them in the foyer, taking over for the flustered butler. "Oh, Your Grace, you're home so early!"

"As usual, London failed to keep me entertained. Would you please have one of the maids draw a bath for the young miss? She's dirty and ill."

"Of course." Mrs. Langingham signaled to a maid, who scurried off.

"I'll see you later," Derek said to his cousin as he followed the footman carrying the woman up the stairs. At the doorway to the room he'd assigned her, he hesitated. It wouldn't be proper for him to be in her bedchamber. Even though he had no idea who she was or where she'd come from, he worried about her reputation, nonetheless.

The footman set her on the bed and came to the door.

"Thank you," Derek said, his eyes on the woman. He stood watch over her until the maids had her bath ready in the bathing room he'd recently installed.

Mrs. Langingham bustled into the room after them,

barking out orders and taking command. "Now off with you, Your Grace. We'll take good care of her."

"If she comes to," Derek said, acting on instinct, "don't tell her where she is or who found her."

"As you wish."

"I'll check on her later."

"We'll take good care of her," Mrs. Langingham said again as she ushered him out the door. "Don't worry yourself."

Derek left the room, but he didn't want to. For some odd reason, he wanted to stay and care for her himself. To peel the filthy clothing from her petite body and bathe what looked to be weeks of grime off her, to wash her long hair and towel it dry by the fire. He wanted to crawl into bed next to her and hold her until the fever broke and she could tell him why she'd been digging on his land. So far all she'd done was growl at him, but the desperation he'd heard in that growl had touched him deeply.

He could go back, clear the room and take over. But Mrs. Langingham had helped to raise him, and he'd never shock her that way. Walking toward his own bedchamber at the other end of the long hallway, Derek decided he'd go back as soon as they had her settled in bed. Hopefully by then the doctor would have arrived.

An hour later, Derek returned to check on his new ward and stopped dead in his tracks at the bedchamber doorway. The woman was propped against a small mountain of pillows, her damp golden curls forming a halo around her freshly scrubbed face. A porcelain complexion, pretty pink lips and a button nose completed a rather captivating picture. He'd been oddly drawn to her when she was dirty and smelly. But now he needed her to awaken so he could find out everything there was to know about her.

While he stared at her, she began to thrash in the bed as if in the midst of a frightening dream.

"What's wrong with her?" he asked, riveted by the fear he saw on her face.

"She's been terribly agitated, Your Grace," Mrs. Langingham said, wringing her hands.

"Can't you do something?" he asked the doctor. Reeking of whiskey, the old man had clearly been dragged from the village pub. Derek moved to the foot of the bed for a closer look.

"She's quite ill, Your—"

"Don't call me that," Derek snapped. "Until I find out more about what she's after, I don't want her to know who I am or where she is."

"I doubt she's paying much attention to what we are saying, *sir*."

"Regardless, can't you do something to make her more comfortable?"

The doctor shook his head. "If she doesn't wake in the next day or two, we can bleed her."

"Absolutely not."

"But Your, I mean, *sir*, there may be no other choice."

Derek had yet to hear of anyone who'd been better off after bleeding than they had been before. "No talk of bleeding. For God's sake, no one does that anymore."

"It can still be highly effective," the old man huffed.

Derek decided then and there it was time for a new doctor in the village. He'd begin the search as soon as possible.

"I can't help but notice," Mrs. Langingham said to Derek, "that she seems to calm somewhat when she hears your voice."

He moved to the side of the bed, took the young woman's work-roughened hand and held it between both of his. "There now, you're safe here. Try to rest." Before his astounded eyes, she relaxed into the pillows, but her fever-reddened cheeks worried him. Turning to the doctor, Derek said, "Will she recover?"

The doctor picked up his bag of useless tools. "She's young, and though she's somewhat malnourished, she's strong. There's no reason to believe she won't recover. Try to get some tea or broth into her."

Mrs. Langingham, who'd been hovering at Derek's shoulder, nodded vociferously. "I'll see to it personally."

"I'll do it," Derek said.

"But, sir," Mrs. Langingham protested, "it's not proper!"

"You said yourself that my presence calms her. And besides, who will know?"

She wilted under the intensity of his gaze. "As you wish. I'll have the tea sent up." She bustled from the room.

As the doctor prepared to leave, Derek stopped him. "Not a word of this in the village. Do you understand me?"

"Yes, sir. I'll check on her tomorrow."

After closing the door behind the doctor, Derek went to stand by the bed. Hands in pockets, he studied his guest so intently that he never heard Mrs. Langingham's return. She set the tray of tea and broth on the bedside table.

"I'll take it from here," Derek said.

"Your Grace," she whispered, her expression scandalized.

"That'll be all, Mrs. Langingham." He sent her a warm smile. "Thank you for your assistance."

"You'll need to put a towel under her chin."

"I can handle it. I'll see you in the morning." Derek waited until the housekeeper left the room before pouring the tea and waiting for it to cool. Once it had become somewhat tepid, he sat on the bed and arranged his patient so she reclined against his chest. Remembering the towel Mrs. Langingham had recommended, Derek tucked it under the woman's chin and over her shoulders and then reached for the tea.

The heat from her feverish body seeped through their clothing to warm him. "Come now," he said softly. "Let's have a little sip."

She strained against his tight hold and turned her head away from the cup he held to her lips. Her mouth opened, and he was able to get her to drink a small bit without her choking. It took more than half an hour, but he managed to get most of the cup into her. He wiped her face with the towel and started to settle her back in bed.

But she turned into him, her head on his chest, and began to murmur in her sleep.

Now this, Derek thought, *was* definitely *improper*. Regardless, he couldn't seem to bring himself to leave her, even though her fever was making him overly warm.

"No," she muttered. "Don't. Please *don't*." She stiffened, as if in pain, and let out a low moan.

"It's all right," Derek said, combing his fingers through her glorious mane. "I've got you. You're safe here."

"Don't hurt me. Please don't."

Derek tightened his hold on her. "You're safe. No one will hurt you." He realized his shirt was damp and looked down to see tears on her fever-brightened cheeks. Brushing them away, he ached to know who she was, who had hurt her, and what had brought her to his corner of Essex.

He spoke softly to her until she once again relaxed into a deep sleep. The long, eventful day finally caught up to him, and his eyes drifted closed. His next conscious thought was one of struggle. Someone was fighting him with everything they had. He startled awake to find his patient battling her way out of his embrace.

"Wait," he said. "I won't hurt you."

"Release me this instant!" Her voice was low and cultured, and the sound stirred him profoundly.

Derek did as she asked, and she sprang from the bed.

Arms folded across the front of the thin night rail Mrs. Langingham had found for her, she glared at him as she wobbled on unsteady legs. "Where am I? Where is my clothing? Who undressed me?"

"You're at Westwood Hall. The housekeeper bathed and dressed you."

Her face flaming with embarrassment, she grabbed a blanket from the foot of the bed and wrapped it around herself. "And who resides here?"

"The Duke of Westwood."

She made a face of supreme distaste.

Derek bit back the urge to laugh.

"I have no desire to be the guest of a duke. If you'll find my clothes, I'll be on my way."

"I believe they were burned."

"*I beg your pardon?*"

"They weren't fit to be rags."

"They're all I have!" Her pale face lost what color it had left as she swooned.

Derek bolted from the bed to catch her and settled her back in bed. "You're ill. You can't go anywhere until your fever breaks and you regain your strength."

Dark blue eyes filled with tears. "I can't stay here."

"What has the duke ever done to you?"

"Not a thing."

"Then why are you so opposed to being his guest?"

"I'd feel the same about any peer of the realm," she said with a haughty lift of her delicate chin.

"And why is that?"

"I have my reasons. Who are you anyway?"

Derek's brain froze.

"Have I asked a difficult question?"

"Of course not," Derek said, recovering. "I'm Jack Bancroft, the duke's estate manager."

"You're not a peer?"

"No, ma'am." Derek wasn't sure why he lied, except that he wanted to know more about her and already understood that he'd get nowhere with her as the Duke of Westwood. That, alone, made her different from every other woman he'd ever met.

"Good," she said, visibly relieved.

"Now that I've given you my name, will you return the favor?"

She rolled her plump bottom lip between her teeth. "Catherine."

Derek lowered himself into the chair next to the bed. "Pleasure to meet you, Catherine."

"How did I get here?"

"I brought you. Do you remember our encounter in the woods? You were digging."

"And you took my shovel."

"The duke tends to frown upon strangers digging on his land without his knowledge or permission."

Her eyes flashed with anger. "Oh, what does he care? He has *thousands* of acres. What's one small hole to him?"

"It's still his land, and thus his hole. Why don't you tell me why you were digging?"

Her eyes widened. "My bag! Where's my bag?" Clawing at the blankets, she tried to get up.

"Stay there. It's right here." He crossed the room to get the threadbare valise and brought it to her.

She did a quick inspection and then clutched it to her chest, eyeing him warily. "Did you look inside?"

"I did not." Dropping back into the chair, he propped his feet on the foot of the bed. "You haven't answered my question. Why were you digging?"

"I was looking for something that belongs to me," she said, her gaze darting to his feet on the bed and then back to his face. Her expression told him that if it were up to her, he and his feet would be expelled from the room immediately.

Confused, Derek said, "So, you've been here before?" He was quite certain he'd remember her.

"No. My grandmother has."

"And she left something behind?"

"I don't wish to discuss it any further."

"I can't help you if I don't know what brought you here or why you were willing to risk your health and well-being in pursuit of it."

"Why would you want to help me?"

With every passing minute Derek grew more fascinated by her. He forced himself to project a sense of calm when he was anything but. "The duke has gone abroad to America for the summer." Even though he surprised himself with the easy lie, his face remained neutral. "I've nothing much to do in his absence. If you're looking for something, I might be able to help."

"I don't require your assistance. If I could just borrow some clothing, I'll be on my way."

"I'm afraid I can't allow that."

"You can't, or you won't?"

"As the duke's estate manager, I oversee everything involving the land. I can't permit a stranger to dig un-supervised." He sent her his most charming smile. "You wouldn't want to cause me trouble with my employer, now would you?"

"I don't see why you can't just let me go and forget you ever met me."

Derek gave her his most charming smile. "My lady, you are quite unforgettable."

"And it is quite unseemly for us to be alone together in a bedchamber."

"No member of this household will speak of it." He would see to that. "You were sick. I thought you'd be more comfortable waking up to someone you recognized, even though our association was brief."

"And how precisely did you end up in bed with me?"

"I fed you some tea and then you fell asleep. I didn't want to disturb you. And you seemed . . ."

"What?"

"Frightened. Has someone hurt you?"

Catherine gasped. "Of course not. Why would you say such a thing?"

"You were speaking in your sleep."

She put a hand over her mouth. "I wasn't."

Derek leaned forward and rested his elbows on the bed. "Who hurt you, Catherine?"

Shrinking back from him, she sank deeper into the pillows. "No one," she said in barely more than a whisper.

"Let me help you."

"I can't stay here. I won't accept charity from the aristocracy."

"The way I see it, you don't have much choice. You're sick, weak, most likely far from home, alone, unprotected. Need I go on?" When she only glowered at him, he continued. "I can help you, but only if you're honest with me."

"And what will you tell the duke?"

"He is to be away for some months and trusts me to manage his affairs in his absence."

"I can't stay in his home. I just can't."

"We may be able to make other arrangements, so you wouldn't have to stay under his roof, per se."

She stared at him, mouth agape. "Why would you do such a thing for someone you barely know?"

"I told you. It's all too quiet around here when the duke is away. Helping you will give me something interesting to do."

She gave him an arch look, which, along with her fever-reddened cheeks, only added to her overwhelming appeal. "And what, pray, will you expect in return?"

He feigned shock. "My dear lady, I may not be a peer, but I *am* a gentleman."

"A gentleman who somehow found his way into my bed the day we met."

Derek couldn't help but smile at her witty retort. "For that I would offer my most heartfelt apologies if I hadn't so enjoyed holding you while you slept."

"You're outrageous," she huffed.

He shrugged. "I speak only the truth. I have a proposition for you." Was it his imagination or did she shrink farther into the mountain of pillows?

"What kind of proposition?"

"You're looking for something that's clearly important to you. I can provide access to the area in which you wish to look as well as food and shelter for as long as you're a guest on the estate."

"In exchange for?"

"The truth. Tell me who you are, what you're looking for, how you managed to get so sick and dirty, who you're running from and anything else I should know in order to justify my actions to the duke."

She rolled that plump lip between her teeth once more, sending a sharp bolt of lust straight to Derek's cock. Had he ever envied another's teeth before? Not that he could recall. He watched an array of emotions cross her expressive face—fear, trepidation, longing, desperation, distrust and despair. That last one made him feel small for forcing himself on her when she clearly wanted nothing more to do with him.

Even though he'd been less than truthful with her, he hadn't lied about wishing for something interesting to occupy his time. Since he was supposed to be in London for another few weeks, his schedule was open, and his regular duties delegated to others.

He extended his hand. "Do we have a deal?"

She glanced at his hand and then at his face. "Do I have any other choice?"

"Not if you wish to continue digging on the duke's property."

Scowling, she held out her hand. "Fine."

As Derek enclosed her soft hand between both of his, a charge traveled through his limbs to settle in his groin, and he wondered just who was fooling who.

Chapter Three

Catherine continued to nibble on her lip as she studied her handsome benefactor. *Jack*. The name suited him. Strong and competent. The two words came to mind before she could come up with anything better. His dark hair had a tendency to slip down over his right eye, which meant he had a tendency to use the fingers on his left hand to clear it away. She wondered if he had any idea how often he had cause to do so. Sharp lines and planes made up a face distinguished by soft brown eyes, high cheekbones and just a hint of a beard along a chiseled jaw. His face remained expressionless as he waited expectantly.

Energy all but reverberated through him, reminding her of pictures she'd seen of panthers preparing to pounce. It occurred to her that she ought to be quite frightened of the power that simmered just below his civilized exterior. Instead, she was rather exhilarated.

"Catherine?"

Jolted out of her reverie, she brought her gaze back to find his trained on her. Hearing her name uttered from a mouth that conjured up thoughts of sinful kisses made her forget every other thought that had been running through her mind and brought her back to the problem at hand:

How much did she dare tell him? Just enough to ensure his assistance, she decided. Once she'd found what she'd come for, she would slip into the night with the duke none the wiser. If only she had more time to determine whether the man called Jack could truly be trusted with her most treasured secrets.

"Must we speak of it now?" she asked, flavoring her voice with a dose of exhaustion. "The fever makes me weary."

A look of genuine dismay crossed his handsome face. "My apologies. Please, by all means, rest."

But instead of getting up to take his leave as she'd expected, he only settled more deeply into the chair.

"Do you intend to remain there all night?"

"What if your condition should worsen?"

"I'll call for a maid."

"If I am right here, you won't need to call for anyone."

Why the thought of needing him sent a shiver of anticipation rippling through her was something she could ponder later when he wasn't so close.

She tugged the covers up to her chin. "It's quite improper for you to remain here when we are without a chaperone."

"I assure you that your virtue is quite safe with me."

Catherine wasn't sure whether to be assured or insulted. "At any rate—"

"Shhh. You need rest." He tipped his head back and closed his eyes, crossing his arms over a broad chest. Through the sleeves of his linen shirt she could make out the distinctive shape of well-muscled arms. Her eyes fixated on the column of his throat—

"You can't sleep when your eyes are open," he said, his voice husky with sleep.

Aroused beyond measure, Catherine tingled from head

to toe with a most inappropriate longing to have his long, muscular frame wrapped around her, to sleep in the embrace of his strong arms, to nuzzle her nose into the very spot where neck met shoulder.

He sat up suddenly and leaned forward to rest a hand over hers. "You're trembling. Does something hurt?"

"No," she managed to say.

"Then you must be cold." Before she could reply, he was up and out of the chair, tossing a log on the fire and stoking the flames, even though the room wasn't particularly cold.

Riveted to his every move, she stared at his long legs and taut backside as he tended the fire.

He spun around and caught her staring. A hum of awareness crackled along with the fire as something urgent and alive passed between them in a moment more charged with excitement than any she had ever experienced.

Her mouth suddenly dry, Catherine ran her tongue over her lip.

Jack set his gaze on her mouth as a raw, hungry expression took the place of his usual guarded look. "Is that better?" he asked.

"Oh," she said, startled. "What?"

"Are you still cold?"

"No." She wasn't sure if it was the fever, the fire or the sudden awareness that the man who'd decided to watch over her wanted her fiercely, but Catherine burned from the inside out.

He came closer to the bed. "You're still trembling."

"I am a little chilled," she said, settling on the less troublesome explanation for her body's reaction to him.

Rounding to the far side of the bed, he lifted the heavy blankets and slid in beside her.

Shock reverberated through her body as he drew her close to him. "Sir! Whatever do you think?"

"Let me warm you." His sweet-smelling breath caressed her cheek, sending odd bolts of awareness coursing through her, not unlike the sensations wrought by the fever. However, unlike the fever, these bolts settled into tingles between her legs.

Catherine lay rigid as he shaped his much larger body around hers.

"The fever has caused you to be chilled," he said.

"Your cure is most unconventional."

He laughed softly, and Catherine wanted to turn into his embrace and cling to the comfort he offered. When had she last been held so sweetly? Not in longer than she could recall—and never by a man in a bed.

"If anyone were to see us, I'd be ruined."

"No one will see us."

"You wield such power in the duke's home?"

"I am in charge when he is not here." His arm tightened around her, drawing her in even closer, until their bodies were aligned from shoulders to hips. "You're still trembling."

"I'm no longer certain it is caused entirely by the fever."

At that his body seemed to tense beside her. "No?"

"I've never been so close to a man."

"And what do you think so far?"

Catherine swallowed the small amount of saliva that remained in her mouth. "It is rather provocative."

"Is it now?"

She elbowed him. "You know it is."

He released a gasp that was half laughter when elbow connected with belly. "It's supposed to be restorative."

Catherine surprised herself by laughing. She also couldn't recall when she'd last laughed. "That is quite possibly the most outrageous thing you've said yet—and that is saying something."

"Mmm."

Was he actually going to *sleep*? How could he possibly sleep when they were *in a bed together*? And what, pray, was pressed against her back? Reaching between them to investigate, she encountered something hard and throbbing and—

"Keep that up," he muttered, "and you'll find out just how *provocative* I can be."

Catherine realized she had her hand wrapped around his manhood and released a squeal of dismay.

Jack laughed as she strained to break free of him. "Easy. You can't get warm all the way over there."

"I can't remain near you and that, that *thing*."

Another soft laugh rippled through his big frame, and Catherine decided she'd never been more riveted by anything in her life. He was so big and vital and aroused. By her. Despite being scandalized, she was also full of her own power.

"I've been told my *thing* is quite nice."

He was also the most outrageous person she'd ever known. "I'm sure you're rather accomplished in matters of fornication," she sniffed.

He raised a rakish eyebrow. "Want to find out?"

"I do not! Remove yourself from my bed at once, or I shall call for someone."

"Everyone is asleep by now, which is what you should be as well."

"How do you expect me to sleep with a big, rutting beast in my bed?"

"Have no fear, my dear lady. Your shrewishness has caused my 'thing' to wither and die, so if you'd like me to warm you, I can assure you that you're entirely safe from my fornicating tendencies."

Shrewishness? "I'll rely on the blankets to warm me, thank you very much."

"Mmm."

"Are you *sleeping?* You can't sleep here!"

"Hmm." He kept his eyes closed as his breathing settled into a steady cadence. "Since you're wide awake, why don't you tell me what brings you here and from whence you came—and remember, you promised me the truth."

Since he didn't seem compelled to remove himself from the bed, Catherine sat up and reached for the mountain of pillows behind them to form a line down the center. Satisfied that she had at least a small barrier in place to protect herself from the big, rutting beast, she settled back against her own pillows.

"Feel better now?" he asked in that sultry, sleepy tone that sent shock waves rippling through her. And what, exactly, was that tingle between her legs? She didn't dare ask him for fear of what outrageous thing he might utter in response.

"I'm quite comfortable, thank you." His hand snaked beneath the pillows to rest on her belly. Shocked to her core by his audaciousness, Catherine didn't dare move as the heat from his hand branded her sensitive skin. "Whatever are you doing now?"

"Testing your fence."

"Apparently, I'm unable to keep the riffraff out." She pushed his hand away. "If you won't remove yourself, at least remain on your own side." But even as she pushed him away, she wanted him closer. As unnerved as she was to awaken inside the home of a duke, being in a bed with his estate manager was, without a doubt, the most exciting thing to ever happen to her. And it wasn't like it would matter if he ruined her. He was a fine alternative to the viscount her father had chosen for her. Speaking of rutting beasts. Catherine trembled just thinking of him.

"Are you chilled again?"

"No."

"You aren't afraid, are you? Of me? I mean you no harm."

Somehow, she knew that was true. She knew she could trust him—the same way she'd known instantaneously that she could *not* trust the viscount. Her instincts certainly hadn't failed her there. "I know that."

"Whatever you're running from, whatever has brought you here, I can help."

Catherine turned to find him lying on one of the pillows she'd put between them to protect her. A fine bit of good that had done her. "I still don't understand why you want to."

"Why wouldn't I?" He looped a lock of her blond hair around his finger. "You're a beautiful young lady, obviously far from home, clearly afraid of something, in need of assistance. What kind of gentleman would I be if I didn't offer all the help I have at my disposal?"

"What kind of gentleman finds his way into a young lady's bed without the benefit of marriage?"

"One who has been very lonely for the companionship of a lady who not only stirs his desires but also fires his mind with witty conversation."

Catherine stared at him, mouth agape. "I *stir* your desires?" she somehow squeaked out.

"I believe I've already provided ample proof of that."

Catherine had hoped to forget about touching his manhood, but of course he wouldn't let her. "I've never stirred anyone's desires before." Except for those of the viscount, of course, and that was hardly the same. The passing breeze stirred his foul desires. And poor Ian hadn't lived long enough to share any kind of desire with her.

"What's wrong with the gentlemen where you live? Are they without sense?"

Intrigued by his obvious interest in her, Catherine turned on her side to face him. "They're all mad about my sister, Madeleine. She's the fetching one. They called her the Belle of the Season."

He continued to play with the lock of her hair. "She isn't the fetching one."

"How can you say that? You've never even seen her!"

"I don't need to see her. The fetching one is here. With me."

Heat crept from her breasts to her neck and then her face. No one had ever said such things to her, and after years of being pushed aside by suitors anxious to get closer to her dazzling sister, she rather liked it.

He brushed his fingers lightly over her face. "Have you ever been kissed, Catherine?"

Rendered speechless by the question, she shook her head.

His fingers moved from her cheek to her jaw, sending shivers of sensation straight to that spot she'd recently discovered between her legs.

"Would you like to be?" he asked.

"I believe I would."

For the longest time, he didn't move. While she waited to see what he would do, Catherine's heart beat faster, her mouth went dry and the trembling began anew. Just when she thought she'd go mad if he didn't do *something*, he raised himself up, removed the pillow between them, and cradled her face with his large hand. He leaned in slowly and finally touched his lips to hers.

Catherine couldn't help but feel let down. *That* was it? *That* was kissing? But then he came back for a second taste, this time sliding his lips back and forth over hers, once again setting off that maddening tingling sensation that converged into a throb between her legs. *What was that?* It made her feel itchy and unsatisfied. She tightened the muscles in her thighs, hoping to make it stop, but that only seemed to intensify the nameless urges.

"What do you think so far?" he asked, his face a mere inch above hers.

Finding it hard to breathe, let alone speak, Catherine looked up to find him gazing down at her. "It's pleasant."

"Pleasant," he said with a chuckle. "In that case I must be doing something wrong."

"It's not supposed to be pleasant?"

He feathered kisses over her face and jaw, making her breathless. "Pleasant," he said between kisses, "is how you describe a kiss on the cheek from your father or brother or perhaps a favored uncle. A lover's kiss should be much, much better than 'pleasant.' Shall we try again?"

Before she could process the word "lover," he dipped his head and captured her mouth in an all-consuming kiss. His tongue pressing against her lips shocked her profoundly. She'd had no idea that was part of kissing and wasn't sure if she should pull him closer or push him away.

"Open for me," he whispered as his tongue teased her bottom lip. "Open your mouth."

Still too shocked to speak, Catherine attempted to do as he'd requested.

He shifted so he was pressed even tighter against her. "More."

Moaning, Catherine opened her mouth. As his tongue rubbed against hers, the tingling between her legs became a burning need for something else. She had no idea what.

"Touch me, Catherine," he said between kisses.

Tentatively, she put her arms around him and sank the fingers of her left hand into his silky dark hair.

This time, he moaned. "God, you taste so sweet." His kisses became more carnal as she responded in kind.

Catherine couldn't keep up with the feelings and needs spiraling through her. How was it possible that a man whom she'd never seen before today had her pinned to a bed and clutching his hair while he kissed her madly? The thought brought her back to reality, and she abruptly turned away from Jack's passionate kisses.

Breathing heavily, he pressed his lips to her neck. "I'm sorry if I got carried away. I've never kissed anyone quite so sweet."

"Somehow I doubt that."

"It's the truth, Catherine. Now that I've had a taste of you, I'll think of nothing else until I can have another."

"Nothing at all?" she asked with a coy smile she wouldn't have thought herself capable of before now, before him.

He raised his head so she could see his face when he said, "Nothing."

Overwhelmed by all she saw on his face, she lowered her eyes. "I should hate to distract you so thoroughly."

"I believe I shall enjoy being thoroughly distracted by you."

Chapter Four

Derek told himself it wasn't really a lie. He'd been drawn to her from the first instant her mane of blond curls tumbled from the ridiculous cap she'd worn to dig in the grove. And now that he'd had the exquisite pleasure of her kisses, he had no doubt the ruse was essential to getting another taste.

If he told her the truth, that *he* was the Duke of Westwood, she'd be gone long before he ever got a chance to explore the attraction simmering between them. For once in his life, he had the opportunity to be a regular man and not a duke with more land and money and privilege than most people knew in a lifetime. Nothing could keep him from pursuing the opportunity that had literally landed in his arms when she fainted dead away the day before. Maybe he'd come to discover that she actually liked *him*, Derek (or rather Jack), and not the damned Duke of Westwood, and maybe, just maybe he'd found the answer to his deadline problem.

That was why he'd assembled the household staff at dawn's first light. Glancing to the back row of gathered servants, he spotted Nathan from the stables, who'd been summoned when he had failed to appear. Satisfied that everyone was there, Derek nodded in greeting. "Thank you all for getting up early. Our guest is resting comfortably, and I believe her fever has broken."

"That's a great relief," Mrs. Langingham declared.

"Indeed," Derek concurred. Now for the sticky part. "Lady Catherine is going to remain a guest for the immediate future. Mrs. Langingham, I'd like you to open the dowager duchess's home and see to its cleaning."

"But we could keep her plenty comfortable here."

"For a number of reasons, I believe she'd prefer to be elsewhere." He took a deep breath before he continued. "She believes I'm Jack Bancroft, the duke's estate manager."

Mrs. Langingham gasped. "But Your Grace—"

Derek set his jaw and pressed on. "No one is to refer to me by my title until further notice. I'm Mr. Bancroft or sir. Am I understood?"

"Yes, Your . . . sir," Rutledge said.

The others murmured their acquiescence, but Derek watched the shock register on their faces.

Mrs. Langingham trained a steely stare on Derek, letting him know he'd answer to her the moment they were alone. He expected nothing less.

"And I, sir?" a male voice intoned from the far right. "What's to become of me in light of your, ah, situation?"

Derek turned to face off with his estate manager. "My apologies, Mr. Bancroft, for absconding with your name."

Jack smiled broadly. "No harm, Your Grace, er, *sir*. I'm flattered."

"I believe this would be an excellent time for you to visit your mother in Kent. Do you agree?"

"I'll be off by sunset," Jack said with another smile.

"With my most humble appreciation." Derek cleared his throat. "As far as our guest is concerned, the duke has gone abroad to America for the summer, and I am in charge in his absence. Are there any questions?"

When he was met with silence, Derek dismissed them to their duties with his thanks. He had no doubt he'd be the topic of their scandalized whispers below stairs as they went about their work.

As expected, Mrs. Langingham followed him into his study and closed the door. Hands on broad hips, she stared him down with sharp eyes that missed nothing. "What are you about, Derek Eagan?"

He lowered himself to the chair behind the desk. "An opportunity has presented itself. I intend to take full advantage."

"Explain yourself."

"I've been a duke since I was six years old. I've never had the chance to be anyone else. I find myself intrigued by our guest, and I'd like to get to know her better. If she knew I was the duke, that wouldn't happen."

"What has she against the aristocracy?"

"That's one of many things I hope to discover."

Mrs. Langingham's eyes narrowed with displeasure. "You play a dangerous game, young man."

"It's no game. I assure you that once her business here is finished, she'll return home, and I'll resume my regular, mundane life with her none the wiser that she deigned to lower herself to befriend a duke."

"And what exactly is her business here?"

"She is looking for something on the southeastern quarter. I don't know much more than that. Yet."

"It's not like you to be dishonest in your dealings. That's not how you were raised."

"You're quite right, madam," Derek said, making some effort to control a flash of temper. "I was raised to be exactly who and what I am, but for once, just *once*, I am going to take something for myself. For however long it lasts, I am Jack Bancroft. Now, will you see to the arrangements for opening my grandmother's home?"

She stood before his large desk studying him shrewdly. "As you wish, *Mr. Bancroft*."

"And when my uncle returns, you'll inform him?"

"*That* you can handle on your own, *sir*."

Apparently, even the most faithful of servants had her limits. "Very well."

"Will Lady Catherine require a lady's maid or cook in her new home?"

"I don't believe so, but I'll inquire and let you know." Derek suspected she'd rather fend for herself than be fawned over by servants.

Mrs. Langingham headed for the door but stopped just short of it and turned back to him. "I urge you to be cautious with your affections, Mr. Bancroft. As someone who has watched over and cared for you all your life, I'd despair to see you harmed in any way by an untruth that went too far."

"While I appreciate your concern, I have no intention of being harmed."

He had no doubt she wished to say more but wisely took her leave and left him to wonder if a couple of torrid kisses really had the power to send him over the bend into madness.

Catherine woke alone in the big bed and reached out to the other side while trying to decide if she'd dreamt the whole thing. Finding herself alone, she brought fingers to lips that were swollen and sensitive. Not a dream. She had kissed Jack Bancroft like a brazen hussy and lain abed with him all night long. He'd bathed her face with a cool cloth

when her fever had returned in the predawn hours and held
her through the chills. While she knew she should be scandalized by the liberties she'd allowed him, rather she was
far more concerned about where he'd gone and when he
might return.

Glancing at the fireplace, she noticed he had stoked
the flames to ensure she'd wake to a heated room. The
gesture warmed her inside as well as out. Her body ached
as she eased herself up and reached for the dressing gown
the housekeeper had left at the foot of the bed. When the
floor moved beneath her feet, she quickly lowered herself
to the edge of the bed to get her bearings.

That's where Jack found her when he knocked and entered with a breakfast tray. As memories of their passionate
kisses the night before swirled through her mind, Catherine found it difficult to look at him. It was just as well that
the tantalizing aromas coming from the tray caused her
empty stomach to growl, which made them laugh, cutting
the tension in the room.

"Feeling better?" he asked with a kind smile that made
his sun-browned face crinkle attractively in the corners of
his eyes. His was a face that had smiled often and laughed
freely—discoveries that comforted her.

"Yes, a little."

"I didn't know what you like, so I asked our cook,
Amelia, to make you some of everything." He put the tray
down and removed covers from dishes to reveal eggs, bacon,
toast, jam and pastries—a veritable feast for someone who
hadn't eaten regularly in weeks.

Her stomach growled loudly again.

He laughed and held out a chair for her. "Well, come on."

Not trusting her own legs, Catherine got up slowly only
to gasp when the room again shifted under her.

Jack rushed to her side and put his strong arms around her.

She sagged into him, closing her eyes against the sickening swirl of the room.

"I'm afraid the fever has weakened me." Before she could recover herself, he swept her into his arms and settled her back into bed. "What are you doing?" she asked. "I need to get up."

"I'll bring breakfast to you."

"But I need . . ." Heat scorched her face. One didn't discuss such things with a man.

He turned to her. "What do you need? I'll get you anything you desire."

"I, um, desire the chamber pot."

Jack tossed his head back and laughed. "I can do you one better. The duke had indoor plumbing installed in all his homes several years ago." He carried her to the en suite water closet.

"Do you mind?" She gestured to the door.

"Oh. Right. I'll wait for you outside."

"Thank you." Even though she was still dizzy, she attended to her personal needs and then used a silver-plated brush she found on a chest of drawers in an attempt to tame her unruly hair before she called Jack to come back in.

"Are you all right?" he asked, concern etched into his stunning face.

Catherine had never seen a more attractive man in her life. He was so beautiful that he apparently rendered her mute.

He moved to her side. "Catherine?"

"I'm fine. Just hungry."

"Do you feel up to sitting at the table?"

"Of course."

Jack held her chair and helped her get settled. "May I serve you?"

Her heart fluttered with awareness of him—his large, muscular frame, the clean scent of leather and citrus that clung to his skin, the dusting of dark hair on the back of his hand as he reached for the first covered dish. "Please," she managed to say. It was all she could do not to devour everything he put on her plate. Instead, she waited until he was seated across from her before she began to eat slowly. "Have you broken your fast?" she asked when she noticed he hadn't filled his own plate.

"Hours ago." He poured something with a robust scent into a delicate china cup. "I'm used to waking early."

"What is that you're drinking?"

"The duke has introduced me to American coffee, and I confess I've developed quite a taste for it. Have you had it?"

She shook her head. "The aroma is certainly unique."

"Would you like to try it?"

The scent of coffee was another that she'd now forever associate with him. "I prefer tea, but I'll try it."

"It's somewhat of an acquired taste. May I suggest adding some milk to sweeten it?"

"I defer to your judgment."

Catherine was aware of Jack watching her out the corner of one eye as he deftly prepared the coffee and placed the cup before her. He continued to observe closely as she took a first tenuous sip of the bitter brew.

"What do you think?"

"It has a strong flavor." And she instantly detested it but vowed to never let him know that. Not after he had taken such pleasure in introducing her to something new.

"Like I said, it's an acquired taste."

Catherine endured another sip, acutely aware of his eyes riveted to her mouth. "You're staring, Mr. Bancroft."

He startled. "My apologies."

Catherine couldn't help but giggle at his befuddled expression.

Jack sat back in his chair, propping one foot on the other knee, the pose relaxed even as tension marked his shoulders. "You find me amusing?"

She nibbled on a second piece of toast. "Enormously."

"I'm glad you're feeling better," he said drolly.

Retrieving the napkin from her lap, she blotted her lips. "I very much appreciate your help and hospitality, however I should probably be on my way."

His relaxed pose disappeared as he leaned forward on the table. "To where?"

"I don't belong here. I need to go home."

"What about your grandmother's property?"

Dejected, Catherine cast her eyes down. "It's a key. What is the likelihood that I'll actually find it?"

"A key to what?"

"A chest belonging to the duke," Catherine said. "She once told me if I ever found myself in need of money, I should come here, to the duke's property where she'd buried a key twenty paces from the grand oak in the south-eastern corner. Only she failed to say twenty paces in what *direction*."

"And what would this key open?"

Catherine's face blazed with color. "Apparently, there was a chest in the duke's bedchamber where she hid money and jewelry that were gifts from him. She was forced to flee the house and buried the key, intending to return someday for her belongings. She never made it back. When she was dying, she told me about the key and said I should come find it if I was ever in need of resources. It's a fool's errand, though. The key could be anywhere. I should probably just forget about it."

"But you've only just begun to look. Why would you want to give up so soon?"

Catherine rested her chin on her closed fist. "I fear it's a frivolous search, at best."

"So then why begin to look in the first place?"

Studying him, she wanted to tell him everything but still she hesitated. "I'm afraid that is a very long story."

"I've nothing but time."

"Wouldn't it be easier to find me some clothes and let me walk away?"

"Perhaps."

"But?"

"I'd rather you didn't walk away."

"Why?" she asked, astounded by the intensity of his gaze.

"I'm not sure, really. All I know is that it's been far more exciting around here since you arrived than it ever was before."

Catherine had no idea how to respond to such a startling statement.

"When you do take your leave, I'd wish for you to take with you what you came to find," he added without an ounce of guile.

She looked around at the opulent room that she had barely noticed in her weakened state the day before. "I can't stay here."

"So you've said. That's why I've ordered the dowager duchess's home reopened and prepared for you."

Catherine tilted her head, wondering if she had heard him correctly. "I beg your pardon?"

"The duke's grandmother passed away a decade or so ago. She had her own home on the property, rather near where you wish to conduct your search. I believe you'll be quite comfortable there for the remainder of your stay."

Catherine stared at him, wondering if he was truly as sincere as he seemed.

"Will that suit you?"

"I, um, I don't know what to say."

"You could say, 'Why yes, Jack, that sounds lovely,' and I could have you settled there by noon."

Almost against her will, her face lifted into a small grin. It was simply impossible not to like this charming, kind man who seemed to want only what was best for her. Later she could take the time to examine his ulterior motives, but for now she wished to bask in his kindness. It had been so very long since anyone had been kind to her.

"I'm waiting."

Catherine met his gaze. "Why yes, Jack, that sounds lovely."

He rewarded her with a dazzling smile that stopped her heart. "Now," he said, "are you going to tell me that really long story?"

Chapter Five

The moment Catherine mentioned the key, Derek had known what it would open. His grandfather had left behind a small Hepplewhite chest that Derek still kept in his bedchamber. The key had been missing for years, and family lore had it that his grandfather's mistress had taken it. Derek was astounded to realize his grandfather and Catherine's grandmother had probably been lovers.

Now he wanted to find the key as badly as she did. How many years had he wondered what he'd find inside that chest? How many times had he considered whether it would be worth destroying a priceless piece to get inside? How often had he resisted the urge?

"I grew up in Hampshire," Catherine said tentatively. "My father was the local blacksmith, and I all but lived in the stables. Horses were my whole life when I wasn't reading."

Derek watched, transfixed, at the soft glow that lit her face when she spoke of the animals she loved. "Did you have one of your own?"

She nodded. "A bay named Sunny. I never knew how my father came to own her, but there she was one day, and he said she was mine."

"Where is she now?"

"I left her with an innkeeper on the outskirts of Essex. She's old, and she'd gone as far as she could."

Alarmed, Derek said, "How did you travel the rest of the way?"

"Mostly on foot, but I got a ride here and there. It helped that I looked like a boy."

"You could never pass as a boy."

"I fooled you," she said with a saucy grin that set his blood to racing.

"For about two seconds." He'd never admit to another living soul that he had been attracted to her curves even when he'd thought her a boy. "I'll send someone after Sunny."

She inhaled sharply. "You will?"

"Of course."

Catherine's big eyes filled with tears.

Derek moved his chair closer to hers. Careful not to startle her, Derek cradled her hand between both of his.

"You are so kind," she whispered.

Humbled, he had no idea what to say. He tried to remember the last time a woman had tongue-tied him. "Sunny is important to you. You'll want her with you."

"She's my very best friend." Catherine wiped the tears from her eyes. "They didn't want me to bring her."

"Who didn't?"

"My parents." She sighed. "I'm getting ahead of myself. Nine months ago, my father's brother, the Earl of Brisbane, died of smallpox. His son died, too."

Derek had, of course, heard about the earl's untimely demise while he was in London. "I'm so sorry."

"Don't be. They were awful people. We despised them and everything they stood for."

Ahhh, Derek thought. *Here is the reason she disdains the aristocracy.*

"My father was a second son. His brother, the earl, could have ensured that his brother shared in the family's wealth. He chose not to. We went there once, to his estate, Hedgerow, in Norfolk, about ten years ago. My parents were disgusted by the earl's self-indulgent, hedonistic lifestyle, and my father said as much. We were dispatched back to our cottage in Hampshire, and we never heard from them again until footmen from the estate showed up to tell my father he was the new earl."

"And how did you feel about that?"

"I was *horrified*. I liked my life just as it was. I didn't want to move and leave my friends, my house, my books."

"You couldn't take them with you?"

She shook her head. "They were in the village library. I had read all six-hundred volumes at least once. Many of them twice."

Derek stared at her, astounded. "*Six hundred?*"

"At last count."

"You've read *six-hundred* books?"

"I taught all the village children how to read, too. That's what I do—or rather what I *did* before everything changed."

He tightened his hold on her hand. "I'm so impressed."

Her shy smile touched his heart. "Do you read, Jack?"

"Some." He couldn't exactly tell her of his studies at Oxford. "The duke has a vast library you're welcome to use while you're here."

Eyes widening, she gasped. "Really?"

"Absolutely." As the delight danced across her face, Derek realized he could sit right here and talk to her for the rest of his life and never get tired of the sound of her voice, of the way her face betrayed her every emotion, of the simple pleasure she took in the most basic kindnesses.

Here was what had been missing in every other woman he'd ever met. "What is your surname, Catherine?" He couldn't let on that he'd known Terrance McCabe, the Earl of Brisbane, and had shared her sentiments on his character.

"McCabe."

"Madeleine McCabe is your sister?"

She nodded.

He had a vision of one of the more attractive and seemingly sensible debutantes. "I met her," Derek said before he caught himself. A jolt of panic reminded him of the lie he'd told her.

"Where?"

"In London when the duke went for the beginning of the Season before he left for America. We met her on the street in Mayfair one day."

"What did you think of her?"

Derek knew he had to tread carefully here. "She was quite lovely, but I never gave her another thought after we parted."

"And the duke? Was he impressed by her?"

"Not overly. He's not easily swayed by a pretty face."

"I think I'd like him."

Derek experienced another pang of conscience over the lies he'd told her. "He's a good man." At least he usually was. "So your parents packed you up to move to Norfolk?"

"With a stop in London for the social Season so they could debut their middle daughter, Madeleine, into polite society. Much to my surprise and dismay, my parents fully embraced their new role as members of the *beau monde*. The same people who'd scorned that lifestyle all my life are now strutting around like proud peacocks, spending money like wildfire. Their behavior sickened me."

Not wanting to rush her, Derek waited expectantly for her to continue.

"My sister, Madeleine, was presented into society, but I, at five and twenty, am apparently 'on the shelf,' too old to be a formal debutante, which was fine with me. My other sister Hillary is only sixteen."

"So you ran away?"

"Yes," she said softly. "I packed my grandmother's journals and stole some of my brother's clothes. I got Sunny from the stables, and I left."

"How long had you been traveling when I came upon you?"

"About three weeks."

"And no one is looking for you?"

"I'm sure they're searching."

"I was in London with the duke, but didn't hear anything about a lady going missing."

"It wouldn't be unusual for my father to go to enormous lengths to keep our family's troubles private."

Derek stared at her, confounded. "His daughter is missing, and he keeps that quiet?"

Her face curled into an ironic smile. "It would be a different matter altogether if one of my brothers went missing. Especially Stuart."

"His heir."

Catherine nodded. "Back when we were no one special, he loved us all equally. Once he was elevated to the aristocracy by the deaths of his brother and nephew, everything changed."

Derek could see that the loss of her father's affections had hurt her. "That must've been so hard for you."

"We were always very close, thanks to our mutual love of horses."

"You miss him."

"I did until he decided he needed to find me a husband *post haste*."

Riveted, Derek hung on her every word. "And did he make a match?"

She shuddered with revulsion. "An appalling match with a viscount thirty years my senior. He's fat and smells bad and drinks."

Derek couldn't help but chuckle quietly at the picture she painted.

"You find my predicament funny? Can you imagine being in bed with such a rutting beast?"

He made an effort to squelch his laughter. "No, I most definitely can't imagine such a thing."

"You mock me."

Derek found her pique adorable. "I do no such thing, my lady. I begin to understand you better."

"I couldn't stay there and be forced into marriage with a man who sickens me."

"Who is this man who sickens you?"

She glanced at him, uncertain. "Viscount Lindsey," she said softly.

Derek had to fight to hide his shock from her. Lindsey was indeed despicable, and the thought of this glorious, delicate creature married to him sickened Derek, too. However, Lindsey's title was one of the oldest and most revered in all of England. He was not a man to be trifled with. "May I ask something that's perhaps none of my business?"

"If you must."

"Did Lindsey harm you in some way?"

Catherine's hand clutched her throat as color crept into her cheeks. If Derek had found her adorable before, now she was positively dazzling. "My father forced me to spend time alone in the viscount's presence."

"And what happened?"

"He, he tried—"

Filled with rage, Derek said, "Did he hurt you?"

"He held me down and forced himself on me." Her face flamed with shame and embarrassment. "He touched me. Afterward, I had bruises everywhere, but so did he."

Derek contained his rage by clasping his hands together tightly as he absorbed the real reason she'd run away. "What did you do?"

Once again, her exquisite discomfort fired Derek's protective instincts. He hoped Lindsey was looking for her and that he found her at Westwood Hall. Derek hoped that most fervently. The viscount would find out what happened to men who overpowered defenseless women.

"I kicked him in a place I'm told is most sensitive to a man."

Derek winced. Well, maybe not entirely defenseless.

"He called me vile names and vowed to make the consummation of our marriage as painful as possible."

"Swine," Derek muttered under his breath, understanding at last the nightmares that plagued her sleep.

Her cold hand clutched his sleeve. "He can't find me," she whispered, her face gone ashen. "I believe he intended to defile me in my father's parlor. Had I not grown up in the company of rambunctious brothers, he might've succeeded. I left London the very next day."

Derek warmed her frigid hand between both of his. "I can assure you, my lady, nothing of the sort will happen while you're under my protection."

"Even though I've ventured to spend as little time as possible in his company, I'm told he's rather besotted. I don't believe he'll give up easily. I have no doubt he is searching for me." A shudder rippled through her. "If he finds me—"

"He'll have to get through me and my men."

"You're so confident. I've never known anyone quite so confident."

Derek told himself to be careful. He spoke with a command far more in keeping with a duke than a duke's estate manager. If she'd grown up among the *ton*, she might be suspicious of such a powerful estate manager. "You can trust that you are safe here."

"I'd still rather not be the guest of a duke. As soon as I locate the key and retrieve my grandmother's belongings, I'll be on my way."

She had nothing, not even the clothes on her back, but her pride dictated that she be beholden to no aristocrat.

Derek stood. "Until then, I'll arrange transport to the dowager duchess's cottage. I believe you'll be quite comfortable there. I'll also send for the village seamstress to provide you with new clothing."

"I can never adequately thank you for your many kindnesses."

He left her with a small bow. "I am at your service, my lady."

In the hallway, Derek took a moment to gather himself. The idea of someone attacking her, threatening her with rape, sickened him. A surge of nausea caught him off guard. He'd met her only yesterday and already he'd kill to protect her.

"Sir?" Mrs. Langingham said.

Derek snapped out of the state he'd slipped into. "Yes?"

"The dowager duchess's home has been cleaned and aired, and the icebox filled. It is ready for your guest."

"Very good. Thank you. Please ask Rutledge to gather every man on the staff at the stables in an hour."

"Is something amiss?"

"I've learned that Lady Catherine may be in some

danger. I wish to arrange for regular patrols and to make the household aware of her concerns."

Mrs. Langingham brought a hand to her heart. "What kind of danger?"

"Her father has betrothed her to a man who sickens her and who once attacked her. He is indeed an odious pig of a man whom I've had the displeasure of meeting on several occasions."

"Oh my! Whatever shall we do?"

"We will provide her with shelter and protection for as long as necessary."

"Your Grace," she whispered. "Should you be involved in such a mess?"

"Perhaps not, but involved I am. Please see to her transport. I shall speak to Rutledge and the others myself."

"Very well." She bustled off while Derek descended the stairs, his head spinning from everything Catherine had told him.

Hours later, after taking every step he could think of to ensure Catherine's safety, Derek saddled Hercules and set off along the well-worn path he'd once traveled daily to visit his grandmother. After the loss of his parents, his uncle Anthony had seen to the many needs of the duchy, while Derek's grandmother, his father's mother, had showered him—and Simon—with love and care until they left for boarding school.

She'd been gone more than ten years now, and Derek still missed her. As he rode, he wondered what she had known of her husband's earlier dalliance with a woman in service to the household—Catherine's grandmother. Even though it had happened well before their marriage, he was certain, knowing his grandmother, that she'd been well aware of the affair that had no doubt caused quite the scandal at the time.

Outside the cozy little cottage, Derek tied the horse's lead to a tree and was felled by nerves that made him laugh softly to himself. When was the last time he'd been nervous because of a woman? Probably the night Kitty made a man out of him—and that had been more than a decade ago.

In the hours they'd spent together, Catherine had touched him deeply. Her vulnerability struck at his protective nature, but her strength and determination had been just as compelling. He only wished he didn't have to keep his identity hidden from her. Just long enough to get to know each other and to keep her safe from Lindsey, he told himself as he approached the front door and knocked.

She answered wearing a pale pink silk dressing gown. Her golden locks fell past her shoulders in waves of curls.

The sight of her pushed the air from his lungs. She looked so pretty and pure and perfect.

"Hello, Jack."

Chapter Six

Derek told himself he was supposed to say something, but with all his focus on her loveliness he found it nearly impossible to form a coherent thought. "I just, I, um wanted to make sure you were comfortable."

"I am more than comfortable. This house is absolutely adorable!" Without an ounce of guile, she ushered him inside where a fire in the hearth cast an amber glow over the small sitting room. The sight brought back his grandmother in a rush of memories—the happiest memories of his young life. "It reminds me of our home in Hampshire," Catherine said. "Cozy and quaint."

Derek gripped his hat in both hands, feeling like a hulking lout in the small room. "And you have everything you need?" He took a quick look around, noting the homey touches Mrs. Langingham had probably seen to personally.

"Indeed. Would you like to sit?"

He eyed the high-backed chair adjacent to the settee. "Um, yes, thank you."

"Are you all right?"

"Of course," he said, startled. "Why do you ask?"

"You seem different. Tense."

Tense. He wanted to laugh. His skin suddenly felt too tight for his body as every inch of him was painfully aware of her fresh scent, the way the silk clung to curves he hadn't fully appreciated earlier, and how at home she seemed in his grandmother's home.

He'd no sooner sat than he surged to his feet. "I should probably go."

"So soon?" Disappointment radiated from her.

"It is not proper for us to be here alone."

"And yet it was proper for you to spend most of last evening in my bed?"

"That was different," Derek stammered. Had he ever been so undone by a woman? No. Never. "You were ill."

"You said yourself no one would know we were alone together when we were in the manor. Who will know now?"

Derek stared at her, riveted by the movement of her plump lips. "My, ah, Hercules is out front, announcing that I am here."

She looked up at him with those dark navy eyes. "Announcing to whom?"

"Anyone who happens by."

Those amazing lips curved into a small smile. "Doesn't anyone who happens by happen to work for you?"

Beginning to be amused—and embarrassed—by her questions, Derek rubbed at the stubble on his chin. "Yes, I suppose they do."

"And you have requested their discretion?"

"I have."

"So why then must you leave so soon?"

Cornered, he rolled the brim of his hat between his hands. He looked around, taking in the fresh flowers and wood piled on the hearth. "Are you hungry? Can I fix you something to eat?"

Her expression conveyed suspicion while her mouth quirked with amusement. "You know how to cook?"

He released a jagged breath. "Are you intentionally trying to provoke me?"

Laughter burst from her in rolling waves that captivated him. "Not intentionally."

He tossed his hat on the chair. "I never said anything about cooking. I can, however, put cheese and bread on a tray."

"That I'd like to see."

"Fine." With exasperation warring with amusement and desire, he stalked into the small kitchen to search the icebox for provisions, counting on Mrs. Langingham to be predictable. Sure enough, he found a hunk of fresh cheese. He also found a loaf of crusty bread, still warm from the oven, added a bunch of grapes and poured glasses of red wine. When the spread was ready, he carried it into the sitting room.

After placing the tray on the table in front of the settee, he bent with a flourish and produced a cloth napkin. "Your repast, my lady."

She eyed the offering, again with the hint of humor he'd come to expect from her. "I am most definitely impressed."

"Not all men are useless clods."

"They're not?" she asked, smiling.

"I fear you mock me."

"Never." Attempting a solemn expression—and failing—she helped herself to a grape.

Watching that grape disappear between those sensuous lips was one of the most provocative things he'd ever witnessed.

Patting the other side of the settee, she invited him to join her.

Derek eyed the seat and glanced at her. Swallowing hard, he lowered himself gingerly.

Catherine hummed softly to herself as she sliced the bread and cheese, offering some to him.

"Thank you." They ate in silence, the crackling of the fire the only sound in the room. "May I ask you something?"

Startled, he looked over at her. "Of course."

"Before, at the manor, when we were together, I was in a strange place with people I do not know, yet I was comfortable with you."

Even though his mouth was suddenly dry, Derek managed to swallow the bite of bread. Not trusting himself to speak, he took a long sip from his wine. "And now?"

"Now I fear you are regretting your offer to help me but don't know how to tell me so."

Derek sat up straighter. "I assure you that is not the case."

"Why then are you so dreadfully uncomfortable?"

He sucked in a sharp, deep breath, amazed by how attuned she was to his moods. "I want to help you. Honestly, I do."

A flash of hurt crossed her expressive face. "You *have* changed your mind."

"That is *not* true."

"Then whatever is the matter?"

Summoning courage and self-control, Derek blotted the wine from his lips and turned to face her. "When I kissed you, I told you I would think of nothing else until I could do it again. It turns out I was quite right about that."

Her face flushed with color that only fueled his desire. "And this makes you uncomfortable?"

"Very."

"Why?"

"Because a gentleman must be concerned about the reputation of the woman he cares about."

"You care about me?"

"Yes."

"Even though we have only just met?" she asked, incredulous.

"We already know each other better than I have known almost anyone." Derek told himself that much was true despite the lies he had told her.

Seeming pleased by that, she reached for his hand and held it between both of hers. "I am five and twenty, Jack. You gave me my first kiss yesterday. I feel like my life is passing me by, and nothing exciting has ever happened. Until now."

Derek forced himself to breathe. "And you find me exciting?"

Her fingers skimmed over his knuckles. "I do."

He leaned in closer to her. "Would it be improper if I kissed you again?"

"Probably."

"Oh," he said, backing off as disappointment flooded him.

She laughed and tugged on his hand to bring him back to her.

Dangling at the edge of sanity, Derek uttered a growl and tilted her face to receive his kiss. This time, she met him with open lips and an eager tongue. He tried to remember this was only the second time she'd ever kissed a man, but her avid response made him forget his good intentions. Her flavor, sweetness tinged with the bite of wine, invaded his senses, making him hungry for more.

"This is highly improper," he whispered against her lips.

"Highly."

"So we should stop." Her fingers sifted through his hair, sending a shiver of delight dancing through him.

"Probably." But rather than stop, he angled his head to delve deeper. "You are certain you have never done this before?"

"Mmm."

"You're a fast learner."

Catherine's throaty chuckle sent a burst of lust straight to his already hard cock.

"Do you still feel uncomfortable?" she asked.

He caressed her face with both hands, gazing into her eyes. "Yes, but for different reasons."

Embarrassment once again colored her cheeks. "That seems to be a frequent concern for you."

"Only since I met you."

She gasped. "You say the most outrageous things!"

"I speak only the truth," he said with a pang of guilt over what he was keeping from her. But every time he was with her he became more convinced the deception was necessary for now.

"Will you come back again tomorrow?"

He kissed both her hands. "Do you want me to come back tomorrow?"

"Yes, Jack," she said, laughter dancing across her face. "I want you to come back tomorrow."

"Then I shall."

"Will you kiss me again?"

"Only if you want me to."

"Do I have to wait until tomorrow for that?"

Derek hung his head, seeking guidance before he did something they might both regret. "It might be best if we waited."

"You don't wish to kiss me anymore? Did I not do it right?"

Derek gasped and looked up at her. "You did it exactly right. That is the problem."

Tears flooded her eyes. "I don't understand."

"I want more of you, Catherine. I want things a gentleman only takes from the woman he is married to."

"Oh." Her eyes met his, and in them he saw courage and determination. "What if I want those same things?"

Derek ached for her. Did she *know* what she did to him? "You have been through a terrible ordeal, first with Lord Lindsey and then with your illness. I do not wish to take advantage."

Her cheeks flamed with color. "If I ask you to bed me, then you are not taking advantage."

Derek nearly swallowed his tongue. "I should speak first to your father, ask for your hand."

She shook her head. "He would never allow it."

"Because I am common."

"You are not common to me."

Derek wanted to laugh at the irony. Her father would no doubt jump at the chance to marry his spinster daughter off to the Duke of Westwood. But *Catherine* would never marry a duke. Here, finally, was a woman who possessed all the qualities he most desired, but he could not have her as his wife. The situation suddenly seemed tragically ridiculous.

"Why have you never married, Catherine? Surely someone so lovely had many suitors."

She crossed and uncrossed her fingers, staring at them

for a long time before she flipped those potent eyes up to meet his. "I was once betrothed. Many years ago."

"What happened?"

"His horse spooked on a jump they'd made hundreds of times before. Ian was thrown. His neck was broken."

Derek grasped her hand. "I'm so sorry."

"It was a very long time ago."

"And there has been no one since then?"

"No," she said sadly. "All the other eligible young men in my village were betrothed to others."

"So he was your one chance."

"Or so I thought." After a moment of charged silence, she added, "I shock you with my candor."

"To the contrary. I find it refreshing."

"I am not a foolish young debutante, Jack. I am a fully grown woman who knows her own heart, who yearns for romance and passion, and who would rather be ruined by a decent, common man such as yourself than be the wife of a boorish aristocrat like Lindsey."

"What of love? Do you yearn, also, for love?"

She shrugged. "I had love once. I am no longer naïve enough to believe it is the most important element of a successful match."

"Prudent *and* practical."

"I have had to be both since my father announced his intention to marry me off to Lord Lindsey."

Derek's head was spinning. The woman of his dreams was offering herself to him with no reservations. Why then did he hesitate to take what she offered? "I would like to court you." The words were out of his mouth before his brain caught up. "As much as it is possible to court someone under these conditions."

"My father and Lindsey are no doubt looking for me."

"If they get close, we will know. I have men positioned throughout the estate. Any outsider will be brought to me immediately."

"And what will we do if they succeed in finding me?"

"Why don't we determine that if it happens? And in the meantime . . ."

"You would like to court me."

"With your permission, of course."

She smiled. "Permission granted. Whatever does courting entail under these circumstances?"

"I imagine we'll find out," he said, squeezing her hand. "Will you be all right here alone tonight?"

"Of course. I managed to survive on my own for three weeks, did I not?"

"I refuse to even imagine how you did that. I will have an armed footman positioned outside with orders to shoot should anyone trespass into your yard."

"That will allow me to sleep in peace."

He rose from the settee, even though everything in him yearned to stay. "I bid you farewell until the morrow."

She did something with her long eyelashes that stirred his deepest desires. "When you return shall we begin our courtship?"

"Indeed." Bending to add more logs to the fire, he turned to find that she had stood to walk him to the door.

"Mrs. Langingham tells me the seamstress from the village will be here in the morning to take measurements," she said.

"Then I shall aim to arrive after your meeting."

"I will await your arrival." At the door, he turned to her, intending to leave her with a quick kiss on the cheek. But she curled her arms around his neck and went up on her toes to better reach his mouth. One taste was all it took to once again make his head swim.

"Get some rest," he whispered when he was finally able to tear himself away.

"You do the same."

As Derek left her standing in the doorway, he wondered how he could possibly sleep with blood boiling in his veins and desire thrumming through his body. He swung up onto Hercules, tipped his hat at Catherine, turned and headed for home.

Chapter Seven

Catherine watched Jack ride off on his black stallion.
After a lifetime spent in stables, she appreciated the skill
with which he handled the high-spirited mount. She
couldn't help but smile when she noticed the way his
breeches hugged his muscular legs and backside. Yes, he
and his splendid horse were both finely made males.

She tempted him. Even an inexperienced woman recognized hunger in a man's eyes, and the knowledge filled her
with anticipation. How would she ever pass all the hours
until he returned?

Taking an anxious look around the yard and woods
beyond, Catherine stepped into the cottage and slid the
wooden lock into place. It certainly wouldn't keep out a
determined invader, but she would rest easier with the door
locked. She carried their tray into the kitchen and put
away the leftover cheese before draining the remnants of
her wine.

Fingering one of the dainty lace doilies on the small
kitchen table, Catherine noted the duke's grandmother had
fussy taste, reflected in the feminine furniture and details
in the small cottage. It was the perfect place to recover and
hide out until Lord Lindsey gave up on finding her.

For the first time since she had lost Ian, Catherine had romance on her mind. If only the infernal fever hadn't left her so weakened. She was anxious to be courted by the dashing Jack Bancroft and to continue looking for her grandmother's key. However, it would be a few days before her strength returned. Until then, she had to rest. Being still and inactive never had sat well with her, especially now that she was being courted by a devilishly handsome man. At least he would keep her entertained until she could resume the dig. The idea of *how* he might keep her entertained drew a nervous giggle from her.

She changed into a clean night rail Mrs. Langingham had provided and brushed her hair until it fell in shiny waves to her waist. Even though it was still early, she slid between cool sheets on the four-poster bed and took deep breaths to quiet her busy mind. What if he decided he didn't want a woman who all but threw herself at him? What if he decided he wanted a real lady and not a woman who pretended to be a lady while fancying travel and adventure and digging in the dirt for ancient artifacts?

Why did she have to be different from every other woman she knew? Why couldn't a home of her own and a husband and children be enough for her? She blamed the six-hundred books in the Hampshire library for opening the world to her. Now she wanted to see the pyramids in Egypt and the Parthenon in Greece and the Coliseum in Rome. It wasn't enough just to *read* about exotic places and people and food. She wanted to *see* and *taste* and *smell*. She wanted to *live*.

Would Jack understand that? Would he consider leaving his home and the duke to whom he was so loyal to go off with her? Catherine chuckled softly to herself. She'd known him two days and was already picturing them standing before the pyramids together. While she knew it was foolish to imagine such things, it had been so long since she'd had a foolish romantic thought that she chose to fully indulge in the fantasy.

In Egypt, they would ride camels and shop in the markets and eat couscous. They would stay in an elegant hotel and make love in the afternoon when it was too hot to be outdoors. Giddy with dreams, Catherine stretched her arms over her head and wallowed in the magic. He would kiss her and touch her and slide his manhood into her. Lost in the fantasy, she let her legs fall open and raised her hips to receive him. She released a ragged breath and closed her eyes, picturing how he would look propped over her, his handsome face tight with tension and strain as he made tender love to her.

The vision was so real that Catherine was certain if she opened her eyes he would be there, hovering above her, seeking entry to her most private place. Just thinking of him and how his naked skin would feel against hers started that odd throbbing between her legs, causing her to shiver and tremble. Reluctant to leave her dream, Catherine sighed and sunk deeper into the pillows. If she kept her eyes closed, she could spend the night in Egypt, lying in Jack's arms, drunk on love and adventure.

Her dream was so much better than the reality of that boorish Lord Lindsey finding her and dragging her off to whatever he had in mind for her. Trembling for different reasons, she closed her eyes tighter and refused to allow the nightmare to invade her dream. Jack would keep Lindsey away from her. He would protect her from the fiend.

Then they would go to Egypt.

Derek dismissed the groom and rubbed down Hercules himself. After filling the stall with fresh hay and refreshing the horse's feed bucket and water, Derek rubbed his nose and kissed him good night.

Hercules nickered in response, drawing a smile from his master.

Thinking about Catherine and what she'd shared with him, Derek walked across the yard to the kitchen door. Inside he wasn't surprised to find his cousin Simon helping himself to what he considered a "snack." The heaping ham sandwich on two slabs of thick bread would've been a meal for a normal man.

"Hey, old sod," Simon said, his mouth bulging. "What's had you out so late, or should I ask *who*?"

"I'm sure you already know perfectly well where I have been."

"For the first time in my life, I find myself anticipating my father's return. I expect the explosions will be quite spectacular."

"I would tell you to go straight to the devil, but I fear you would actually enjoy the trip."

"I'm wounded by your low opinion of me."

Derek laughed. "You can't fool me. I believe you are complimented by my low opinion of you."

Simon grunted out a laugh. "You know me too well, cousin."

Whereas Derek was tall and dark and muscular, Simon was fair and blond and lanky, with dimples the ladies positively swooned over. His lackadaisical approach to life made him one of Derek's preferred companions, but he wasn't the first person Derek turned to in times of need. Which made what he was about to ask of his cousin so hard to fathom.

Catherine's safety was at stake, and there was no one else he could ask. Hoping his cousin would rise to the occasion, Derek turned to him. "I need you to do something for me."

"As much as I adore lying to my father, I fear I don't have the stomach for it these days. He's so bloody concerned about your impending birthday that I refuse to engage in baiting him. It always comes back to bite me in the arse."

"It's not that." Derek leaned into the wooden counter and gripped the edge until his knuckles turned white. "Have you met Lord Lindsey?"

Simon scowled. "I'm sorry to say I have had the displeasure."

"Catherine is betrothed to him."

Simon froze mid-bite. "You cannot be serious."

"I'm afraid I am quite serious."

"I just lost my appetite." With a quarter of his sandwich remaining, Simon pushed away the plate. "What is it you want me to do?"

"Go to London. Do some sniffing around. Use that formidable charm of yours to ingratiate yourself with the *ton* and find out what you can about the Earl of Brisbane's missing daughter. Catherine believes they are looking for her but are keeping her 'disappearance' quiet to protect her reputation. I need to know what they're doing to find her and how close they are."

Simon sat back and studied his cousin. "And what's in this for you?"

"I promised to keep her safe. Lindsey all but attacked her, and she believes he would have raped her had she not kicked him in a most sensitive place."

Simon winced and crossed his legs. "Ouch."

"So he is scorned *and* angry. She is very much afraid of him."

"Pardon me for saying so, Derek, but I have never seen you so *interested* in the plight of a woman."

"I would provide aid and shelter to any woman under similar circumstances."

"If Lindsey discovers you have been harboring his fiancée, it could cause you condemnation in the House of Lords, not to mention a potential lawsuit."

"That is the very *least* of my concerns."

Simon raised an eyebrow, apparently surprised by Derek's lack of concern for the potential scandal. "You find this woman appealing?"

"Enormously."

"That," Simon said, laughing, "is surely a first, and potentially just in the nick of time to save us both, no?"

"Indeed. So you will help me?"

Simon gave him a curious look that had Derek wondering what his cousin could be thinking.

"You never ask anything of me, you know."

"I am aware of that, and I wouldn't ask now except that I don't dare leave her unprotected—"

"Of course I will help you, Derek. I am honored that you would trust me with such an important errand."

"I shall be eternally grateful for any information you are able to uncover. I probably don't have to tell you that time is of the essence."

"I understand. I will be off in the morning and will return immediately with anything that will help your cause."

"Thank you." They shook hands.

"It is high time you realized you don't have to carry your heavy burden alone. There is nothing I wouldn't do for you. You need only to ask."

Touched by his cousin's allegiance, Derek said, "Of course by helping me, you also may be protecting yourself from a fate worse than death."

"Thought hadn't crossed my mind, old chap."

Derek laughed. "Of course it hadn't." Long after Simon left the room, Derek stood there marveling over the amazing man his cousin kept hidden behind that lackadaisical façade. He finished the last of Simon's sandwich and then went to find one of the grooms to send him after Catherine's horse.

Chapter Eight

After seeing Simon off, Derek spent the morning reviewing tenant farm reports and considering several new investment opportunities. His practice was to read over the proposals and then set them aside for a few days until one or two nagged at him with their potential. In the years since he'd reached his majority and taken control of his holdings, Derek's investments had nearly tripled his already sizable fortune.

In fact, he would daresay he'd become one of the wealthiest men in all of England, not that adding to his fortune really mattered to him. Investing was all about the excitement of risk and the potential for tremendous benefit—along with spectacular failure. However, he hadn't experienced much of the latter, thanks to what some referred to as a golden touch, or as Simon liked to put it, a golden gut. Whatever you called it, it rarely led him astray.

Lately, he'd ventured into more esoteric areas by funding Sir Walter Green's expedition to Africa to dig for ancient civilizations. While a find would yield Derek no significant return on his sizable investment, the publicity and ensuing books would bring him much acclaim for his forward-thinking approach to investing. Besides, the expedition interested him, and he had the money to pursue a few interests even if he didn't have the luxury of accepting Sir Walter's very tempting invitation to join the dig.

Derek's uncle Anthony, who'd been furious over his interest in the Wright brothers and their "flying deathtrap," called the investment "another foolish waste of good money." Derek had long ago stopped letting his uncle's strong opinions influence his investment decisions. If he was to remain tethered to the land and his many obligations, then he intended to live vicariously through others who were doing the living and exploring.

At midday, he stood up from his chair and stretched. The remainder of *this* day was not about work, however, but about courtship, and his heart skipped with excitement. He had spent considerable time in his library, choosing volumes he thought she might enjoy to help pass the time during her recuperation. Amelia had packed a luncheon that, judging from the aromas wafting from the bags he'd strapped to Hercules's saddle, promised to be sumptuous.

Tying Sunny's lead to Hercules's saddle, Derek directed Hercules toward the cottage. After an all-but-sleepless night spent remembering the sweetness of her kisses, Derek couldn't wait to see Catherine again. As he approached the cabin, he slowed the horses, not wanting to seem too eager. His stomach fluttered with nerves and excitement and desire. In all his life, Derek Eagan, the Duke of Westwood, had never experienced all three of those emotions at the same time.

When he arrived in the yard, he waved to the footman he'd assigned to watch over her and signaled him to be off. The man scampered onto one of the stable horses and left the yard, tipping his hat at Derek as he went past.

Catherine must have heard the stampede of horse hooves because the door flew open, and there she was, wearing an ill-fitting pale green day dress and a welcoming smile. Her curls fell to her waist, a curtain of spun gold made more brilliant by the sunlight when she stepped outside to greet him. He loved that she had left her hair down rather than containing it the way fashionable women always did.

She let out a happy cry at the sight of Sunny and ran to her, hugging the horse as she wept with joy. "Thank you so much for finding her for me, Mr. Bancroft. I missed her terribly."

Sunny whinnied with pleasure at being reunited with Catherine.

Derek swung down from Hercules and secured both horses. "She seems to have missed you just as much."

"Did you sleep well?" she asked, looking up at him with those spectacular navy-blue eyes that caused his belly to flutter in awareness and his cock to harden.

Clearing his throat, he shook his head.

Alarm transformed her pretty face. "Why not?"

"Thoughts of a beautiful young lady invaded my sleep, making it impossible to do anything but think of her."

Catherine's pretty mouth twisted into a coy smile as she slipped her hand into the crook of his arm to lead him inside.

"Wait," he said, stopping her. "I come bearing gifts."

"Oh! I love gifts!"

"I figured you might." He untied the bags from his saddle and offered her his arm again. "That is a pretty dress, but it fits you rather poorly. Do I need to have words with the village seamstress?"

Catherine laughed at his scowl. "Oh no, she was most lovely and accommodating. Mrs. Langingham asked that she bring me several day dresses to wear while my new clothing is being made."

"In that case, I shall not chastise her, but rather hope that she works quickly to provide you with something that . . ."

"Better showcases my attributes?" Catherine asked with a saucy grin.

"From your mouth to God's ears."

"Why Jack Bancroft, that is a highly improper thought for a gentleman to entertain, let alone express to the lady he is courting."

He put his bags on the kitchen table and turned to find her right behind him.

Seeming to have a mind of their own, his arms encircled her narrow waist and brought her in close to him. "I find that most of my thoughts where you are concerned are highly improper."

Her eyes widened, her breath caught in her throat and her lips parted in anticipation.

Derek zeroed in on that pretty mouth. "I told myself I wouldn't kiss you the minute I arrived."

"Whyever not?"

"I wish to court you properly, the way a lady deserves to be courted."

Her arms wound around his neck, and her fingers sifted through his hair, sending a thrill straight to his cock. "If you were courting me properly, we'd have a chaperone, and your arms would most certainly not be around me just now."

Spurred by her encouragement, he drew her in closer to him. "We would cause a scandal," he whispered, bending his head to touch his lips to hers.

"Mmm," she whispered in reply, her eyes closing, "I so adore a good scandal."

He took her mouth then, intending to be gentle, until she tightened the fingers in his hair and thrust her tongue into his mouth. Derek's groan rumbled through him and echoed into her. His hands traveled from her back to her taut bottom, which he cupped to bring her in tighter against his arousal.

"Oh," she said, breathlessly, when they came up for air, "this is *highly* improper."

"Do you want me to stop?" he asked, fearing her reply.

"Absolutely not. Please do not stop."

"Catherine—" Whatever he was about to say was stolen when she initiated another torrid kiss. If he were thinking clearly, he'd have been surprised by such a passionate lady. The ladies he had known in his life tended to be tentative and prim when it came to kissing. He'd never yet met one who willingly used her tongue—at least he hadn't until now—and the impact all but knocked him off his feet. Emboldened by her response, he ran his hands over her ribs, stopping just below the swell of full breasts.

Needing to breathe, he tore his lips free and trailed kisses over her jaw and neck.

"Jack," she whispered, her tone urgent.

"Yes, my love?"

"Touch me." Her entire body vibrated beneath his hands. "Please touch me."

"I told myself I wouldn't rush this, that I would court you properly and marry you before I took anything more from you."

She drew in a ragged, deep breath, placed her hands over his on her ribs, and urged them up to cover her breasts.

With his hands full of plump, fleshy mounds, Derek's cock surged painfully. In all his many trysts with Kitty, he had never experienced this kind of wild desire. He ran his thumbs over the hardened tips, and Catherine's legs seemed to collapse beneath her. Derek scooped her up and carried her into the bedroom, stopping short when he realized he was about to make love to her in his grandmother's bed.

Pushing that unsettling thought from his mind, he rather hoped she would approve. She had wanted so badly for him to find his own true love, and he had ample reason to believe he had finally done just that.

Catherine clung to him, her arms wrapped tight around his neck, her face resting against his chest.

He laid her gently on the bed, hovering above her. "We will be married right away."

"Yes," she said, her eyes shining with unshed tears. "Yes, Jack, we will be married."

Every time she called him *Jack* a knife twisted in Derek's gut, setting off warning bells in his conscience. The gut he trusted and followed so diligently when investing didn't like this deception. It didn't like it one bit.

"And you are certain that this is what you want? To be married to me? To lay with me now the way a woman lays with a man?"

"I have never been more certain of anything in my life. When you touch me, my entire body becomes inflamed."

Her words were almost as seductive as her actions. When she tugged him down for another sensuous kiss, Derek abandoned any thought of waiting. He simply had to have her—in his bed, in his heart and in his life. He had known almost immediately that she would be different, that she would change everything. To resist her now would be foolish. Only she could fill the gaping emptiness inside him.

Hopefully, once she learned the truth about him, she would understand that he had hidden his identity to protect her from Lord Lindsey and to give them a chance to find out what they might have together. If she knew who he really was, she certainly wouldn't be unbuttoning his shirt and setting *his* entire body on fire with the brush of her fingers against his skin. She wouldn't have told him her secrets or trusted him with her fears. Had she learned his identity, she would have fled Westwood Hall and perhaps run right into the arms of her unscrupulous fiancé.

Perhaps he had been wrong to deceive her. Perhaps he would pay mightily for that deception when she learned the truth. But as she pressed delicate kisses to his neck and chest, he told himself it was a deception he didn't regret, for he had never experienced anything that could compare to the thrill of lying atop Catherine's lushness.

His lips found the curve of her neck, and he summoned the gentleness he would need for her.

She combed her fingers through his hair, firing his desires to a fever pitch. "Are you very experienced at this?" she asked shyly.

Startled by the question, he raised his head to find her eyes. "I have been with women, though not many."

"Good."

Derek smiled. "What is good? That I have lain with women or that I have not lain with many?"

"Both. I should hate for neither of us to have any idea what we are to do, but I am glad to have only a few of whom to be jealous."

"You need not be jealous of any other woman. I have never wanted any woman, or *anything*, for that matter, more than I want you."

She gazed up at him, her heart in her eyes. "How can that be when we have only just met?"

"I cannot begin to understand it myself. I only know that after the first time I kissed you, I knew I would never again want to kiss anyone else."

"Oh, Jack," she sighed, her hands moving with provocative intent over his chest. "You say the sweetest things."

"You are certain you wouldn't rather wait to have relations until after we are married?"

"Is it possible to be married soon?"

"I will apply for a special license today, so perhaps by tomorrow, the next day at the latest, we can have the local vicar marry us." There would be hell to pay with Lindsey, but Derek would worry about that later. He couldn't yet think of the hell he'd have to pay when his wife discovered whom she'd really married. That, too, was a thought for another day.

"If that is the case," she said, trailing a finger from his chest to his belly, "does it really make a difference if we wait?"

"I wish to treat you only with the utmost respect and decorum, but I seem to keep failing in that regard."

Her eyes narrowed with what seemed to be despair. "How can you say that? You have provided me with safety and shelter and more affection than I have received in longer than I can remember."

"But I have also been forward and improper at times."

"And I have encouraged your forwardness and impropriety, so we are equally guilty."

Derek smiled. How could he not? He had never been happier or more content. Finally, he had found a woman whom he could not only talk to, but who endlessly entertained him and fired his desires like no one else ever had. Since they had worked out as many of the details as they could at that moment, he decided to attend to those desires. He reached for the first button to her dress.

Catherine gasped at the brush of his fingers over her sensitive skin.

"I don't wish to hurt you," he said, kissing a trail from her neck to her upper chest.

"You couldn't."

"The first time can be painful for a woman. Have you, did you, your mother . . ." Sighing, he rested his head on her shoulder. "You turn me into a bumbling fool."

She giggled softly at his distress. "You wish to know if my mother ever spoke to me about what transpires between a man and woman in their marriage bed."

"Yes," he said, relieved that she had been able to express it so eloquently.

"She did not speak to me for she had no reason to. Ian was killed weeks before our wedding."

"So you don't know what to expect?"

"I never said that." She flashed that coy smile he was beginning to love. "I have read. Somewhat extensively."

"Ah, yes, the six-hundred books."

Her cheeks flushed to a delightful shade of pink. "And I have worked with horses."

"Well, then, you are as prepared as any lady can be."

Her stern expression made him want to laugh. "Are you mocking me?"

"No," he whispered, returning to the sweet succor of her mouth. "I am most assuredly not mocking you."

"Jack," she said, sighing, "when you kiss me that way, my entire body trembles."

"Then I suspect you will like when I kiss you elsewhere." Derek yearned to hear his real name whispered from her lips in the throes of passion, but he reminded himself that he couldn't tell her. Not yet. Not until he had assured her safety. He finished unbuttoning her dress and helped her up so he could slide it off her shoulders. The thin muslin of her shift did little to hide her enticing curves, and once again, Derek had to remind himself to savor when he would've preferred to devour.

They worked together to remove her dress and his shirt.

She stared at him with reverence in her eyes. "You are so beautiful."

"Men are not beautiful," he said, embarrassed by her effusiveness.

"You are the exception." Running her hands over his chest and arms, examining each muscle in detail, she had him on the verge of release within seconds.

Desperate to regain control, Derek helped her up to remove her shoes and roll the stockings down her legs, leaving her covered only by the shift and thin drawers. He took her delicate foot in his much larger hand and pressed a kiss to her arch.

She giggled uncontrollably.

"Is my darling ticklish?" he asked.

"Terribly."

"Then I shan't torment you any further." He moved his mouth to the inside of her ankle before turning his attention to her calf. By then she was no longer laughing, but rather panting and squirming. Derek loved her responsiveness and was delighted to know that she desired him every bit as much as he desired her.

"You have found a new way to torment me," she said as he paid homage to the back of her knee.

He chuckled softly. "I have only begun to torment you, my love."

"Am I your love, Jack?"

"I do believe you could well be the love of my life, Catherine. The very reason I was born."

A shudder rippled through her entire body as she attempted to blink back tears. "I had despaired of ever finding you."

"I have been right here," he whispered against her trembling thigh, "all this time. Waiting for you to find me." Moving slowly, so as not to startle her, he slid her drawers down past slender hips and long legs and flung them over his shoulder. He smoothed his hands along the creamy skin of her thighs, pushing the shift up as he went. When he uncovered the thatch of pale blond hair at the apex of her thighs, his mouth went dry and his heart all but leapt from his chest.

She watched everything he did with eyes open wide with passion and shock and what he hoped was pleasure. He wanted nothing more than to sate her with more pleasure than she'd ever imagined possible. Pushing the shift up farther, he revealed her a bit at a time by laying a path of hot, openmouthed kisses on her belly. Just as he was about to uncover her breasts, she stopped him, and he noticed she was suddenly breathing hard.

"Do you wish me to stop, Catherine? We don't have to—"

"No, I don't wish to stop. I just need a moment to catch my breath."

He pressed his lips to the softness of her belly. "Take all the time you need, my sweet."

She surprised him a minute later when she reached for the hem of her shift and tugged it over her head, leaving her completely bare to his worshipful gaze.

"I have never seen anything more beautiful." His eyes skimmed over her, settling on her copious breasts with pretty pink nipples. He cupped the satin mounds and ran his lips in circles around the crowns, denying her the contact she craved. Her hips surged against him, driving him mad with desire. Finally, when it seemed that neither of them could survive another minute of teasing, he dipped his head and sucked one nipple deep into his mouth while rolling the other between his fingers.

She cried out, but held his head tight against her chest, letting him know he was to continue. It was just as well since he couldn't possibly stop now. Not after sampling her sweetness. He sucked and licked and lightly rolled her nipple between his teeth. By the time he raised his head to sample the other side, her well-loved nipple had turned a deep, dark pink. Derek blew on it, drawing another cry from her.

"Oh, Lord," she whispered as he gave her other breast the same attention. "I had no idea it would be so . . ."

"So what, love?"

"Consuming. *All*-consuming."

"It isn't always. Not like this."

"Then we are a good match?"

"We are a *very* good match," he said, eager to prove to her just how good a match they were. "Do you trust me, Cat?"

"Oh yes. *Yes!* I trust you with my life, Jack!"

"Then let me show you how truly all-consuming it can be."

Chapter Nine

As Jack suckled and licked the tips of her breasts, Catherine was quite certain she had died and gone straight to heaven. That this big, beautiful, thoughtful man wanted her so desperately still came as a shock after living most of her life in the shadow of her younger and much more attractive sister. Wait until Madeleine feasted her eyes on the man who would be Catherine's husband!

Her husband! Jack Bancroft. Mrs. Jack Bancroft. Catherine Bancroft. *Oh God*, she thought, as he continued to cup her breasts while kissing his way to her belly.

Did she trust him? Good Lord, she had never trusted anyone more than this fine, wonderful man who had been so incredibly good to her. She would give him anything he asked for, anything at all. But surely he couldn't mean to . . . *"Jack!"*

"You trust me, remember?" This he said as his broad shoulders forced her legs farther apart than Catherine had ever had them. What a shameful and sinfully good feeling to have his chest hair tickling her most sensitive region.

"Yes," she stammered. "I trust you, but certainly you

can't . . . Oh! Oh *God!*" His tongue scorched a trail between her legs—long, sensuous licks of heat and fire. "*Jack!*"

"Relax and let me love you, Cat."

She *loved* that he had chosen a nickname for her that no one else had ever used. Kate and Katie, yes, but never Cat. That belonged only to him. She tried to heed his advice, but the sensation of his tongue, licking her *there* . . . How did one *ever* relax when that was being done to them? And then he found a spot that seemed to be the very center of her, a place she hadn't even known existed until she met him and began to feel those odd twinges and tingles and throbs right *there*. Oh, yes, yes, *yes!*

At this point she no longer cared that she must resemble a total wanton. Her legs flew open even wider, her hips came off the bed to get *closer*. Oh what, *what* was happening to her? "Jack! *Jack!*"

And then he slid a finger deep inside her, and Catherine imploded, shattering into tiny glimmering pieces of the person she had been before him, before them, before this. As aftershocks ricocheted from her hands to her feet to her breasts to her core and everywhere in between, her body glistened with sweat, her heart galloped relentlessly and she was reborn. Here, in the stark light of day, he had changed her forever.

"Jack," she whispered.

He kissed his way from her belly to her breasts and then her mouth. "I am here, love. I am right here."

She tasted her essence on his tongue as he kissed her deeply. "Wh-What happened to me?"

"You experienced fulfillment, my sweet."

"It was *so* . . ."

He laughed at her fumbling attempt to describe the indescribable.

"Spectacular," she decided. "It was spectacular."

"Yes, it was."

She was finally able to bring herself to make eye contact with him, and heat flooded her overly sensitive body. "Did you too?"

"Not yet."

"But you said it was spectacular!"

"Watching you reach your fulfillment was perhaps the most spectacular thing I have ever experienced."

Imagining how she must have appeared to him caused her face to go hot with mortification.

"Don't be ashamed, Cat. Don't ever be ashamed of how we express our love for each other. Promise me."

"I promise, Jack." She reached for him and ran her hands over his back, coming to a stop at the waist to his breeches. "Can we, are you, do you want to—"

He kissed the words off her swollen lips. "Yes, I want to." Reaching for the buttons, he freed himself and kicked off his remaining clothing. "I really, really want to."

At the sight of his straining member, Catherine's eyes widened and her heart quickened. "But it will never fit!"

"Oh, believe me, my love," he said, laughing, "it *will* fit."

"How?" She squirmed about in an effort to get free of him. "How in the world will it fit?"

He lay on his side and turned her to face him. "You said before that you trusted me?"

She met his gaze and nodded, even as a surge of fear nearly took her breath away.

"Then trust me when I tell you it *will* fit, and it will only hurt for a brief moment before it feels very, very good. I promise."

Though she wanted so badly to believe him, Catherine shook from head to toe. Nothing had ever seemed more tempting or more off-putting at the same time. While she anticipated the pain, he seemed to be in no particular hurry, starting all over again with carnal kisses that began the throbbing between her legs anew.

The sensation of his much larger, much stronger body pressed tight against hers, the feel of his hands caressing her breasts, his warm, clean, masculine scent overwhelmed her. Her every sense was on full alert, waiting and anticipating. Now that she knew what to expect at the end she wondered if it would happen again. He hooked her leg over his hip, opening her to questing fingers that slid in and out of her effortlessly.

"Do you feel that?" he whispered. "Your body is ready for me."

Catherine tried to believe she was ready for him, but still she trembled uncontrollably. "You will be gentle?"

"Always." He shifted them so he was poised between her legs.

The blunt head of his shaft pressing against her swollen flesh made her tense up. "Relax, love," he whispered in her ear. "Let me in."

Catherine took a deep, ragged breath and tried to force her lower body to relax.

Jack pressed harder this time, and her body burned and stretched as it accommodated him.

When he retreated, Catherine knew a moment of relief before he entered her again, surging deeper this time.

"That's it, my love," he whispered. "That's it."

His face was rigid, his eyes closed tight, his lips parted. To Catherine, he had never been more fiercely attractive.

She framed his face with her hands and brought his

mouth to meet hers as he pushed forward before retreating again. Just as she became accustomed to the pressure below and the thrusts of his tongue into her mouth, he pressed into her again, farther than before, and a deep, searing pain stole the breath from her lungs. She tore her lips free and cried out, tears seeping from her eyes.

He held her tight against him. "That was it, my darling. That was the beginning and the end of the pain."

By now, Catherine was drenched with sweat, some hers and some his, as he slid into her again before retreating almost completely. When he didn't come back the way he had before, she forced her eyes open to find him gazing down at her. "Why did you stop?"

"I can't bear to hurt you. It hurts me almost as much as it does you."

At that moment, Catherine was certain that she loved him. She found his waist and shifted her hands lower, cupping his muscular buttocks and encouraging him to continue.

With a low growl he entered her fully.

"Oh!" she cried. "Oh you were right. It does feel wonderful!"

Her confession seemed to shatter what remained of Jack's control. He pumped into her, urging her up again to that place he had taken her once before. The crisis grew and multiplied until there was nothing left but him, deep inside her, taking her where she could only go with him. Catherine raised her hips from the bed and met his final thrust, the one that completed her transformation and made her his forever.

* * *

Derek knew he should move, that he must be crushing her, but nothing in his body seemed to work anymore.

Her hands moved languidly over his back in light caresses that made him feel loved and cared for and finally, finally *home*. She was his home, and he was ever more grateful that he had never buckled under the enormous pressure to marry someone acceptable to everyone but him. For now he knew that no one but Catherine McCabe would have sufficed.

Dragging himself out of the stupor, he remembered that he needed to care for her. Somehow he managed to raise his head. Her eyes were closed, and her lips curved into a satisfied smile that warmed his heart.

Derek bent his head and kissed that smile.

Her eyes fluttered open, and for a long breathless moment, they simply absorbed each other.

"Are you all right?" he asked.

"I am divine."

"Do you hurt?"

"It was worth any discomfort."

"Was the discomfort substantial?"

Her fingers danced over his face, as if she were memorizing every plane and texture. "The *pleasure* was substantial."

Despite her moan of protest, he finally withdrew from her and kissed her again. "Stay here. I will be right back."

"Where are you going?"

"Do not fret, my love." Still unclothed, he went to the fireplace in the sitting room to heat a pan of water. When it was warm, he moistened a towel and carried it back into the bedroom, wishing he'd had a water closet installed here when he'd done so at the main house. Catherine had covered herself and rolled onto her side.

Derek brushed the silky strands off her face and kissed each closed eye. "I need to tend to you."

Her eyes flipped open. "How do you mean?"

He eased the covers down.

She tried to stop him.

Reaching for her hands, he moved them to her sides. "A little late for modesty now, is it not?" Chuckling, he watched a blush color her fair skin as he finished uncovering her and eased her legs apart.

"Jack, honestly. This is not necessary."

Derek applied the warm compress to her tender flesh.

"Oh, *oh*. That is *heavenly*." He smiled, transfixed by her ardent reactions to every new experience.

"Open for me, love."

Catherine eased her feet farther apart, and Derek bathed her with loving care. "You are never to be embarrassed by how we express our love for each other, remember?"

"I never imagined we would express our love in this particular way."

"I have only just begun to express my love for you."

She reached for his free hand and brought it to her lips. "I must be the luckiest woman in all of England. Perhaps all the world."

"I am surely the luckiest man." Her smile faded, and her eyes shifted away from him.

"What just occurred to you?"

"I fear it can't last. Nothing this lovely and perfect can possibly last."

"Of course it will last. We will laugh and love and live together and bring children into the world and live to be old and gray and never stop laughing and loving."

"You are so certain."

"I have never been more certain of anything in my life."

"You make me believe it is possible."

"It is entirely possible." Turning the compress, he pressed the warmth against her.

"I must leave you now to obtain the special license we will need and to make arrangements for our nuptials."

"How long will you be gone?"

"Several hours. I will hasten to return to you with all due speed."

"I don't want you to go. I fear you will leave and you won't come back. Somehow I will lose you."

He caressed her soft cheeks. "Is that what happened with Ian?"

Her small nod tugged at his heart. "His brother Giles invited him to go riding, and he promised he would be back before tea time." She focused on the curtain billowing over the open window but was far away, lost in her memories. "I waited for him. I didn't have my tea because I wanted to dine with him. It got dark, and still I waited."

"How did you learn about the accident?"

"Giles came. I could see right away that he had been crying."

Derek gripped her hand. "It must have been a terrible shock."

"I didn't believe it. They had to take me to him, so I could see for myself."

"Catherine," he whispered. "I am so sorry."

She turned her gaze on him. "It was a very long time ago."

"That kind of pain never goes away entirely."

"You seem to know all too well."

"I lost my parents when I was very young." The words were out of his mouth before he remembered that he hadn't planned to tell her Derek's story. He was wading into dangerous territory here.

Her eyes softened with sympathy and concern. "What happened to them?"

"They were in a carriage accident. Their horses were spooked by a gunshot. I take comfort in knowing they died in each other's arms."

"Who cared for you?"

"My grandmother, uncle and aunt, though my aunt has been in poor health for many years."

"But you missed having a family of your own."

Her perception sliced through him, cutting him to the quick and loosening his tongue. "I was a twin."

She gasped and tightened her hold on his hand. "Oh, Jack."

"I never knew him. My brother, I mean. He died at birth."

"But you've always missed him."

He stared at her. "Yes. How is it possible to miss someone you never even knew?"

She brought his hand to her lips and kissed each knuckle. "He was a part of you."

"All my life, I have had an aching, empty hole inside me that nothing could ever fill." Brushing a light kiss over her lips, he added, "Until now."

She still clutched his hand. "If I let you go, do you promise to come back?"

"I promise to come back. As soon as I can." Derek got up to find his breeches and pulled them on. "In the meantime, I brought books and food."

"You brought me books."

He held his shirt against his chest. "Is that all right?"

"That is the nicest thing you could have done for me."

"You are very easy to please." Derek finished dressing and sat on the bed to put on his boots. "I find it difficult to leave you."

"I will be right here waiting for you."

"In that case, I shall go and hurry back."

"Please do."

He bent down to leave her with one last kiss. "My whole life, Catherine," he said, caressing her cheek, "has led to you. I *will* be back."

Chapter Ten

Derek, Hercules and Sunny emerged from the wooded thicket just as two men on horses turned away from the manor and headed down the long driveway. "Whoa, boy." Derek brought Hercules to a halt, so he could watch them depart. They had gotten past the guards he'd positioned on the property, a realization that filled him with fear for Catherine's safety.

He waited until they were farther down the lane before he spurred Hercules forward, bypassing the stable on the way to the main entrance. He swung down off the horse and took the stairs two at a time while both horses looked on.

Rutledge met him at the door. "Oh, Your Grace. Thank goodness you are here."

"Who was that?" Derek asked, even though he already knew.

"Lord Lindsey is searching for his missing fiancée." Rutledge's wise old eyes surveyed Derek. "Judging from his description, she bears a striking resemblance to Lady Catherine."

Derek swore under his breath. "What did you tell him?"

"That no one meeting her description has been here."

"Good. Thank you." Derek paced the foyer, his heart racing as he realized there was no time for a special license. They had to leave right away for Gretna Green in Scotland where they could be married under less restrictive rules. Derek rattled off a list of what they'd need, and asked Rutledge to see to the carriage.

He thought of Catherine, waiting for him at the cottage, and of Lindsey being so close by. "When everything is ready, send the carriage to the cottage. I can't leave her there unprotected. Not when he's nearby."

"Very well, Your Grace."

"Hurry, Rutledge. I need to get her out of here. Tonight."

"I understand."

"Please ask one of the footmen to see to Catherine's horse Sunny. Return her to the stables."

"Yes, Your Grace."

After stopping in his study to grab his pistols and ammunition, Derek sprinted out of the house and swung up onto Hercules as a footman led Sunny to the stables. Almost as if he understood his master's urgency, the horse took off at a run to the cottage. Every minute it took to cover the short distance felt like a year to Derek. What if Lindsey hadn't left the estate? What if he and his henchman had ventured off the road and discovered the cottage? What if he got there and she was gone?

"Hurry, boy. Please hurry." With the horse giving him everything he had, Derek held on tight to the reins and gave him his head.

When the little cottage came into view, Derek jumped from the horse and took off running. Oh God, the door was open.

"Catherine! *Catherine!*" He tore into the house. It took no time at all to discover she wasn't there. "No, no. *No*, God, please." His stomach surged with revulsion as he imagined what she might endure at the hands of that monster. "Catherine."

He ran back into the yard just as she emerged from the garden carrying an armful of wildflowers. Derek blinked her into focus, not sure if she was real or a dream. Either way, he ran to her. Only when she was crushed to his chest with her sweet fragrance and that of the flowers invading his senses did he believe she was real.

"Jack! What is it? You're back so soon!"

Overwhelmed with relief, Derek could barely breathe, let alone speak. Still holding her, he focused on pulling air into his lungs.

She drew back from him and raised her hand to his face. "What is it?"

"Lindsey." A breath that resembled a sob shook his body as he tried to gather himself. "He's been to Westwood Hall looking for you."

The flowers dropped to her feet, and the color drained from her face. "He can't find me."

He swept a hand over her long hair. "He won't. We're leaving. Tonight. We'll go to Gretna Green and be married right away. Once you're my wife, he'll have no claim on you. You'll be safe. I promise."

"He's a powerful man. If you cross him—"

"I am not the slightest bit afraid of him. We will be legally married. He won't be able to touch you."

"I haven't any clothing, certainly nothing I can be married in."

"We'll go through the dowager duchess's belongings. I'm certain there will be something you can use."

"I can't use her things. They don't belong to us."

"The duke wouldn't mind. He would want me to use everything at my disposal to protect you." Derek tugged her hand to lead her into the house. "We have to hurry, though. Something brought the viscount here today, so he must know you are in the area."

He kept a firm grip on her hand until they were in the bedroom. In the closet, he found a carpetbag and was grateful he'd insisted that his grandmother's things be kept exactly where she had left them. For years, he'd intended to clean out her belongings, to make the cottage available to one of his employees, but he'd never been able to bring himself to actually do it. Maybe he'd somehow known that one day he would need to borrow from the past to enable the future.

He found shifts and stockings and several gowns that looked as if they might fit Catherine passably. In the back of the closet he located several more dresses that he dragged out to examine more closely. Between a burgundy velvet evening gown and a yellow day dress was an antique lace dress. "Oh, look! I'll wager that this was her wedding dress." He held it up to get a better look. "What do you think?"

Derek turned to find Catherine sitting on the edge of the bed, her hands tightly clasped in her lap, her face devoid of color. "Darling, what is it? Do you not like the dress? You don't have to wear it if you do not like it." He reached for her hand, which was icy. "Catherine?"

"You don't have to do this," she said softly.

"What don't I have to do?"

"Marry me. Just because we had relations doesn't mean—"

He silenced her with a kiss. "I *want* to marry you. I want that more than anything. I'm not just doing this because of Lindsey."

She looked up at him. "You're not?"

"Cat, I *love* you. I want to sleep with you and wake up with you and have children with you and talk with you and eat with you and be with you every day for the rest of my life."

"You're sure?"

He sat beside her, put his arm around her and brought her head to rest on his shoulder. "Unless you don't want to marry *me*."

"Of course I want to marry you."

Derek closed his eyes tight against the surge of emotion. "And you won't be sad not to have your family there?"

"They're caught up in the Season at the moment."

"We can do it again later." Derek told himself they *would* do it again when she knew *exactly* whom she was marrying. Right now, all that mattered was her safety. That she would also be solving his biggest problem was of little concern to him when stacked against her safety. "You can invite anyone you want to our real wedding."

She forced a smile.

"We have a long trip ahead of us." He held up the lace dress. "Shall we take it?"

"As long as you are sure the duke won't mind if we borrow his grandmother's clothing."

He tipped his head to kiss her. "I'm quite certain he won't mind."

Catherine wanted him to ride in the carriage with her, but Derek was leaving nothing to chance. With his pistols loaded and one of them lying across his lap, he and Hercules followed the carriage. Derek eyed every bush and tree, expecting Lindsey to come bursting through the brush line at any moment, demanding that Derek turn Catherine over to him. The very thought of it made Derek's skin crawl.

By the time they stopped at an inn to have a meal and acquire a new team of horses, Derek was ready to snap from the strain. His every muscle was on fire after hours of sitting rigidly in the saddle, and his eyes burned from the trail dust as well as from barely blinking in his vigilance.

Only the sight of his betrothed could calm him and remind him of why they were making this journey to Scotland. This time tomorrow she'd be his wife, for better or worse. That thought settled his racing heart as he ducked his head into the carriage to see to Catherine.

"Jack, honey?" She brushed the hair from his brow. "You're so tired. Why don't we stay here tonight so you can get some rest?"

He shook his head. "We have to keep going. I'm sorry, my love."

"Whatever for?"

"Certainly no woman dreams of a wedding that requires hours in a carriage and no time for a decent bed in which to rest."

Her lips fluttered with amusement. "I believe every woman would dream of running away in the night to marry a handsome man who thinks of her safety before his own comfort."

"You flatter me, my lady."

"I adore you, kind sir."

Derek smiled and swore his heart did a full somersault in his chest. "In that case, let me feed my fiancée while the stablemen see to the horses." He extended his hand to help her from the carriage. Her fingers closed around his, and she gazed up at him with a look of love that reminded him of why they were doing this. Was it really only three nights ago that he'd stood in a stuffy ballroom despairing of ever finding exactly what he now had with her?

His stomach ached when he thought of the deception that stood between them, threatening everything. Hopefully, by the time she learned whom she had really married,

Derek would've made himself essential to her. Even if she were furious, she would still be his wife.

Ushering her into the cozy inn, he told himself everything would be just fine. It had to be. The alternative was no longer imaginable.

Arriving in Gretna Green early the next morning, they went directly to the home of the local magistrate. While Catherine changed into his grandmother's wedding dress, Derek pondered the surreal aspects of this momentous day. All his life, he had been groomed and prepared for the moment he would take a wife, begin his family and ensure the continuation of the dukedom. He'd expected that once he chose his bride, the banns would be read and a wedding would occur a month hence in the stone chapel where generations of Eagans had been baptized, married and sent to their final reward.

Never had Derek imagined a five-minute exchange of vows in a dark room without even a ring to give his new wife. The room might have been dark, but a glow of love and excitement surrounded Catherine. Listening to her vow to love, honor and obey Jack Bancroft, Derek realized he would've given everything he owned to hear her pledge her undying love to him, Derek Eagan, the Duke of Westwood.

The very minute they returned to Westwood Hall, he would rectify the ring situation. The other situation, however, would be far more complicated to rectify. In the meantime, Derek ensured that Catherine signed the register before him. Once she moved to the parlor where the magistrate's wife was pouring tea, Derek signed his real name next to hers and then stood there staring at their two names, filled with relief and satisfaction and dismay, before joining his wife.

Catherine let loose with a lusty laugh that settled him.

She looked over at him just then, beckoning with her sweet smile and an outstretched hand.

As the very sight of her calmed the storm brewing inside him, Derek went to her and took the hand she offered. For the first time since he had lost his parents so suddenly, he felt whole again. The empty places within him had been filled, and there was nothing, nothing at all, he wouldn't do to keep her by his side for every one of his remaining days.

"What is it, my love?" Catherine asked, looking up at him a short time later as they prepared to leave the magistrate's home. "You're tight with tension." Adding a coquettish smile, she said, "You aren't already regretting your hasty marriage, are you?"

He brought her hand to his lips. "I will *never* regret my hasty marriage."

The comment was rewarded with the bright smile he'd come to crave. "Tell me, my dear husband, will we have an equally hasty honeymoon?"

Gazing down at her, Derek's blood boiled with lust at the look of blatant desire he saw on her lovely face. "The honeymoon shall be so hasty that if you blink, you might just miss it."

Catherine laughed, and he covered the hand that clutched his arm so tightly. "I definitely do *not* want to miss it."

Derek swallowed hard as anticipation and desire all but took his breath away. His coachman had taken charge of finding a suitable place for the newlyweds to spend the night—nothing fancier than an estate manager might be able to afford—and the man was waiting for them when they emerged from the magistrate's residence. After offering his heartfelt congratulations to the newly married couple, the coachman led them down a side street to a cozy inn that he said came highly recommended. Since being alone with his new wife was Derek's top priority at the moment, he slipped his man a guinea and patted him on the shoulder. "Check in with me tomorrow afternoon."

"Yes, Your—"

Derek scowled at him.

"Mr. Bancroft," the man mumbled before he scurried off, no doubt to find a pub in which to spend the tip.

The innkeeper was so delighted to welcome the newly married couple into his humble establishment that Derek suspected his man had informed the innkeeper of his true identity. "My wife would enjoy a hot bath after our long journey," Derek said, delighting in saying "my wife" for the very first time.

"Right away, *sir*." The man sent him a conspiratorial wink and grin to let him know he was in on the secret, forcing Derek to scowl at him, too.

In a matter of minutes, a bevy of maids had appeared, carrying a large metal tub and steaming pots of water, while Derek wished he'd instructed his man to find a place with actual plumbing. He'd gotten spoiled having it at home.

Watching the goings-on intently, Catherine nibbled her bottom lip and pulled the pins from her hair, sending ropes of blond silk cascading down her back.

Derek sat to remove his boots but kept one eye on his lovely bride. When the flurry of maids departed, Catherine seemed suddenly shy and uncertain. Derek got up and went to her.

"What is it, my love?"

"Your duke must be very powerful if his employees receive this type of treatment."

Of all the things he thought she might say, that wasn't one of them.

"I'm sure the word rippled through the village when the duke's carriage arrived." He leaned in to kiss her softly.

"Now how about we get you into that tub before the water cools."

She turned her back to him. "Would you mind?"

Derek stared at the daunting row of buttons that joined two panels of delicate lace and reached for the top button. "How in the world did you get into this so quickly?"

"The magistrate's wife was quite handy."

"I'd say so." He nuzzled the smooth skin on her neck as his oddly clumsy fingers fumbled with the buttons. Derek groaned, which made her giggle. "How can I find the man who first decided to put so many confounded buttons on a wedding dress and throttle him?"

"Do you suppose the duke's grandfather once asked that very question on his wedding day?"

The question stopped Derek mid-button. He swallowed hard. "If he found his wife half as delightful and desirable as I find mine, I'm certain he was equally frustrated."

She released an impatient sigh. "Hurry, Jack."

Hearing her call him Jack brought back the hollowed-out feeling he'd lived with for so long and reminded him once again of his deception. Telling himself it was worth it to keep her safe from Lindsey, he pushed those unsettled thoughts aside to concentrate on the task at hand and quickly finished with the buttons. With his hands on her shoulders, he nudged the dress into a puddle at her feet, leaving her in only a serviceable shift.

She turned to him, arms folded across her breasts, cheeks pink with embarrassment. "I wish I had something prettier to wear for you tonight."

Derek vowed in that moment that she would have the finest of everything—silks and satins and velvets. One day, he hoped she'd embrace her new standing as his duchess. Until then, unadorned muslin was as enticing as anything he'd ever seen, he thought as he bent to retrieve the priceless dress from the floor. "You need nothing more than you yourself to please me tonight, my lovely wife." As if it were something they had done hundreds of times before, he helped her out of the shift and into the tub.

Slipping into the warm water, she let out a satisfied moan that sent a jolt of desire straight to his already hardened cock.

He knelt down next to the tub. With his eyes fixed on her face, he rolled up the sleeves of his white linen shirt.

She watched his every move, her lips parted in anticipation. Raising her arm from the side of the tub, she ran her fingers languidly through his hair, the gesture so loving and tender it brought a lump to his throat. How long had it been since anyone had touched him so lovingly? More years than he cared to count.

"What are you thinking, my darling?" she asked softly.

"That since my grandmother died, no one has caressed my hair or called me their darling."

Her eyes softened with emotion. "Then I shall do so every day for the rest of your life."

Taking her roving hand, he pressed his lips to the palm. "Nothing would please me more." Would he still be her darling when she learned he was the duke? God, he hoped so, but deep inside a terrible coil of fear sent chills up his spine. Now that he had found her, how would he ever do without her? And it wasn't enough to just *have* her. No, he wanted her heart, her soul and her love.

She ran a finger over his furrowed brow. "So very serious."

Startled from his thoughts, he smiled at her imitation of his serious face.

"Your face is utterly transformed by that rakish grin."

"Is that so?"

"Mmm."

He helped her to wash her long hair and then dried it with a towel by the fire before dipping into the tepid water to wash the dust and road dirt from his own body. In the candlelight, his wife watched him from the four-poster bed. Her eager expression had him rushing through a quick shave.

She looked so trusting, so certain of the enormous step they had taken together that day—just the third day since they had first set eyes on each other—and suddenly, Derek couldn't bear the deception a moment longer. He couldn't bear that trusting expression on her face when almost everything he'd told her had been a lie. Wrapping the damp towel around his waist, he forced his gaze to meet hers.

"There is something I must tell you."

Chapter Eleven

Catherine had watched his expression become deeply troubled. Whatever was bothering him, however, tonight was not the time for such worries. They had a lifetime ahead to contend with whatever concerns might arise. She had no doubt that he loved her and was pleased to be married to her. Tonight, that was more than enough for her.

She sat up in bed, let the covers drop to her waist, and held out her arms to him.

At the sight of her naked breasts, an expression of needy hunger stole the furrow from his brow.

"Come to me, my love," she whispered.

Jack released the towel and slid naked between the cool sheets. Reaching for her, he wrapped his strong arms around her and buried his face in her hair.

As a light dusting of chest hair tickled her nose, she breathed in the clean scent of citrus and leather that only added to his overwhelming appeal.

"We need to talk," he said.

"Tomorrow." She ran a hand up and down his muscular back, wanting to memorize each detail of her husband's magnificent body. "We'll have all the time in the world to talk about whatever has you so troubled."

He looked directly at her. "I haven't the first regret about marrying you, Cat. I hope you know that."

The heated erection pressing against her provided adequate proof that he spoke the truth. "Of course I do. Nor have I any regrets." She ran her fingers through his hair in a gesture of comfort more than seduction. "None at all."

As they lay on their sides facing each other, his lips moved on her neck, sending desire darting through her, while his hands stroked her back and cupped her bottom.

"Jack," she gasped, tightening her arms around his neck, overwhelmed by the feel of his warm skin against hers. How was it that just a few days ago she had never known such desire, and now she could no longer conceive of a life without it?

He turned them, so he was on top, gazing down at her. "I never imagined this, Catherine."

"What didn't you imagine?"

"That I would find a wife whom I love and desire the way I do you."

The softly spoken words brought tears to her eyes. "And I never imagined that my father's elevation to the aristocracy, his boorish behavior and my hideous alliance with my former fiancé would lead me to you."

Jack's smile transformed his face. "One never knows, does one?"

Catherine returned his smile. "Certainly not. How so many bad things can lead to the very best thing."

He dipped his head to tease her nipple with his lips and tongue. "The very best thing indeed." Continuing the sensual torture, he said, "I had planned to kiss you everywhere and make you moan the way you did yesterday, but

I find that I want to be inside you more than I want my next breath."

Stirred by his words and the emotion behind them, she reached for him. "Then don't wait, Jack. Don't wait."

As he slid his pulsating member through the dampness between her legs, his face tightened with tension. When he pushed into her, the tension seemed to leave him. "Nothing has ever felt better than this."

If she could have spoken, Catherine would have agreed.

"Does it hurt, my love?" he asked, concern once again marking his features.

Catherine reached up to caress the worry from his face. "It feels heavenly." That seemed to spark something primal in him, and he began to move with more purpose. The tingling sensation between her legs began anew, but this time, knowing it would lead to paradise, Catherine welcomed the intense rush. Gripping his broad shoulders, she encouraged his fierce possession by lifting her hips to meet each thrust. Just when she thought he was going to drive them both over the precipice, he slowed, hovered above her and gazed down at her.

Undone by all she saw in that intense gaze, Catherine trembled.

He dipped his head and caught her nipple between his teeth, sending a charge directly to that sensitive place between her legs. She cried out and tumbled over the edge. Jack drove into her, finding his own release in the midst of hers.

Simon Eagan made use, as he often did, of his illustrious cousin's name and title to gain entry to Lord and Lady Crenshaw's ballroom. As the nephew and cousin of a duke, Simon operated happily on the outer fringes of the *ton*, accepted—when he chose to be—by a society too polite to risk alienating the duke by casting disfavor upon his cousin and close confidant.

Since Lord Crenshaw was a distant cousin to Lord Lindsey, Simon had figured he was most likely to find the odious viscount here as opposed to some of the other equally disagreeable Society events being held this week.

Simon's reputation for carousing, womanizing, gambling, drinking and a variety of other pastimes that kept him entertained preceded him into the glittering ballroom, and he felt the eyes of everyone in the vast room on him as he sought out friendly faces. He had worked hard to cultivate his less-than-stellar reputation as well as the air of indifference he wore as easily as a waistcoat. Both usually served him quite well by keeping him far, far away from ballrooms such as this, where his hard-won reputation was nothing but a dreadful liability.

Relief swept through him when Justin, Lord Enderly, waved to him from across the dance floor. On the way to join him, Simon nodded politely to a number of people he recognized but couldn't name if a pistol were pressed to his temple. Lady something or other tittered with distress when Simon brushed past her, as if his filthy reputation might actually rub off on her and her debutante daughter. Simon fought back the urge to press a kiss to the woman's doughy cheek, chuckling to himself as he imagined her succumbing to the vapors if he dared to actually kiss her.

"Thank goodness you're here," he said to Justin once he finally reached him. Simon had been a year behind Derek and Justin at Eton, and the three of them had been fast friends.

"Better yet, what the devil are *you* doing here?"

Simon nodded to Aubrey Nelson, the American, a newer

friend of his cousin's whom Simon had met once before at Tattersalls. "I'm here on Westwood's behalf."

Enderly stared at him in amazement. "Is that so? I thought he had taken his leave of the city."

"Indeed, he has. I'm looking for Lord Lindsey. Have you seen him?" The question was met with silence and perplexed stares.

"Whatever do you want with that swine?" Enderly asked.

"I'm interested in his whereabouts at the moment."

"I couldn't tell you. I haven't seen him in weeks."

Simon's hopes fell at that news. Deep inside he'd hoped to be able to report back to Derek that Lady Catherine's fiancé couldn't give a fig that she had fled the city and was carrying on with the Season as if nothing at all were amiss. Simon should've known better. Of course, Lindsey was out looking for her. It would be a matter of pride. "And the Earl of Brisbane? Is he in attendance tonight?"

Enderly's sharp blue eyes traveled up and down the length of Simon. "What are you about, Eagan?"

"The duke has asked me to gather some information. I am merely tending to his request."

"The last time we saw the duke," Nelson interjected, "he was running for his life from this very scene. You'll have to pardon us if we find your *inquiries* curious at best."

"There have been some developments." Simon chose his words carefully. Even though Enderly was one of Derek's closest friends and Nelson a favored acquaintance, Simon had decided he would tell no one about Catherine and what had transpired since Derek left the city. Not, at any rate, until he knew more about the situation his cousin found himself in.

"What kind of developments?" Enderly asked.

"I'm not at liberty to say. Could you please, if you are so inclined, point out the earl?"

Enderly studied Simon for another long moment before he nodded his head. "There. With his wife and daughter."

Simon looked to where Enderly indicated and felt the air seep from his lungs in one sharp gasp. For there, standing next to the gray-haired earl, was the most exquisite creature Simon had ever beheld. Blond hair, so light and bright it might've been spun from gold itself. Almond-shaped eyes that were dark blue or maybe even violet. A pretty, pink bow of a mouth and a button nose. Tall, with a hint of generous curves beneath the bodice of an icy-blue silk gown, she fairly shimmered.

The observations came at him, one after another, a new one before he could begin to process the previous one. Never, in all his twenty-nine years, had he noticed more than one thing at a time about any woman, and never had he taken such particular notice of a lady of the *ton*. They were always far more trouble than they were worth. But this one . . . *This one* . . .

"Simon? What is it?"

Enderly's voice invaded the stupor into which Simon had been drawn as he gazed at the face of an angel. She spoke, he noticed, with her hands, a habit her mother apparently didn't abide as she corrected her daughter twice in the short time Simon stood transfixed. Admonished, the angelic creature hooked her index fingers together in front of her in an obvious attempt to contain her enthusiasm. *No!* Simon wanted to shout. *How dare you smother the life out of such a glorious creature?* But he could say no such thing. He could only stare and hope that, at some time in the distant future, his heart would begin to beat normally again.

"Ahh," Nelson said with a knowing smirk. "Young Simon has noticed Brisbane's daughter, the very enticing Lady Madeleine."

"Who is only the belle of the Season," Enderly added with dry amusement.

Before Simon could disabuse them of their observations, Lady Madeleine glanced in his direction. Their eyes met, and again Simon felt the air leave his lungs in a great whoosh. Navy. Her eyes were most definitely a dark navy blue, and at the moment, they were studying him with curiosity. Catherine's sister, he realized. If Derek had experienced anything near the same reaction to meeting Catherine, Simon could well understand why she was now under his cousin's protection.

"You can't be serious, Simon," Enderly said in tone rife with disdainful laughter, but Simon pretended not to hear him. He was already on his way to the other side of the dance floor. He was already on his way to her. About halfway there, it occurred to him, in the midst of the fog he'd fallen into, that he couldn't just approach her without a proper introduction.

Panic-stricken at the thought of her getting away, Simon glanced back over his shoulder at Enderly. Rolling his eyes, Enderly shook his head. Simon pleaded silently. With a growl, Enderly strode across the floor to meet Simon. Taking him by the elbow, Enderly said, "I'll introduce you, but not until you tell me what Derek wants with Lindsey."

Simon searched her out again. There, right where he'd last seen her, surrounded by her parents and a bevy of young bucks working up the nerve to approach her. "It's a private matter."

"If you want to meet her, you'll tell me what private matter Derek has with Lindsey." Enderly stopped walking, his usually amiable face set in an expression Simon hadn't seen before. He glanced at Madeleine, who again met his gaze, before he tore his eyes away to meet Enderly's. "It involves Lindsey's fiancée."

"I hadn't heard Lindsey was betrothed. What does she have to do with Derek?"

Simon tugged on his collar. "That's somewhat of a long story."

Enderly gestured to Madeleine. "If you want to meet her, you'll tell me the long story. Quickly."

The young bucks were creeping closer to her while she remained aloof, her eyes still trained on Simon. Desperate, he said, "Derek met her on the way home. She had run away from Lindsey, who was unkind to her, and I believe Derek is quite besotted with her. He asked me to determine whether Lindsey—or her father, the Earl of Brisbane—is looking for her."

"Interesting," Enderly said, scratching his chin. "All of this in just a few days' time?"

"I told you what you wanted to know. Will you introduce me? Please?"

"She's so far above your station, it's comical," Enderly said as they made their way to the earl's group.

"I am the cousin of a duke," Simon said indignantly.

"You are a rakehell of the first order, and her mother won't let you anywhere near her."

Thanks to a generous behest from his late uncle and Derek's winning instincts when it came to growing money, Simon was, in fact, filthy rich in his own right. But Justin was quite correct—Lady Madeleine's parents would hardly care about his money when stacked against his reputation. *Blast it all!* For the first time that he could recall, Simon experienced a tinge of shame over how he'd spent the last ten years. "I'm a successful, wealthy businessman with ties to the highest realm of the aristocracy," Simon said.

"For all the good that will do you when your skirt-chasing reputation makes its way to Lord and Lady Brisbane."

"I've stopped all that foolishness."

"As of when?" Enderly asked with a snort.

"About five minutes ago."

Despite that somewhat shocking statement, Enderly managed to paste a smile on his handsome face as they approached the earl and his family. "Lord Brisbane, Lady Brisbane, Lady Madeleine, may I present Simon Eagan, first cousin to the Duke of Westwood?"

"Westwood, you say," Lord Brisbane said, his chest pumped out as he shook hands with Simon.

Was it Simon's imagination or did Lady Brisbane cringe when he bowed before her. So, she'd already heard about him, had she? "Pleased to make your acquaintance, my lord and my lady."

He felt rather than saw her derision, and it was the very reason he tended to stay away from ballrooms full of judgmental mothers and debutantes such as the exquisite creature who waited patiently for him to turn his attention to her. Simon steeled himself and shifted his gaze to her. This time, her scent was the first thing he noticed, an arresting array of lemon and spice.

Later, he wouldn't remember what he said to her or what she said, nor would he recall signing her dance card or Enderly leading him away when no more polite conversation could occur without causing a scandal. While Simon wanted nothing more than to stand before her and continue to make inane conversation, he was ever mindful of Derek's place among these people and his place with Derek.

"You scored a bloody waltz," Enderly marveled as they walked away. "Only you, Simon. Only you."

Stricken, Simon stared at Enderly. "A waltz, you say?"

"*You* signed the card, man!"

"I had no idea what I was signing!"

"What the devil has gotten into you? *And* your cousin?"

"You know," Simon said, feeling as if something significant had shifted in his world without his knowledge or permission, "I haven't the foggiest idea."

Thirty minutes later, Simon told himself it was just a dance. Except, of course, it wasn't because he avoided scenes such as this like the plague. He couldn't actually recall the last time he had danced with a woman, let alone waltzed. Could it have been as far back as Eton? Good Lord, he'd make a fool of himself and Derek by association. Before he could begin to actively sweat, Lady Madeleine smiled up at him and stopped his heart.

Gazing down at her, Simon vowed to leave his old life behind. He vowed to give up all his vices. Well, maybe not *all*, but most. Definitely most. Whatever it took to make himself a man this exquisite creature might welcome into her life.

"You're staring, Mr. Eagan."

Her softly spoken words startled Simon out of the trance he'd slipped into. "I'm sure you're quite accustomed to that."

"Most are more subtle."

"I've made you uncomfortable. My apologies."

"None necessary." Even though he was acutely aware of her soft hand gripping his through her glove, of the heat of her body under the hand that rested on her back, of her bewitching scent, somehow Simon managed to navigate them through the steps without tripping over his own feet while pondering the changes he'd begin to make imminently.

First, he would quit drinking. Then he'd stop gambling. Other women? A thing of the past. Horse races? Maybe he could continue to visit the track on occasion. Gentlemen did such things, didn't they? Simon honestly couldn't say. He'd never given a fig about the activities of the *ton*. But now . . .

"Lady Madeleine, I wondered if I might, if you would be amenable . . ." He cleared his throat.

"Yes?" Did she sound breathless or was he imagining it?

"I'd like to call on you."

"You would?"

Simon nodded, afraid to speak or breathe. If she said no, he'd die. His heart would simply cease to beat.

Her lips parted, and Simon had to remind himself of where he was. Otherwise, he might've kissed her right then and there, heedless of the scandal such an action would cause.

"I would be amenable," Madeleine said softly.

"Your parents may not be." The moment the words were out of his mouth, Simon wanted to shoot himself. *Way to sell yourself, Eagan.*

She turned those potent navy-blue eyes up at him. "And why is that?"

Simon winced. "I have somewhat of a reputation."

"Ah," she said, laughing. "Are you a bit of a rakehell then?"

"Lady Madeleine, I am truly shocked that you know such a word."

"I know a few others as well."

Maybe it was her saucy tone or perhaps it was the laughter in her eyes, but Simon fell straight off the cliff into love with her. After years of disdaining other men who changed their entire lives for a woman, Simon suddenly understood why they did it.

"Should I be concerned about this reputation of yours?" she asked, affecting a mockingly serious expression.

"You should probably be terrified."

But rather than terror, he saw intrigue in her expression. Interesting. Very, *very* interesting.

"I'll be at home tomorrow afternoon. A walk in the park would be lovely, don't you think?"

"Mmm, lovely."

"Mr. Eagan?"

"Yes?"

"The music has stopped."

Startled, Simon looked up to find the eyes of the *ton* trained on him. He bowed and pressed a kiss to the back of her hand.

"May I escort you back to your family?"

"Yes, please."

He offered his arm and walked her across the ballroom. Delivering her to her mother, he mumbled something unintelligible and had to force himself to walk away. Knowing a dozen other young bucks were waiting in line for their turn to dance with her made him feel sick. How could she dance with anyone else? Didn't she feel the connection between them?

A hand landed on Simon's shoulder, jolting him. "What the devil has gotten into you?" Enderly asked.

"I seem to have developed an affliction."

His friend laughed. "Is that so? What are your symptoms?"

Simon rested a hand on his chest. "Racing heart, trouble breathing, a spot of fever, chills."

"As serious as all that?"

Tearing his eyes off Lady Madeleine across the room, Simon glanced at his friend. "I'm afraid so."

"Never thought I'd live to see the day."

"Nor did I, my friend." Simon sought her out once again, hungry for more. "Nor did I."

Chapter Twelve

"If I ask you something, will you tell me the truth?"

The question sent a bolt of fear rippling through Derek.

"What am I saying?" Catherine asked with a laugh. "Of course, you'll tell me the truth. You'd never lie to me."

"Cat—"

"I apologize for inferring that you'd ever be anything other than truthful with me." She shifted so she was on top of him and pressed her lips to his. "Do you forgive me?"

As the fear gripped him, he ran his hands over her back. He had to tell her. *He had to*. If only he wasn't convinced that telling her would ruin everything—and that was a risk he wasn't ready to take. "I may need some inducement," he said with a playful smile that belied the terror. He'd never been so afraid of anything as he was of losing what he'd so recently found. Now that he'd had it, how would he ever do without it?

Her lips moved softly over his face.

Derek closed his eyes as waves of pleasure washed over him, seeping into the cold, dark, empty spaces within him. "Catherine."

"Hmm?"

"Don't leave me," he whispered, cupping her face in his big hands. "No matter what happens, promise you'll never leave me."

She looked down at him, her eyes filled with confusion and wonder. "How could I leave you when I couldn't possibly live without you?"

Overcome by relief, he brought her down to accept his kiss, sweeping his tongue into the sweet softness of her mouth. His fingers combed through her hair, anchoring her. Derek raised his hips, and she let out a squeal of surprise.

"Easy," he said, arranging her so she straddled him.

A flush crawled from her breasts to her neck to her face. "We can't! Not like this."

"Oh, yes," he said, laughing at her scandalized expression, "I assure you we can." He nudged at her soft flesh with the blunt head of his cock.

"*Jack!*" She squirmed on top of him, forcing a sharp gasp from him.

"You'll like it." He guided her hips. "I promise." Raising her, he took himself in hand, found her heated entrance and had to remind himself to go slow, that this was all new to her.

"Oh! Oh, God. *Jack.*"

He hated, absolutely *hated*, hearing another man's name uttered from her plump lips at such a moment.

"It won't fit," she wailed.

"Yes, it will. Relax and let me in." Her eyes fluttered closed, and her head fell back in total surrender as he lowered her inch by torturous inch. Once she was fully embedded, he stayed perfectly still, giving her time to accommodate him.

"Jack," she panted, her muscles clenching so tightly

around him it was all he could do to keep from losing control.

He skimmed his hands from hips to breasts. Watching her expressive face, he raised himself up to draw her nipple into his mouth and swirled his tongue back and forth over the sensitive bud. Her hips surged, and he bit back a curse as he moved quickly to hold her still, lest this end before it really began.

"I need to move," she said between choppy breaths.

Derek lightened his hold, encouraging her to ride him. At first her movements were jerky and desperate, but then she found a rhythm that made them both breathless as they moved together. Enveloped in her heat, he decided that nothing in the world could compare to the feeling of being inside Catherine.

She rolled her hips in a move he'd expect from a seasoned courtesan and not his recently virginal wife. Derek slipped a hand between them to coax her. The instant his finger made contact with her center she came harder than she ever had before, taking him with her for the most explosive release of his life.

Gasping, they fell into a tangled pile on the bed. As he fought to bring air into his lungs, it occurred to him that she'd never asked her question. Since she expected nothing but the truth from him, maybe it was just as well.

In the light from the fireplace and the candles they'd never bothered to extinguish, Derek watched her doze. She lay facing him with one hand under her face and her golden hair fanned out like a halo on the pillow. Noise from the street and the tavern downstairs filtered into the room. Derek would've preferred to take her somewhere nicer, but he hadn't wanted to make her suspicious about what an estate manager could afford.

He'd never intended for the deception to get so out of hand. Of course, he'd also never intended to fall in love with her. Protecting her from Lord Lindsey had become his top concern, and surely she'd forgive him the deception that had ensured Lindsey could never come near her again. Wouldn't she? A twinge of anxiety worked its way down his spine as he remembered her utter disdain for the aristocracy.

If only he could be certain that she would understand, he would wake her and tell her the truth right now. But the idea of her looking at him with disappointment rather than adoration stopped him. He just needed a little more time alone with her to show her how much he loved her, and then he would tell her.

He leaned over and nudged the sheet aside to place a kiss between her soft breasts.

She shifted onto her back, but didn't awake. He kissed his way up the slope of her breast and nudged at her nipple. "Hmm," she murmured, still asleep. Sliding closer to her, he kissed a trail from her breast to her belly. When he reached the soft blond curls at the juncture of her legs, he felt her stiffen with awareness. Just as quickly she relaxed, but her breathing remained ragged.

"Again?" she asked, running her fingers through his hair as he tasted her hip bone.

"Mmm, again," he whispered, watching bumps rise on her sensitive skin. He moved farther down on the bed, settling between her thighs and arranging her legs so they rested on his shoulders.

"Oh," she said, moaning as his tongue traced her outer lips. "Jack." The fingers that had been caressing his hair tightened, and her hips surged almost of their own accord. "I still can't believe you like to do that."

"I *love* to do it." He slid his hands under her to cup her buttocks, opening her to his exploration. His tongue slipped inside, feasting and devouring. Derek lost all sense of time and place, his entire focus on her pleasure. Withdrawing one hand from her bottom, he teased her with two fingers at her entrance.

When his tongue circled her clitoris, she released a deep moan. Encouraged by her responsiveness, Derek pushed his fingers into her and sucked hard on the pulsating nub.

Catherine raised her hips to meet the thrusts of his questing tongue and fingers. The sounds that came from her, the scent of violets and lily of the valley, the honey-sweet taste of her, the glow of the candlelight on her soft skin. Derek had never been more absorbed in anyone. He slowed the movement of his fingers, then removed them from her channel and pressed one damp finger against her back entrance.

Her eyes flew open in shock and perhaps excitement. "*Jack.*"

He kept up the pressure of his tongue on her clitoris as he pushed more insistently against her tight pucker.

"Oh, oh, *God*," she cried as his finger gained entry to her most private passage. He sucked hard again on her clitoris, and she came with a cry that no doubt woke everyone in the inn and maybe even the houses next door. Her climax went on for what felt like an hour as she shook and trembled and cried out with each new wave.

Derek stayed with her throughout the tumult, keeping up the steady pressure of his tongue and finger.

Finally, she calmed, but her uneven breathing told him how completely undone she was. He withdrew from her and moved so he was on top of her. "Still with me?" he asked, kissing the dampness from her forehead.

She kept her eyes closed when she nodded. "Yes." Even that single word came out on a choppy-sounding breath.

"Look at me, Cat."

It seemed to take tremendous effort for her to comply with his request. When she ventured a glance up at him he saw something new, something different. "What are you thinking right now?"

After a long pause during which she absorbed him with her eyes, she said, "That I might have lived my whole life without ever knowing it was possible to feel like this."

Undone himself by the raw emotion behind her words, Derek touched his lips to her neck and pressed his cock against her sensitive flesh. "And now that you know?"

She wound her arms around his neck and sought his lips. "I never want to be without it again."

"You won't be," he vowed, entering her with one long thrust. "You'll never be without it or me again."

He loved her with everything he had, hoping it would be enough when the time came to give her the truth.

"What did you want to ask me? Before I distracted you?"

Catherine laughed softly. "Is that what we're calling it? Ravished is a *much* better word." Except for her brief nap, they'd been awake for more than twenty-four hours, but neither was in any rush to end their magical day.

He took her hand and kissed each finger. "Distracted, ravished, whatever you prefer."

"I have a different question now." Her face heated when she thought of what he'd done to her, how it had made her feel and what she wanted to know.

"You may ask them both." The words were spoken in

his usual tone, but Catherine sensed rather than heard the hesitancy behind the statement.

She closed her eyes against the tingles of sensations that his fingers combing through her hair aroused in her. "I can't help but wonder where you learned such wicked lovemaking skills."

Jack laughed. "Wicked?"

"Mmm. Very, *very* wicked."

"I believe you rather enjoy my wicked lovemaking skills."

"I never said otherwise. I am, however, painfully curious as to how you came to know such things."

"I had a friend," he said tentatively.

"What kind of 'friend' teaches you . . ." Her face heated with mortification. She couldn't believe she was having such a conversation with a man, even if he was her husband. But then she also couldn't believe the things he'd done to her, things she'd never imagined transpired between a man and woman, even in their marriage bed.

"Wicked things?" he asked with a chuckle.

"Yes," she whispered.

"She was a courtesan named Kitty, and she made a man out of me."

Catherine gasped at the matter-of-fact delivery of such a scandalous statement. "You're making that up."

Beneath her, he stiffened, as if she had insulted him. Catherine raised herself up, so she could see his face. "Aren't you?"

"I'm not making it up. I'm sorry if it upsets you, but it's the truth."

He looked so pained and ashamed that Catherine immediately regretted her questions. "It's none of my concern. Whatever happened before we met—"

"Doesn't matter now. My whole life began the day I found you digging a hole in my . . . Well, in the duke's backyard."

"You're quite proprietary about his estate."

"It's my whole life." That much had been true up to now. "How else would you expect me to be?"

"No other way, I suppose," she said, running a finger over his muscular chest.

"What are you thinking?"

She shrugged. How could she ask him, knowing what his job and the duke meant to him?

"Catherine." His finger beneath her chin forced her to look at him. "I hope you know there's nothing you can't ask me." There, again, a flash of something in his eyes, something that might've been fear or trepidation. What could that be?

"It's just, I wondered . . ."

"What do you wonder?"

Catherine forced herself to meet his intense gaze. "If you'd ever consider leaving your duke for a time to travel."

As he studied her, he swallowed hard as his cheek twitched with tension. "Where would you like to go?"

"Somewhere. Anywhere."

Jack smiled and skimmed a finger over her cheek. "Nowhere specific?"

"Paris, I suppose, and Egypt. I'd like to see the pyramids. And the Coliseum in Rome. I've seen paintings of the Alps, but I wonder what they really look like. Can you imagine taking a ship across the ocean to New York?"

"But nowhere specific," he teased, his face alight with amusement.

Catherine burned with embarrassment when she realized how she must sound to him. If only he knew how many places she wished to go to and things she wished to do. Her wanderlust had made her an oddity at home, and she probably would've been wise to hide that side of herself from Jack until she knew him better. However, after the intimacies they'd shared, it seemed foolish to hide any part of herself from him. She wanted to know everything about him, so how could she expect that he'd want anything less from her?

"I'd give you the world if I could. I hope you know that."

"You are sweet to say so." She cupped his cheek and brought him in for a chaste kiss. "I was foolish to mention it. I'm happy to just be here with you, to be married to you. Please don't think that I require anything more—"

He rested a finger gently over her lips. "I always want you to tell me your fondest hopes and dreams. How am I to make them come true if I don't know about them?"

Catherine studied his handsome, earnest face and wondered—not for the first time—how she'd ever gotten so lucky as to have landed such a husband. Surely there was not a man among the vaunted aristocracy who could compare to her estate manager. When her day of reckoning came with her parents, she would hold her head up high and proudly introduce them to the best man she had ever known. Lord Lindsey, on the other hand . . . She shuddered at the memory of his filthy hands pawing her the way they might a side of beef.

"What?" he asked, concerned. "Something just frightened you."

"I am deeply afraid of what Lord Lindsey will do to you once he learns we are married."

"I am not the slightest bit afraid of him. If he so much as raises a finger to either of us, I will make certain that all of London and Parliament know that he attacked a young woman in her father's parlor and would have raped her had her rambunctious brothers not taught her how to defend herself against such scum."

"And your duke will have no problem with you making such a public spectacle of yourself?"

"I assure you that my duke has absolutely no patience for men who bully or attack women."

"I think I'm going to like your duke," she said with a sigh of contentment.

"I'm quite counting on that." He twisted her curls around his fingers. "So where would you like to spend your honeymoon? Here or the cottage?"

"The cottage," she said without hesitation. "I want to cook for you and play house and look for my grandmother's key for as long as we possibly can before you have to return to work."

"Then we shall set out for home tomorrow." Pausing, he added, "Although, now that you are under my protection, you no longer need the resources your grandmother made available to you."

"Perhaps not, but I'd still like to find the key and recover her property."

"Then that's what we shall do. I wondered, though, did your grandmother and the former duke conceive a child together?"

"Oh, no. She didn't have children until much later, after she married my grandfather." Propping her chin on his chest, she studied him. "Tell me more about this courtesan friend of yours."

Jack surprised her when he rolled them, so he was once again on top of her. Catherine pushed back the shank of hair that covered his forehead. "Rather than tell you about her, how about I show you some more of what she taught me?"

Catherine released a most unladylike squeal. "There's *more?*"

His rakish grin lit up his face. "My love, we've only just begun."

Chapter Thirteen

Simon presented his card to the Brisbanes' butler and wiped sweaty palms on his pants as he watched the man ascend the staircase to the second floor. He'd worn the most elegant clothing he owned and had asked his valet for the velvet waistcoat that his tailor had insisted was all the rage. The tight fabric gave the feeling of confinement, like a wild tiger would feel inside a cage. A hot ball of nerves had settled in his throat, giving him the sensation of being strangled since he walked away from Lady Madeleine the night before. Leaving her at the ball with scores of other admirers, Simon had experienced a most uneasy—and unprecedented—sensation.

Some might call it jealousy. Simon couldn't say for sure as he'd never before experienced the emotion. And Simon Eagan knew himself as well as it was possible to know anything.

He was painfully aware of his sordid reputation and less-than-stellar behavior with the fairer sex. In fact, until the night before, his awareness of his failings had never been painful. Now, for the first time, he had cause to worry that his past might stand in the way of something he desperately wanted.

Just how much did Brisbane know about him? That was anyone's guess.

All night long, Simon had lain awake, pondering the mysteries of fate. If you had told him a week ago that Derek would be considering marriage to a woman with whom he was besotted to protect her from a vile lord, Simon would have laughed. If you had told him two days ago that he, Simon Eagan, would abandon his hedonistic pursuits after being in the presence of a young maiden exactly once, he would've challenged you to meet him at dawn with your pistols drawn. And that the two women were sisters only made the situation that much more comical—and fitting.

A gentleman—if you could call him that, and many would not—didn't call on a marriage-minded young miss unless he had marriage on his own mind. Simon knew that, of course, but even the thought of that dreaded institution had not kept him from his promise to call on Madeleine today. In fact, it had never occurred to him *not* to keep their appointment. That alone should've been disconcerting but wasn't.

Muffled voices filtered down the stairs from the drawing room. He tilted his head to better hear them. A woman and a man. No, two women and a man. One of the women was young, her voice higher than the other's. It was her. *Madeleine*. Simon's heart quickened in response to being so close to her, to hearing her voice, even if it was muted by a door.

"I absolutely *forbid it*!" The earl's voice—and his anger—was loud and clear even through the closed door.

Simon took a step back, astounded by the fury behind the statement. Well, that solved one mystery. Clearly, Brisbane had asked around about the man his daughter had shown an interest in the night before—and not liked what he'd heard.

". . . a rakehell of the highest order."

Simon winced at that one. Not the *highest* order. Close to the top, maybe, but London certainly boasted worse rakes than him, or so he thought. How could one really know for sure?

". . . believing idle gossip."

Thank you, Madeleine. If he weren't already falling madly in love with her, he would have been after hearing her defend him.

". . . not idle gossip. Fact."

The sheepish-looking butler descended the stairs. "May I offer you some refreshments while you wait, sir?"

"That's quite all right, but thank you."

The butler glanced upward. "It'll be just another moment. My apologies for the delay."

"No need to apologize."

". . . *whether you like it or not!*"

Simon felt a charge similar to that he often experienced at the track when his favored horse surged into the lead. Winning always thrilled him. *Go, Madeleine. Go.*

A door upstairs was flung open and then slammed shut.

The butler, who'd resumed his post by the front door, winced as the sound echoed through the foyer like a shotgun blast.

"Come back here this instant, young lady," the earl shouted.

And then there, at the top of the stairs, his Madeleine appeared.

Simon sucked in a sharp breath of surprise at her sudden appearance. Behind her, a lady's maid watched the scene with wide eyes. In a most indelicate fashion, Lady Madeleine stormed down the stairs, seemingly fueled by fury. If Simon had fallen for her docile, ladylike side last night, today's hellcat would be the very ruination of him.

When he went to swallow, he discovered all the saliva had drained from his mouth. She wore a pale green silk gown with a portrait neckline that showcased her spectacular bosom. Not that he was looking. The day before yesterday, he would have taken a good, long—some would say *indecent*—look. But as the changed man he now was, he took only a fleeting glimpse and then turned his gaze to her face, which was stained with red. Apparently, when her dander went up so too did her color. Good to know for future reference because he fully intended to get her dander up as soon and as often as he possibly could.

"I apologize for making you wait, Mr. Eagan," she said when she reached the foot of the stairs.

"No need for apologies, my lady." He took her gloved hand and placed a chaste kiss on the back. "You look absolutely lovely this fine day."

"Thank you."

Was she flustered by him, or was that just wishful thinking on his part? Probably wishful thinking in the wake of the row with her parents.

Speaking of her parents, they appeared at the top of the stairs, their stormy expressions leaving little to the imagination.

Lady Madeleine turned to her maid, who wrapped a light shawl around her shoulders, and then turned back to Simon wearing a magnificent smile. "Shall we?"

Simon started to offer his arm, but then glanced at the pair upstairs. The day before yesterday, he would have spirited her out of there before her parents could stop them. Today, he knew what he had to do, no matter how unpleasant it might be. He glanced at Madeleine, who seemed completely uninterested in doing the right thing, and beseeched her with his eyes to allow him to at least *attempt* a proper courtship.

She released a rattling, resigned breath, and he admired her restraint. Her lady's maid seemed to quake in anticipation of the coming battle.

Lord and Lady Brisbane came down the stairs arm in arm, a regally united front.

Simon bowed to each of them. "My lord, my lady, it is a pleasure to make your acquaintance once again."

"Eagan," Lord Brisbane said without preamble. "If my associates at White's are to be trusted, you are not the kind of man a father wants courting his daughter."

"I'm afraid your associates are quite correct."

Madeleine and her mother gasped.

"However," Simon said, glancing at the woman who had changed his life in one fateful instant, "that was before."

"Before?" Lord Brisbane said, his expression rife with confusion and disdain.

"Before I laid eyes on the exquisite Lady Madeleine. If any woman can reform a man like me, I believe she can." He called upon his most charming smile and directed it at her. "I'd certainly like to find out."

The pulse at the base of her neck beat frantically, which Simon took as a sign that his most charming smile was still quite formidable, even when used on the most important of women.

"Well," Lady Brisbane harrumphed, "I never."

Simon turned again to Madeleine. "My lady, I believe I promised you a walk in the park." He extended his arm. "May I?"

As he waited to see what she would do, whom she would choose, Simon was acutely aware that his future happiness hinged, for the very first time, on the whims of someone other than himself. He didn't dare breathe or blink or swallow while a seemingly endless moment passed in which the ticking of the grandfather clock in the hallway beat in time with his rampaging heart.

Finally, when he'd begun to assume that all hope was lost, Madeleine curled her hand into the curve of his arm and sealed her fate along with his.

"You may," she said with a demure smile, all signs of the hellcat long gone.

Simon hoped she'd be back. He hadn't seen nearly enough of her.

Behind them, her lady's maid released a sigh that sounded, at least to Simon, like approval.

Her mother, on the other hand, continued to glower at him as he led Madeleine to the door.

"Eagan."

Simon turned to face the earl.

"If you step one inch out of line while you are courting my daughter, you will never see her again. I promise you that."

"And I promise you I shall never even approach the line of which you speak while I am courting your daughter, my lord."

Shockingly, that seemed to pacify the earl, if not his wife. Simon decided to get the hell out of there while the getting was good. He ushered Madeleine through the door that the butler, whom Simon now thought of as his partner in crime, hastily opened for them. Simon nodded to him and swore the old man winked. Or was that, again, wishful thinking?

Once they were outside, Madeleine released a long, tortured sigh. "That was highly unpleasant and utterly mortifying."

Simon laughed at her acerbic tone, already charmed by her. "I'm sure I've faced worse. I'm just not sure when."

"It was ridiculous and unnecessary. I'm hardly a blushing maiden in the throes of adolescence without a shred of judgment when it comes to gauging another's character."

Simon swallowed hard. "And what, pray, does your judgment tell you about my character?"

"That I should stay far, far away."

"And yet you are here with me after putting up a fight that Napoleon himself would admire."

She flashed a saucy grin. "You think so?"

"Most assuredly."

"That's about the nicest thing you could say to me."

Right then and there, Simon realized he had fallen for no ordinary female. Most of them cared more about their clothing and hair and dance cards than they ever would about their ability to stand toe-to-toe with their disapproving parents. His respect and admiration for her, already through the roof, went up a few more notches.

"Do you often wage war with your parents?" he asked as they strolled toward Hyde Park.

"I never used to," she said wistfully. "Ever since everything happened, they've changed. They've become people I barely know or recognize. They used to trust me and my judgment. Now I'm treated like a dunderheaded female who hasn't a lick of sense or an original thought in her head."

Oh, how he loved her. With every word she spoke he fell harder.

"Why are you staring at me? Oh heavens, I've shocked you with my candor. When will I ever learn to keep some of my thoughts to myself?"

He wanted to kiss her. God, he wanted to kiss her until she could no longer think or speak. But then he remembered the promise he had made to her father not even five minutes ago and reined in his baser desires. "I hope that you will never learn to keep your thoughts to yourself. I rather like hearing them."

"Do you?"

"Indeed."

"But you've heard only one of them!"

"I want to hear *all* of them."

She flashed the same saucy grin that he wanted to awake to every day for the rest of his life.

"Well, I hope you have a lot of time, because I have many, *many* thoughts."

"I have all the time in the world to give to you, my lady."

Behind them, her maid sighed with what definitely sounded like approval.

Simon smiled. All was right in his world. For now.

The next day, Simon sent word via a footman to Derek, letting him know that he'd discovered Lord Lindsey was not in the city. Simon also mentioned that he would be detained in London by a personal matter that might lead to more information about Lady Catherine. Simon was intentionally cryptic in his message to his cousin. During his afternoon stroll with Lady Madeleine, she hadn't mentioned her missing sister, and Simon didn't wish to bring up what might be a sore subject. He'd decided to wait for her to confide in him.

He was due to see her again that afternoon and couldn't wait. They'd drawn curious stares and mumbling comments during their stroll the day before, but neither had bothered to pay attention. They'd been far too absorbed in each other to be concerned with idle gossip.

Simon wondered how long he had to court her before he could ask for her hand. He wished Derek was about to give him advice on such things. God knows Simon had never paid much attention to these rituals in the past. He'd have to ask Enderly about the rules. He would know.

Whatever it took to make Lady Madeleine his forever. Suddenly, she was the only thing that mattered to Simon.

The door to the morning room burst open and in strode Simon's father, Lord Anthony, a stormy expression on his lean face. *Oh dear.*

"What in the devil are you doing here?" Lord Anthony asked his son.

Simon paused in applying marmalade to his toast. "Nice to see you, too, Father. Wherever have you been?" That his father kept a mistress was no surprise to Simon, but he suspected his mother retained her illusions when she was aware enough to wonder where her husband might be.

"None of your concern." He accepted a cup of tea from the footman who had hurried to tend to Lord Anthony the moment he entered the room. It amused Simon, and Derek, too, when he was in residence, the way the London staff fawned over his father as if he were still the head of household. Simon suspected that was one of two reasons his father spent much of his time in the city. "Where is your cousin?"

"He has retired to the country."

Anthony looked up with surprise. "Is that so?"

"It is."

"Well," Anthony said with a satisfied smirk, "he'll never find a bride in time at this rate."

"I wouldn't be so certain of that," Simon mumbled. His father's naked ambitions sat poorly with him. Simon's loyalties would always remain firmly with Derek.

"What did you say?"

"I wouldn't count Derek out just yet, Father. He still has a week in which to marry."

"And who, pray, will he find to marry in seven days' time if he is not here in London?"

"I can't imagine." Derek might already be married, but

no way in hell was Simon's father going to hear that news from him.

"You know something." Anthony's shrewd eyes zeroed in on his son in a frosty stare that used to reduce Simon to a sniveling fool. Not any longer, however. Simon had long ago outgrown the need to please his father that had driven him during his formative years—and Anthony knew it.

Simon shrugged. "I know a lot of things." The veiled threat was clear: *push me on this, and I'll start to pick at where exactly you've been for the last three days.*

Anthony retreated—for the moment.

Simon had no doubt Anthony would interrogate the staff at the first opportunity. Blotting his mouth and placing the linen napkin on the table, Simon rose. "I must be off."

"To where?"

In truth, Simon had nowhere to be until three and had planned to wile away the time at home this morning. But now that his father had returned, he preferred to be anywhere else. "I'm meeting Enderly at White's."

"Very well, but if I find you are keeping things from me—"

Simon told himself to keep walking, to not engage, but the temptation was far too great. He turned. "You'll do what exactly?"

"I expect your loyalty. You are my son, after all."

"And Derek is my cousin and best friend. I won't stand idly by and watch you bring him harm or dishonor."

"You dishonor me by suggesting I'm capable of either."

Simon eyed him shrewdly. "Do I?"

The tendons in his father's neck bulged, a sign of his growing fury. In the past, Simon would've run for his life at the first sign of those bulging tendons. That was then.

"Your impertinence knows no bounds," Anthony said, snarling.

"Nor does your ambition. Tread lightly, Father. I'll be watching you. Derek may not have asked to be the duke, but he won't stand by and watch you take from him that which is rightfully his."

"If he doesn't soon marry, I won't have to *take* anything."

Simon decided to give his father the last word, because frankly, he'd grown bored by the tedious conversation. Hopefully by now Derek's title was safe and out of Anthony's reach. His father would find out soon enough that he'd been denied his fondest desire once again. A knot of fear lodged in Simon's chest. What would happen then?

Chapter Fourteen

Derek allowed himself seven days and seven nights of total bliss. He'd decided that on the first day of their second week of marriage, he would tell her the truth and then bear the consequences. In the meantime, he devoted every minute of that first week to her.

Once they were back at the cottage, the search for her grandmother's key framed their days. They spent several hours each morning investigating a new area of the glade, working until the heat of the day forced them inside for a midday meal followed by a leisurely afternoon in bed. They took Hercules and Sunny on long rides, returning to the glade in the early evenings during which they worked until dark.

On the seventh day, rather than take their midday meal at the cottage, they raided the icebox that Mrs. Langingham kept well provisioned and took a picnic to the small lake near the dig site.

"I'm so hot," Catherine said as they spread a plaid blanket under a tree. She'd worked as hard as he had on the dig, and more than once he'd encouraged her to rest. He worried incessantly about her fever returning, but she'd dismissed his concerns and continued to work by his side.

"I can cool you off," Derek said, hugging her from behind.

"I'm all sweaty!" She attempted to wiggle out of his embrace. "I must smell terrible!"

He kissed his way up the damp skin on her neck to roll her earlobe between his teeth. "You smell delicious."

She leaned back against his chest. "I'm so easily enchanted by you," she sighed. "I need to start making you work a little harder to earn my favor."

"Don't," he whispered, reveling in the tremor his words sent rippling through her body. "I like you just as you are." His hands coasted over her belly to cup her breasts. He pinched her nipples between his fingers, drawing a gasp from her. While one hand continued to stimulate her breasts, his other hand got busy unbuttoning her simple day dress. Only when he nudged the dress from her shoulders did Catherine become aware of what he'd done.

"Jack! We can't! Not out here."

"Yes, we can." He'd directed his staff to keep everyone away from this corner of the estate until further notice from him. "There's no one around for many miles, except for Hercules and Sunny, and they won't tell anyone."

She clutched the dress to her chest. "You can't know there's no one else about."

"I do know it." Moving around so he was in front of her, he eased the dress from her clutches and let it fall to her waist. He continued to release the buttons until it landed in a pool around her feet.

Catherine's fair skin flushed with color that only fueled his desire for her. "We can't," she said again, more softly this time.

"I promise no one will disturb us." Watching the excited rise and fall of her chest through the thin lawn of her chemise, Derek tugged off his boots and removed his clothes.

She licked her lips at the sight of his aroused body.

"Take off your chemise," he said, his voice rough and hoarse.

"I can't." She crossed her arms demurely over her chest.

That she could still be shy after the many intimacies they'd shared over the last week amused him. Reaching for her hands, he drew them down. "Take it off."

Her hands trembled as she reached for the hem and did as he asked. When he scooped her up into his arms, she released a surprised squeal. "Relax, my sweet, I've got you."

"We'll cause a scandal traipsing through the woods in our all-together."

"No one will ever know." He pressed a kiss to her soft lips. "It'll be our secret."

She tightened her arms around his neck and held on as he walked them to the lake. "Wait! Where are we—"

He strode to the end of the short dock and, still holding her in his arms, jumped into the water.

They emerged sputtering and laughing. "You're not hot anymore," he said.

She splashed water into his face. "I can't believe you did that!"

Derek retaliated by reaching for her waist and dunking her.

Once again, she resurfaced sputtering. "That, my love," she said as she pushed sopping strands of hair from her face, "was a declaration of war."

Swimming swiftly away from her, he called over his

shoulder, "Catch me if you can." Derek knew he shouldn't have been surprised to feel her hand clamp around his ankle. She'd shown herself to be his equal in more ways than one over the last week.

A clamp of a different kind closed around his heart, stealing the breath from his lungs when he imagined how tomorrow might go. But he couldn't delay the inevitable for another day, if for no other reason than his uncle would soon appear at Westwood Hall, hoping to make a claim on the dukedom. Derek would need to be there to disabuse him of his lofty ambitions.

Slowing his strokes, Derek let Catherine catch up to him. Hand in hand, they floated on the surface in contented silence for many minutes before Derek let his legs fall to the marshy bottom. He drew her into his arms and sighed with completion when she wrapped her arms and legs around him. Tipping his head, he found her mouth and feasted on her sweetness. "I love you," he said between kisses. "I love you so much. I have no idea how I survived before I found you."

"And I love you. Just as much." She clung to him, returning his kisses with the ardor he'd come to expect and crave from her.

"I have a confession to make," he said.

Drawing back from him, she met his gaze. "And what is that?"

"Today is my birthday."

She gasped. "I had no idea! Why didn't you tell me before now?"

"Birthdays are just another day."

"Since your parents died, you mean," she said, her expression grave. She cut him to the quick with her astute summary. It was all he could do to offer the briefest of nods. "Well, birthdays will no longer be just another day," she declared. "They will be celebrated. How old are you today?"

"Thirty," he said with a sheepish grin.

Again, she gasped. "Well, we must have a party!"

Laughing, he said, "And whom shall we invite to this party?"

"Do we need anyone else?"

"No." He shook his head and bent to kiss the drops of water off her lush lips. "We don't need anyone else." Pressing his tongue into her welcoming mouth, he guided his cock to the sweet warmth of her entrance and brought her down on him. The combination of the cool water and her heated channel took his breath away. He released a tortured groan. "God, that's incredible."

"Surely, you've done this before," she said against his ear.

"No. Never."

"Oh, finally! Something we're doing for the first time together."

He grimaced at the reminder that there'd been other women. "There will be many, many things we do together for the first time." As he spoke, he walked them to the far side of the lake where a rock formation extended into the water. One of the larger boulders formed a ramp.

"Where are we going?" She squeezed him with her internal muscles, drawing another tortured groan from Derek.

"You'll see," he somehow managed to say. Withdrawing from her, he turned her and arranged her so the top half of her body was facedown on the flat, sun-warmed stone. "Does the heat feel good against your body?"

"Mmm," she said, squirming.

Derek moved behind her and smoothed his hands

over her back, his lips following the same path down her spine. He worshipped her plump buttocks, until she fairly launched off the stone. Under the water, his fingers slid into her slick channel. After seven days of intense lovemaking, he could tell she was close to an explosive release. He replaced his fingers with his cock, sliding into her in one swift stroke.

Catherine cried out from the impact and gripped the edges of the stone as he pumped into her.

He reached around to where they were joined, found the hardened nub of her desire and rolled it between his fingers.

"Oh, oh, *Jack!*" she cried out as she shattered.

As he joined her in exquisite release, Derek would've sold his soul to the devil himself to hear her cry out his real name in her moment of ecstasy. It was the only thing he really wanted for his birthday, and the one thing he couldn't have.

Simon wondered if it were possible for a man to go mad from an overabundance of desire. Surely a body couldn't withstand this amount of yearning for long without suffering some sort of ill effect. As he strolled through the park with Lady Madeleine, everything about her held him captive to her overwhelming allure.

He couldn't help but notice, however, that she lacked her usual verve and vitality today. In fact, she hadn't said much of anything, which was rare indeed. Could she be losing interest in him? The thought struck a note of fear in Simon. She couldn't. He wouldn't survive it.

"Are you well today, my lady?"

The question seemed to startle her. "Why do you ask?"

"You're awfully quiet. Is something troubling you?"

"Tell him," her maid hissed from behind them.

Madeleine sent her a foul look. "Quiet."

The maid scowled.

"Now my curiosity is impossibly piqued," Simon said, stopping to look at Madeleine, then her maid and back to Madeleine.

"You tell him, my lady, or I will," the impertinent maid said.

"Very well." Madeleine's face flushed as she struggled to find the words. "It's my sister. She ran off a while back to get away from the viscount our father insisted she marry."

Playing dumb, Simon hung on her every word. "This lord," he said, "he is . . ."

"Vile! Absolutely *horrible!*"

"Why in the world would your father make such a match?"

"We aren't sure, exactly. We think perhaps it involved a wager of some sort." Her pretty lips curled with displeasure at the notion.

With every fiber of his being, Simon wanted to kiss those pretty lips. "That's unfortunate," he said, deliberately understating the obvious. "There's been no word from your sister?"

Distressed, Madeleine shook her head. "Not in weeks, and I miss her terribly. I just hope that nothing untoward has happened to her."

"Do you suspect that's possible?"

"She's extremely resourceful, but she's all alone."

Simon reached for her hand. "How can I help?"

"Tell him," the maid growled. Madeleine sent her yet

another withering look. "Her absence has caused a bit of a problem for me."

"How so?"

"If Catherine doesn't come home to marry the viscount, I'll have to."

Simon's world tilted on its axis. "That can't happen! You're going to marry *me!*"

"Am I?" Madeleine asked with a shy smile.

"Of course, you are."

"Not if my father and the viscount have anything to say about it."

Simon's mind raced with ideas and scenarios and schemes. "Your sister ran away to avoid marrying the man," Simon said slowly. "You will do the same."

"See what I'm telling you," the maid said, poking at Madeleine. To Simon, she said, "I told her you'd know what to do."

"Thanks for the vote of confidence, Evangeline," Simon said with a charming smile. "Now would you mind giving us just a minute or two alone to discuss the particulars?"

"Yes, sir." With a pointed look at her mistress, the maid scurried off to a nearby bench—out of earshot, but close enough that she could still keep an eye on her charge.

"Thank you," Madeleine said. "She's been driving me *mad.*"

"She's looking out for you."

"Yes."

"So."

"So."

Simon took a good look around at the mostly deserted park. The unusually warm day had kept the crowds inside.

Seeing that they were mostly alone, he dared to trail an ungloved finger over her rosy cheek.

Madeleine gasped. "*Simon*."

"Yes, my love?"

She looked up at him, her heart in her eyes. "Am I your love?"

"Oh, yes. You are my dearest love." In a brazen move, he cupped her cheek, discovering her skin was as soft and silken as it appeared. "I knew the moment I first saw you that you would change my life forever. Will you do me the great honor of being my wife?"

She hesitated for a moment, long enough to stop his heart. What would he do if she said no?

He cleared the fear from his throat. "Lady Madeleine?"

"May I ask you one question before I give you my answer?"

"Certainly."

"If I hadn't told you about the viscount, would you still have asked me to marry you?"

Simon pondered that for a second and decided to go with the truth. "Maybe not today but soon. I'd been waiting for the right opportunity to present itself." He glanced at the maid. "I was hoping for a moment alone in which to declare myself." Reaching for Madeleine's gloved hands, he added, "I have no title, but I also have no obligations to anyone other than myself. I'm wealthy in my own right, so you'll never want for anything. We can travel the world if that is your wish or never leave our home. There is nothing I wouldn't do to make you happy, nothing I wouldn't give to have you as my wife."

Tears shimmered in her beautiful eyes. "And children?"

"As many as you want. I am your humble servant."

She surprised him when she threw herself into his arms. "Yes," she whispered. "Yes, yes, *yes*."

Overwhelmed with relief and gratitude as well as the miraculous sensation of having her soft curves pressed against him, Simon closed his eyes tight against the rush of emotion. "We must act quickly," he said as he reluctantly released her and stepped back from her bewitching scent. "I want you to go home and feign illness. Pack only what you need for a couple of days for yourself and Evangeline. I'll meet you at the servant's entrance at midnight."

"*Tonight?*" she squeaked.

He nodded. "We can't risk your safety by giving your father and the viscount time to scheme. We must get you out of there immediately." Her expression was one of fear and reticence. "Do you trust me, Madeleine?"

"Oh, yes, Simon. I do. I trust you."

"Then do as I say and meet me at midnight." He brought her hand to his lips. "I'll take care of you."

She released a deep, shuddering breath. "I'll be there."

"There is something else I must tell you."

"What?" she asked, her eyes wide with alarm, as if she worried he might take it all back.

"I know where your sister is."

On the evening of his nephew's thirtieth birthday, an elated Lord Anthony returned to the family's home in Mayfair to prepare for the journey to Essex to finally claim what was rightfully his. Derek had never returned to town to choose a wife and was in default of the family's primogeniture. The former duke had been very clear about his expectations for future generations of heirs, and Derek had failed to live up to those expectations.

Not that Anthony was surprised. His nephew had always been a loner and would continue along that lonely path as he handed over his title to the uncle who'd done everything for him and had never been given the credit he rightfully deserved.

Now Anthony would finally get *everything* he deserved. He was filled with anticipation and plans, the first of which was to end the ridiculous investments his nephew continued to make in frivolous projects, squandering money that could be spent on far better things. A flying machine? Anthony laughed at the sheer madness of it.

After a knock on the door, his valet, James, entered the bedchamber. "My lord, you've returned. It is nice to see you."

"Likewise."

"My lord . . ."

A sense of foreboding had Anthony turning to look at the man who'd been by his side through it all, the most loyal person in Anthony's life. "What is it, James?"

"There has been news from Westwood Hall."

"What kind of news?"

"I'm afraid I must tell you that your nephew was married in Gretna Green one week ago. John Coachman saw the registry with his own eyes."

Anthony was rarely speechless, but he had no words. Once again, his birthright had been snatched out of his hands. Filled with fury that threatened to consume him, Anthony cleared his throat. "Who?"

"My lord?"

"*Who* did he marry?"

"Lady Catherine McCabe, the daughter of the Earl of Brisbane. She had been missing these last weeks."

"Missing?"

"From what I heard from the earl's groom, the earl lost

a steep wager to Lord Lindsey, and betrothed his eldest daughter to the viscount. She ran away rather than marry the man."

"I can't say I blame her, but how did she end up married to my nephew?"

"Apparently, he encountered her on his property and took her in. I haven't heard the particulars of how they came to meet, but when Lindsey went to collect her, the duke immediately took her to Scotland."

"He ran off with another peer's fiancée?" Anthony asked, his wheels turning. If he had his nephew brought up on charges in the House of Lords, perhaps the marriage could be discredited.

"From what I was told, she never accepted Lord Lindsey's proposal and refused her father's directive that she marry the viscount."

The case would be difficult to make, but it was something. Anthony should've broken the boy's neck and left him under a tree to make it look like an accident when he'd had the chance. If he'd done that, he wouldn't be once again on the outside looking in as his brother's family took what was rightfully his. Even from the grave, his brother was still winning.

Anthony wouldn't stand for it. It was time to end this madness once and for all.

"That'll be all, James."

"Good evening, my lord."

For a long time after James left the room, closing the door behind him, Anthony didn't move. He barely breathed as he considered his options.

Then he walked over to the decanter that contained his whiskey of choice, poured several fingers and took a healthy sip, letting the heat of the liquor burn the bile that had settled in his throat. He wrapped his hand around the neck of the decanter.

Imagining his nephew's smug, satisfied face made Anthony see red.

Tightening his hand on the crystal, he picked it up and hurled it into the stone fireplace, watching with satisfaction as it shattered into a million pieces.

By the time Anthony was finished with him, his nephew's life would resemble that shattered decanter.

Chapter Fifteen

After they'd dined by candlelight and devoured the small cake Catherine had baked for his birthday, Jack held her close to him in their bed. Catherine could honestly say that she'd never in her life imagined that such contentment was possible. After she had lost Ian, she hadn't expected to find love again. And if she were being honest with herself, the love she'd felt for her dear, sweet Ian paled in comparison to the fiery passion she shared with her handsome husband.

He was everything she'd ever wanted in a mate: generous, loving, affectionate, passionate and interested in that which interested her. He made her laugh, and he made her think. In the dark of night—and every other time of day, for that matter—he made her scream with the intensity of the releases he coaxed from her body.

Just thinking of their intense connection made her want him again. She slid her leg between both of his and caressed his chest. He'd taught her how to tell him without words what she wanted from him.

His arms tightened around her, infusing her with a feeling of safety and security.

Her hand took a lazy journey from his chest to his belly

and below. When her fingers closed around his manhood, he released a long, tortured breath. Since she'd been unable to shower him with gifts for his birthday, she decided to give him something far more special and intimate than any gift she could have purchased for him.

Raising herself up, she kissed his chest, focusing her attention on the flat nipples that jumped to attention under her ministrations.

Jack combed his fingers through her hair.

Kissing her way to his belly, Catherine kept up the gentle strokes of her hand over his member. He had shown her how he liked to be touched, and she reveled in the short gasps she drew from him.

"Cat," he whispered, his hips lifting off the bed, seeking. "Come up here."

"Not yet." Continuing to caress him, she bent her head and touched her tongue to the sensitive crown.

Jack sucked in a sharp, deep breath.

Encouraged by his response, she took him into her mouth. She wasn't sure if she was doing it right, but judging by his rapid breathing and the tightening of his fingers in her hair, she sensed he was enjoying it. Running her tongue along his length, she kept up the steady movement of her hand.

"Cat, *honey*."

She heard the note of warning in his voice and knew what he was trying to tell her, but she continued undeterred. Opening her mouth wider, she took as much of him as she could, but he was so big.

Jack groaned, and his hips surged. When a tremble rippled through his body, Catherine glanced up at him and found his face tight with tension, his eyes blazing as he watched her every move. Taking him deep one more time, she lashed him with her tongue and sent him into release.

His seed filled her mouth. She swallowed frantically, but some still escaped from the corner of her lips. She wiped it away and stretched out on top of him. His eyes were closed, his breathing ragged, his face damp with sweat.

Catherine brushed her lips over his. "Happy birthday."

A sound that was half grunt, half laugh escaped from him. His arms encircled her, and he settled her head on his shoulder. "Best birthday ever."

"Did I do it right?" she asked softly.

"So right. Any better and you might've stopped my heart."

Smiling, Catherine closed her eyes and began to drift off to sleep.

A shotgun blast shattered the peaceful night.

Jack startled and eased her off him so he could sit up.

Catherine sat up, too, and tugged the sheet over her breasts. "Jack?"

He listened intently. "Shh."

"Westwood!" A voice called from the yard. "Show yourself!"

Something about that voice was familiar to Catherine, and a ripple of fear traveled through her.

Jack reached for his breeches.

"Where are you going?" she whispered. "He's not looking for you. He wants the duke, and he has a gun!"

He pulled on his shirt and bent to kiss her. "No matter what happens tonight, never forget how much I love you."

"Jack!"

Another gunshot. "Westwood! Show yourself before I come in after you."

Catherine got out of bed and fumbled her way into a wrapper.

"Stay here," Jack said as he left the bedroom. "I'll be back."

"*Jack!*"

He turned, and the hard expression on his face stopped her cold. "Stay here, Catherine."

Her heart raced with fear and dread. If she lost him now . . . Even though he'd told her to stay in the bedroom, she moved to the front room to better hear and watch the proceedings in the yard. Through a crack in the curtains she could see three men on horseback illuminated by the full moon.

"You have something that belongs to me, Westwood."

That low, sinister voice sent shock waves through her. *Oh God, Lindsey!* And why was he calling Jack Westwood?

"I have nothing of yours, Lindsey. You would do well to remove yourself from my property."

His property? Whatever was he saying? He would lose his position when the duke found out.

"Where is Lady Catherine?" Lindsey asked as he dismounted from his horse.

"That is no business of yours."

"She is my fiancée!"

"Not anymore she isn't."

The look on Lindsey's face sent a shiver of fear through Catherine. "Explain yourself."

"Lady Catherine is my wife."

"*That's impossible!*" Lindsey roared. "She's mine! She belongs to me!"

"She never belonged to you."

Catherine watched, horrified, as Lindsey reached for his sidearm. "*No!*" she cried, rushing through the door. Blinded by fear, she threw herself at Jack, ready to take the bullet for him.

"Catherine, I told you to stay inside," he said tightly, as he drew her in close to him. "I'll handle this."

"I won't let him kill you."

"He wouldn't dare kill me."

Lindsey glared at Jack. "Don't be so certain, Westwood."

Clinging to her husband, Catherine glanced up to find his face taut with tension.

"Why does he keep calling you that, Jack?"

Ignoring the question, Jack addressed Lindsey once more. "I'm not going to tell you again to remove yourself at once. You are trespassing on private property."

Lindsey sent his eyes on a lascivious journey over Catherine's barely clad body.

"As are you."

"Take your eyes off my wife this instant, or I shall see you at dawn."

Lindsey snorted. "Your *wife* doesn't seem to know who exactly she married. Is it possible that you deceived her?"

"You have no idea what you're talking about, Lindsey," Catherine said. "You're an evil, reprehensible man, and I'd rather be married to a toad than to you."

Lindsey's expression went from arrogantly amused to dark and sinister in the blink of an eye. "For someone who claimed such *disdain* for the aristocracy, you've certainly settled into your new role as a duchess rather quickly, *Your Grace.*"

The words sent a jolt of shock through Catherine. "Why is he calling me that, Jack? What is he saying?"

Jack's posture was rigid. As if she hadn't spoken, he kept his attention fixed on Lindsey. "Get out of here," he said in a low, menacing tone she wouldn't have thought him capable of.

Lindsey stared him down for a long, breathless moment before he turned and remounted his horse. "I'll go, but only because there's nothing here that interests me any longer."

Catherine released the breath she hadn't realized she was holding and felt some of the rigidity leave Jack's posture as well.

"I'll be on my way to meet with your father, Lady Catherine. He'll honor our agreement one way or the other. From the way he was speaking last week at White's, it doesn't much matter to him if it's you or your luscious sister Madeleine who becomes my bride. I hear that Madeleine is the amenable sister, which is much more to my liking anyway. Not to mention, she's untouched. I prefer an obedient, docile, *chaste* woman to a shrew like you."

An almost inhuman growl erupted from Catherine at the thought of her lovely, precious sister married to that beast. When she would've run after Lindsey, Jack held her back.

With an evil laugh, Lindsey spun his big horse around and galloped out of the yard. His men followed, leaving a cloud of dust in their wake.

Catherine struggled against Jack's tight hold. "We have to stop him. We can't let him near Madeleine. She'll never be able to fight him off the way I did. *We have to do something!*" Catherine knew she was on the verge of hysteria, but the thought of that evil monster touching her sister had caused something inside her to snap.

"We will go after him, Cat. I promise you, he won't lay a hand on your sister. But before we go, there is something I must tell you."

Chapter Sixteen

Catherine sat very still on the sofa in the cottage's sitting room. The man she had loved with her whole heart and soul stood before her as a stranger. Snippets of conversations raced through her mind.

I'm certain the duke won't mind if we borrow his grandmother's clothing.

I think I'll like this duke of yours.

I'm quite counting on it.

Oh God, she thought as she began to tremble beneath the thin layer of silk covering her.

"Cat, please. Say something."

"My name is Catherine," she said, her tone frosty. "I don't even know yours."

"It's Derek." He knelt before her and reached for her hands. "Derek Eagan."

She pulled back her hands. "Don't touch me."

His face twisted into an expression of agony that might've broken her heart if it hadn't already been shattered beyond repair. He'd lied about *everything*. The days since she met him, the most blissful days of her life, had been built upon so many lies she wondered how she'd ever believe anything he said to her again.

"I did it to protect you from Lindsey. If you'd known who I was, you wouldn't have married me. You would've left that first day, and God knows what might've happened to you. I couldn't let him get to you. I had to protect you."

She stared at him. "And there was nothing in it for you?"

"I *love* you. I have never lied to you about that. I've loved you from the first night I held you in my arms, when you were ablaze with fever. If you'd known the truth, you never would've given me the chance to show you what we could have together. You wouldn't have allowed me to protect you."

"So you *lied to me* and *tricked* me into marrying you?" An appalling thought occurred to her, sucking the breath from her lungs. "Is our marriage even legal?"

"Yes," he said, tightly. "I signed my real name in the register. It's legal."

"Excellent. I am legally married to a man who has lied to me every minute since the day I met him."

"You are legally married to a man who has *loved* you every day since the first instant he laid eyes on you."

"When I was dirty and smelly and feverish?"

"The first instant."

She stood abruptly. She had to get away from him and that face, those eyes, that persuasive voice.

"Cat," he said. "I mean Catherine, we need to go home. To the manor. There are things I must see to there before we set out to find your sister."

"And here I thought we were home."

"I'm sorry."

"I don't wish to go with you. Sunny and I will leave for London in the morning."

A nerve in his cheek pulsed with tension. "I can't leave you here alone with Lindsey in the area."

"Post some of your footmen, *Your Grace*."

He winced. "For better or worse, you are my wife and my duchess, and I won't leave you here unprotected, nor will I allow you to travel unaccompanied."

Duchess. If she hadn't been so devastated by his deceit she might've laughed at the title. Had anything ever been more preposterous?

"Do you wish to get dressed before we set out for home?" They engaged in a silent battle of wills that ended when she stepped around him and went into the bedroom, slamming the door behind her. Fuming, she grabbed a chemise and one of the day dresses the seamstress had made for her. She removed her wrapper and gasped when the bedroom door opened. Catherine scrambled to cover her naked body.

"A bit late for modesty, isn't it?" he drawled.

"A bit late for the truth, isn't it?"

Taken aback by her retort, he stared at her. Clearly, the *duke* wasn't used to being spoken to so harshly. Well, he'd better get used to it.

Trying to dress while keeping all the important parts covered turned out to be more complicated than she'd expected. When she was finally clothed, she waited for him to tell her what he expected her to do next. If she had her way, she'd take her meager belongings and be gone. But the fact that they were legally wed gave him the right to tell her what to do. She wondered if it were still possible to request an annulment.

While she stood rigidly still, he jammed her clothing into a carpetbag he unearthed from the closet. Holding out his hand to her, he said, "Please come."

Catherine folded her arms.

"If I have to toss you over my shoulder, I'll do it. Either you can walk out of here under your own power or under mine, but I am *not* leaving you here. What will it be?"

Blinking back tears, she let her eyes wander to the rumpled bed they'd so recently occupied. In this tiny house, she'd known true happiness for the first time in so many years. Until it had been yanked away from her, exposed as a lie of such epic proportions she might never fully understand it or how she'd been such a gullible fool. A glance at his handsome, intractable face reminded her of how she'd been so easily swept away by him.

She stalked past him through the living area and into the yard. He followed and walked over to Hercules, who waited patiently for his master. Sunny had been delivered to the stables earlier in the day to get the older horse out of the heat. Before Catherine had the presence of mind to object, her husband took her by the waist and lifted her onto the horse.

"What do you think you're doing?" Catherine sputtered.

He swung up behind her, hooked an arm around her and drew her in close to him. "Taking my wife home."

Catherine struggled against his tight hold and nearly unseated them both.

"Sit still," he growled.

The heat of his large body seeped through her clothing, making her skin tingle with awareness. That he still had such power over her, in every possible way, rankled and appalled her. He'd played her for a fool from the day they met. She refused to allow him to play her anymore.

Derek's heart and mind raced with worry and fear. He'd expected her to be angry, but deep inside he'd hoped and prayed she'd understand that he'd done it for *her*, to protect *her*. However, judging by the rigid way she tried to hold herself apart from him, it was clear that she'd rather be anywhere else than in his arms, stealing through the dark of night on the back of his horse.

To think, just an hour ago, she'd brought him such overwhelming pleasure with her mouth and tongue. Remembering it sent a surge of lust straight to his cock, which thrust against the confines of his breeches.

Catherine let out a most unladylike squeal. "Don't touch me with that thing!"

Even though his heart ached at the rancor he heard in her voice, he chuckled. "Where do you expect me to put it? There's not exactly a lot of extra room up here."

"Put it anywhere but against me!"

He pressed his lips to her ear. "That's not what you said when you had it in your mouth."

A shudder overtook her body. "Don't be vulgar."

Brushing his tongue over her earlobe, he said, "It's hardly vulgar to speak of lovemaking with one's own wife."

Catherine shifted her head away from him.

"I understand you are angry with me—and with good reason. We will have ample time to discuss that after we've seen to your sister's safety. When we arrive at Westwood Hall, I would appreciate it if you made an effort to hide your feelings of enmity toward me from the servants unless you wish for our marital strife to be the talk of the village by morning."

"You're already speaking differently," she said so softly he had to strain to hear her.

"I beg your pardon?"

"You sound nothing at all like my Jack."

"Whom do I sound like?" Derek asked, genuinely baffled.

"The aristocrat you are."

"How is that so different from whom I've been?"

"It's as different as night and day."

"And you so preferred the penniless estate manager to the wealthy duke?"

She nodded. "I understood him and his world."

"Maybe if you give the duke a chance, you'll come to understand him and his world as well."

"I know enough about his world to last me a lifetime, and none of it appeals to me."

"You do a disservice to us both by judging me based on your experiences with your uncle, your father and Lord Lindsey. Not all aristocrats are created equal."

Apparently, Catherine had nothing to say to that.

They rode the rest of the way to the manor in silence, but Derek was acutely aware of her body pressed against his, the fragrance of her hair, the softness of her belly under his hand. He wanted to move his hand up to cup her breast and toy with her nipple but knew such an advance would be unwelcome. The knowledge made his heart ache from the loss of her love.

On the short ride home, it became abundantly clear to Derek that he was going to have to start all over to win her heart. And this time would be far more difficult than the first time had been. His every word would be treated with suspicion and contempt until he was able to prove himself to her all over again. The enormity of the task he had before him was unlike any challenge he'd ever faced, and the stakes had never been higher.

When they entered the yard, Derek directed Hercules to the front portico. As Rutledge rushed out to meet them, Derek experienced a sense of desperation. What if she never again felt for him the way she had only an hour ago? After having experienced that kind of love, how would he go on without it?

"Catherine." He tightened his arm around her and pressed his lips to her neck.

She drew in a sharp, deep breath as every muscle in her body tensed.

"I did a terrible thing by deceiving you, but I'm still the same man you fell in love with. The heart that belongs only to you still beats in my chest. I will do everything in my power to make you happy. You need only let me."

Catherine twisted free of his tight embrace and allowed Rutledge to help her down from the horse.

The butler glanced up at Derek. "Mr. Bancroft."

"It's all right, Rutledge. Her Grace is aware of my title."

"Ah," the butler said, obviously pleased by the news. "Very good, Your Grace."

Derek had no doubt the deception had been difficult for his servants, who showed him the utmost respect and decorum at all times. "Welcome to Westwood Hall, Your Grace."

"Thank you, Mr.—" Catherine murmured.

"Rutledge, my lady."

"Mr. Rutledge."

Derek was relieved that her breeding and manners took precedence over her anger.

"Your Grace," Rutledge said to Derek. "If I may, we received word from your cousin that he is bringing Her Grace's sister, Lady Madeleine, to Westwood Hall. It seems they are betrothed, and she is in some sort of danger."

If Rutledge had told Derek that the world was coming to an end at the stroke of midnight, he would not have been more shocked than he was to hear that Simon was betrothed to anyone, let alone Catherine's sister.

"Oh!" Catherine exclaimed, tears sparkling in her eyes. "Then she is safe." She grasped the startled butler's arm. "My sister is safe?"

"I assure you," Derek said to his wife, "if Simon has her under his protection, she is quite safe." He couldn't wait to hear how his rakehell of a cousin had ended up betrothed to the belle of the Season. Recalling his one brief encounter with Catherine's stunning sister, Derek had an inkling of how it might've come to pass, but he would need to see with his own eyes to believe it. "This news saves us a trip to London."

Mrs. Langingham came rushing down the stairs wearing a heavy robe over her nightclothes and a cap on her hair. "Oh, Mr. and Mrs. Bancroft. Welcome."

"Her Grace has been told," Rutledge said.

Mrs. Langingham dropped into a deep curtsy before Catherine. "Your Grace, it is my honor to welcome you home."

"Mrs. Langingham," Derek said. "Please show Her Grace to the bedchamber next to mine."

"Of course, sir. This way, Your Grace." After barking at the maids to draw Her Grace a bath, Mrs. Langingham gestured for Catherine to follow her up the stairs.

At the landing halfway up the grand staircase, Catherine turned briefly to look at him. In the instant before she schooled her expression to one of indifference, he saw fear and anxiety and heartbreak on her beautiful face. Before he could reassure her that none of the most important things between them had changed, she turned and let Mrs. Langingham lead her away.

Chapter Seventeen

As Catherine followed the diminutive housekeeper down long corridors, she wished she had bread crumbs to drop so she could find her way out again. The deeper she traveled into the palatial home, the more anxious she became.

Remembering Mrs. Langingham's kindness during her illness, Catherine made an effort to keep up with the older woman's nervous chatter.

Mrs. Langingham bustled into a warm bedchamber done in rose silks and burgundy velvets. This room was much larger than the one Catherine had been given the first time she stayed here.

The housekeeper yanked open the heavy drapes and threw open the window to let in the cool evening breeze. "We've sent one of the footmen to the village to see if Your Grace's new gowns are finished. Of course, His Grace will want to take you to London to be properly outfitted."

"That won't be necessary—"

"I just had the staff up here day before yesterday to freshen the linens and dust," she said. "Isn't that a stroke of good fortune? Now, let me check on your bath." She went into the attached bathing room, leaving Catherine alone with her thoughts. Her mind raced as she struggled to process her sudden change in station. Married to a *duke*, of all things. Thinking back to the first night, when she'd been so terribly ill, she realized the deception had begun then. Perhaps if she'd been in her right mind, she would've known to question how an estate manager had such authority in the home of a duke.

She thought of the luxurious coach that had conveyed her to Scotland and of their wedding night at the inn when the staff had fallen over themselves to tend to the newlyweds. They'd known who he really was and had given him the respect afforded a duke.

All the signs had been there, but she'd missed them. He'd succeeded in so completely dazzling her with his charm, wit and lovemaking that it had never occurred to her to question anything he told her.

Now she would question every word he uttered. She would always wonder if he was telling her the truth or some version of it. Surely there were laws on the books that would give her a way out of a marriage she'd been coerced into. Images of the blissful days and nights she'd spent in his arms at the cottage flashed through her mind, torturing her with reminders of what could've been.

When her legs would no longer support her, she sank into an armchair. Her hands trembled, and her stomach ached. It would've been better if she'd never known the bliss of his love. Then she wouldn't have to suffer through this agony.

"Off we go," Mrs. Langingham said when she returned.

Weary and overwhelmed, Catherine allowed Mrs. Langingham to take charge. Catherine was led into the bathing room, undressed and shepherded into the tub full of steaming water, which went a long way toward taking away the chill that had settled deep into her bones despite the heat of the evening. While her hair was washed, Catherine focused on a painting on the wall that reminded her of home. Comforted by thoughts of her village, she ached for the children, the books, the stables. She understood that world. This world, the world occupied by her new husband, was entirely foreign to her.

Mrs. Langingham handed her a cake of soap, which Catherine dragged over her skin out of necessity more than anything. Maybe if she scrubbed hard enough, she could clean off the stain his deception had left on her. She was helped out of the tub by strong, competent hands. Her hair was dried and brushed. A night rail was produced.

"Over your head now," Mrs. Langingham said in the cheerful singsong voice she'd used to guide Catherine through her bath. "We'll be needing to find you a lady's maid who can attend to you properly."

"I don't need a maid."

"Of course you do, Your Grace."

When she was dressed, Catherine sat on the edge of the bed, and Mrs. Langingham continued to bustle around the room, cleaning up.

"Can I fix you something to eat, Your Grace?"

"I'd prefer that you call me Catherine."

Mrs. Langingham stopped what she was doing and stared at her. "But I can't, Your Grace. It wouldn't be proper!"

"When we are alone, there should be nothing preventing you from using my given name. I'm no different from you or anyone else who works here."

"But, my lady, that's not true. You're our mistress now. We are at your service."

"It's not what I want."

"It is not my place to speak freely."

Catherine looked up at her. "Please speak your mind."

"Your Grace, the duke is the finest man I've ever known. Anything he did was only with your well-being in mind."

Catherine doubted his motives had been that pure.

"I understand that you have suffered a shock today, but I ask of you, I *implore* you to give him a chance. To let him show you—"

"Thank you, Mrs. Langingham," Jack—or rather *Derek*—said from the passageway that joined their two rooms. He wore a dark blue robe, and his damp hair indicated he'd recently had a bath of his own. "I can take it from here."

"Of course, Your Grace." Mrs. Langingham seemed embarrassed to have been caught extolling her employer's virtues. "Good night to you both." The door clicked shut behind her, leaving them alone.

An awkward silence hung over the room, reminding Catherine once again of what had been lost.

"Do you have everything you need?"

Catherine fisted the counterpane, worried that if she let go she'd slide into a boneless puddle on the floor. "Yes."

As he walked over to the bed and sat next to her, Catherine's heart began to pound, and her mouth went dry. She wasn't sure what she wanted more—to lean away from him or into him.

He reached for her hand, pried it free of the grip she had on the counterpane and enveloped it in his much larger, much warmer hand. His touch and his alluring scent reminded her of what they'd shared in the cottage, and her heart broke all over again.

"I have something I wish to give you," he said, sliding a gold band that glittered with diamonds and rubies onto her finger before bringing her hand to his lips for a soft kiss. "Like this room that's now yours, the ring was my mother's. I've saved it all these years, planning to give it to my wife someday. It pained me on our wedding day to not be able to give you a ring, but there wasn't time to retrieve it from the safe. After Lindsey came here looking for you that first time, all I could think about was getting to you before he did."

Catherine wanted to reject the overture. She wanted to tell him it didn't matter if she had a ring or not, but knowing how painful the loss of his parents had been, she didn't have the heart to take the ring off and give it back to him. Thinking of his parents and the story he'd told her about their horses being spooked made her wonder. "Was what you told me about how your parents died true?"

"Yes. I was six. I went to bed a little boy and woke up a duke. I've been a duke ever since. The only break I've ever gotten from my duties since I reached my majority was the seven days I spent at the cottage with you."

Something in the way he said that told her his position hadn't been without its burdens. "And were you really a twin?"

Nodding, he said, "I swear to you, everything I told you was true—except my name."

Unable to remain seated next to him any longer, she got up and walked over to the fireplace that was cold and empty on this warm evening.

He followed her. "I will do everything in my power to make you happy, Catherine," he said, taking her hands and bringing them to his lips. "If you would only give me a chance to show you how our life could be. It doesn't have to be so different from what we shared at the cottage."

Though she'd intended to remain silent, a snort of disbelief escaped from her lips.

"I understand you find that hard to believe," he continued, undeterred. "I want you to know that I respect your feelings about the aristocracy. In fact, I share many of them. I have no need for society or a life spent flitting from one ballroom to another. I am perfectly content to have a quiet life right here with you and whatever children we may be blessed to have. What you must believe is that I truly love you."

Catherine's mind raced with a hundred thoughts and questions. She wanted—no, *needed*—so badly to believe his love was true, even if nothing else he'd told her was. "I feel the fool," she said softly. "There were so many clues. Why didn't you tell me after we were married?"

"I tried to tell you on our wedding night. I told you there was something I needed to tell you, but you said there'd be plenty of time for that later. You said then you'd never leave me because you couldn't possibly live without me. Do you remember?"

"I remember a lot of things," she said stiffly, "such as the seven days that followed our wedding during which you had ample time to inform me that I had not, in fact, married an estate manager as I'd been led to believe. Rather, I was married to the duke himself, the duke I'd been told was abroad for the summer."

His face was a study in blatant pain, and why that hurt her, as well, would be something she'd ponder later when his large presence wasn't requiring her full attention.

"I have no reason to hope that you will believe me, but I had planned to tell you the truth tomorrow."

Again, she snorted in disbelief. "Then you'll pardon *me* if I *don't* believe you."

"I wanted us to have one week together before I changed everything. I wanted to celebrate the best birthday I've had since I was a very little boy in peace. I was going to tell you in the morning."

"I have no way to know if that is true."

"It is, Catherine. I swear to you—"

She held up a hand to stop him, and the diamonds on the band he'd placed on her finger glittered in the candle-light. "Please. I simply can't listen to any more of your *assurances*."

Judging from the stormy expression on his face, the duke was unused to anyone shutting him down, least of all a woman.

"Let's get some rest," he said, sounding suddenly less sure of himself. "Perhaps things will seem less dire in the morning."

Startled, she looked over at him. "Surely you don't expect . . ."

"We are still married, my love, and I most certainly intend to share your bed."

As her expressive eyes flashed with indignation, Derek told himself he was a heartless bastard. A true gentleman would've given her the night to herself, so she could come to terms with what had happened. A desperate man in love, however, feared if he gave her too much time to think about the many ways he'd done her wrong, he'd have no chance of earning her love a second time. He couldn't let that happen.

"I don't wish to share a bed with you, Your *Grace*."

The utter disdain in her tone wounded him. Didn't she know he'd relinquish his title and everything he owned to see her look at him again with the love she'd given so freely only a few hours ago? Derek would have given up his title and holdings in a heartbeat, if only they wouldn't have gone to Anthony.

"I'm afraid I must insist."

The look she gave him was so full of hatred that

something inside him shriveled up and died, a feeling not unlike what he'd experienced when he lost his parents.

"I'd like to wait up for Madeleine." Her voice wavered with emotion. "I haven't seen her in such a long time."

"They're not due to arrive until close to dawn. There's no need for you to sit up all night waiting for her. You'll have plenty of time with your sister tomorrow." He stood and tugged on the tie to his robe.

She shrank back from him, as if he were going to attack her or something equally unsavory.

Reaching out, he ran a hand over her face, making her flinch.

"I'm not a monster, Catherine," he said softly. "Everything I did was done with your best interests at heart."

"*Everything?*"

"The only thing I ever lied to you about was my name."

Her eyes widened with incredulity. "You honestly believe that, don't you? You honestly *think that was your only lie!*" Pushing past him, she paced the length of the room before turning to face him. In the candlelight, she was magnificent. Her hair shone like spun gold, her blue eyes were hot with fire and her breasts swayed under the thin lawn of her night rail. "*Everything* was a lie! Every word, every kiss, every gesture, every moment of laughter and love. *It was all a lie!*"

Her voice caught on a helpless sob, and Derek went to her. "It wasn't all a lie," he said, putting his arms around her rigid body.

She fought him with everything she had. "Don't touch me!"

Derek feared if he let her go now, he might never get this close to her again, so he tightened his hold on her, bringing his mouth down on hers. At first, her lips were rigid, and Derek again mourned the loss of the warmth and love they'd shared only hours earlier.

Even though he suspected he was fighting a losing battle, he kept kissing her, kept his free hand moving over her curves, kept trying. He cupped her breast and ran his thumb over the rigid peak.

Her gasp provided him entry to the sweet richness of her mouth. While continuing to tease her nipple, he stroked her tongue and almost collapsed from the sheer relief when she gave an answering swipe of her own tongue.

Encouraged, he grasped the linen covering her, tugging it up and over her hips while continuing to ravage her mouth. The hands that had been pushing so hard against his chest were now clutching his robe, as if to keep him from getting away. He pulled her night rail higher, breaking the kiss only long enough to draw it up and over her head. Opening his robe, he brought her in tight against him, the heat of their skin incinerating him.

"Catherine," he whispered against the curve of her neck. "I love you more than anything. I love you more than life." Using his lips and tongue and teeth, he set out to remind her of what they'd shared for so many days in their little cottage. He never broke the kiss as he backed her up to the bed and came down on top of her, capturing her mouth again. "I'll take you to Paris, Egypt, Rome." His lips were soft but firm against hers. "We'll cross the ocean to New York. We'll go everywhere you want to go. I'll get you every book that ever existed."

Her hands fell to her sides as if she were now unwilling to touch him. That was all right, he decided. He had a long way to go in convincing her to forgive him for the deception that had resulted in her being married to a duke. He was convinced that as long as he could continue to please her here in their marriage bed, he might stand a chance at convincing her to give him a chance outside the bedchamber.

With that in mind, he kissed his way down the front of her, cupping each plump breast and paying homage to the sensitive crests. Almost against her will, or so it appeared to him, she whimpered and pushed her hips against him, seeking him. He'd never worked harder to ensure her pleasure. His lips had never been more pervasive, more determined. He used everything in his arsenal to fire the passion that lived within her. It had been his before. It could be his again. Until then, his every breath would be devoted to reaching the day when she would again look at him the way she had before Lindsey had showed up and ruined everything.

"There's nothing I wouldn't do for you," he whispered as he kissed his way to her soft belly. "Nothing I wouldn't get for you should you desire it. Nothing at all. You need only to ask, and it shall be yours."

Her body trembled under him, and he risked a glance up at her face, fearing he'd find tears. Rather, her eyes were closed, and her cheeks were dry. He deduced that the trembling was caused by what he was doing, so he kept it up. Kissing his way to her core, he used his broad shoulders to push her legs apart.

Surrounded by the scent of lavender from her bath, he bent his head to taste her sweetness. His tongue delved between soft folds, drawing a gasp from her as he surrounded the heart of her desire with firm lips. While he stroked her with his tongue, his hands found her breasts, rolling her nipples between his fingers. He sucked hard in time with the pinching action of his fingers until she reached her fulfillment.

Silently.

* * *

Her body had utterly betrayed her. How was she to maintain her distance and think through the implications of all that had transpired if he was going to insist on claiming his marital rights? She could no more resist him here than she could refrain from breathing. And of course, he knew that.

He made slow, sweet love to her, filling her so completely while surrounding her with his scent, his heat and the overpowering presence that had made it so easy for him to deceive her.

Catherine wanted to be immune to him. She wanted to lie there and let him have his way with her without reacting to him, but that was utterly impossible. For she was ashamed to discover that she was no less bewitched by the duke than she'd been by the estate manager. And despite her iron will to resist his overtures, she found herself lifting her hips to better accommodate the large shaft that had brought her such unimaginable pleasure. Against her better judgment, her hands ended up on his back, encouraging him to go faster and deeper. Somehow, she found herself crying out when another shattering peak had her dazzled by the sheer magnificence of the feeling that soared through her heart and body.

The high, however, was brief and fleeting when she remembered how adeptly he'd lied to her. She came crashing down in a painful fall that made her ache all over. Unlike the euphoria she'd come to expect after lovemaking, despondence filled her this time.

As their bodies settled and cooled, he pulled her close to him the way he always did, whispering the words of love and adoration she'd fallen asleep to every night in the cottage. Her eyes burned with tears as she relived every sweet moment with him, thinking of the many clues she'd missed along the way. For one who'd always fancied herself smarter than the average person, she'd been rather easy to fool. Well, she wouldn't be easy to fool again. While she apparently had no control over her body's reaction to him, she could certainly control how her heart reacted.

During that long night, she built a wall around her damaged organ that an army of men wouldn't be able to penetrate. She only hoped her wall was strong enough to keep out one determined duke.

Chapter Eighteen

Derek gave up on sleep just before dawn. He moved slowly so he wouldn't disturb Catherine, who slept fitfully next to him. After taking a moment to drink in her features in the faint light peeking in through the drapes, he reached for his robe, tied it around his waist and went through the passageway to his own bedchamber. His valet, Gregory, appeared almost immediately. Derek swore the older man had ghostlike tendencies in his ability to anticipate his employer's every need.

"Good morning, Your Grace. I trust you slept well."

Since he couldn't very well confess to lying awake all night next to the new wife who was furious with him, Derek said, "Very well, thank you. Did my cousin arrive?"

"Yes, Your Grace. He and Lady Madeleine are in the west wing. He insisted on keeping her close to him in case of trouble."

"Very good. Was there any sign of Lord Lindsey on the road?"

"Not that he mentioned, sir."

Derek was anxious to see his cousin and to make a plan to protect both the women they loved. But the woman *he* loved was his top priority on this first morning after she'd discovered the truth about him. "I could use your assistance with something, Gregory."

"As always, I am at your service, Your Grace."

"The new footman . . ."

"Henry?"

"Yes, that's the one. I need to borrow some breeches about his size."

"Your Grace?"

"I'd appreciate if you keep this between us, but they're for Her Grace."

Gregory seemed momentarily stunned speechless. Then he rallied. "Of course, sir. I will see to it right away."

"Please see to it that he is properly compensated for the clothing."

"Yes, Your Grace." They moved through his toilet with the usual efficiency. As Gregory tied Derek's tie, it occurred to him that Catherine would be disconcerted to see him dressed so formally.

Derek reached up to stop his valet. "I'm going without the tie and collar today."

Once again, Derek could see that he'd shocked his valet. "As you wish, sir."

Gregory helped him into a dark gray coat and brushed any remaining lint from the fabric. "And may I say, Your Grace, my heartfelt congratulations on your nuptials. We are all very pleased for your happiness."

"Thank you, Gregory. I'm quite pleased myself." Or at least he hoped he would be again.

"We are also quite relieved that you married before your birthday."

Right in that moment, Derek realized his staff had been

as concerned about his deadline as he'd been himself. "As am I. Strange how things happen."

"Indeed, sir. And a belated happy birthday to you, Your Grace."

"Thank you, Gregory. Go ahead and break your fast now."

"I'll see to those breeches."

"If you could leave them in here, I'd appreciate it."

"Yes, sir." Gregory nodded and left the room.

Consulting the mirror, Derek adjusted his shirt, feeling naked and unfinished without the tie and collar, but he was willing to do anything he could to make Catherine feel comfortable around him.

He went downstairs, and when he stepped into the kitchen, the staff snapped to attention.

"Your Grace," the cook, Amelia, said. "How may we be of assistance?"

"Good morning, everyone. Could you please prepare a tray for Her Grace? I'll take it up when it's ready."

"Of course, sir," Amelia said. "But we can deliver it, if you'd like."

"I'd prefer to do it myself. I'll be in my study."

"As you wish, Your Grace."

"Thank you." Derek nodded to the others and took his leave. In his study, he found Simon waiting for him.

"Cousin!" Simon said, smiling broadly.

The two men embraced.

"I understand congratulations are in order, Your Grace," Simon said.

"Don't call me that," Derek said, frowning. "It's enough I have to hear it from everyone else. Not you, too."

Simon flashed him a cheeky grin. "At any rate, congratulations on your marriage. I hope you'll be very happy."

Derek hoped so, too. "Thank you." He flipped through

the correspondence that had been left on his desk, giving it a cursory glance. Today was not a day for work, he decided. "And by the way, I sent you to London for information, not to start a scandal for the ages."

"I have been brought low by a woman," Simon said ruefully.

"Never thought I'd see the notorious Simon Eagan hooked and shackled."

Simon winced at Derek's choice of words. "Nor did I, but now that we have both been thoroughly hooked and shackled by the McCabe sisters, I need your assistance to make it official as soon as reasonably possible. No doubt her absence and that of her maid have been discovered by now—along with mine—and her father will be on his way here, possibly with Lindsey in tow."

Derek came around the desk to stand before his cousin. "Have you acquired a special license?"

"Yesterday."

"Then I shall summon the vicar from the village immediately." Derek put his hand on Simon's shoulder and looked him in the eye. "You're sure about this?"

"I've never been more certain about anything in my life."

Derek nodded, pleased for his cousin's obvious happiness. "Catherine is very anxious to see her sister."

"Lady Madeleine was exhausted by the journey and overwrought about leaving home under such conditions. I'm told she is still abed." Simon averted his eyes, and Derek surmised that Simon had looked in on his fiancée to gauge her well-being personally. He would've done the same thing himself.

"We'll have the wedding right before luncheon if that meets with your approval." Even if Lord Brisbane had departed at first light, which Derek highly doubted, it would take much of the day to travel to Westwood Hall.

"It does. Thank you, Derek. All the way here I imagined I'd have to convince you of my sincerity toward Lady Madeleine."

"You need not convince me of anything. If this is what you want, if *she* is what you want, then I shall do everything in my power to see that it is done."

"Even if Lindsey brings you up on charges in the House of Lords?"

Derek shrugged. "Let him. I find that I couldn't give a fig about such things any longer."

"Not that you ever really did."

Derek smiled. "Not that I ever did."

"Pardon me, Your Grace," Mrs. Langingham said from the doorway. "Her Grace's breakfast is ready."

"Very good. Thank you." To Simon, he said, "I need to take breakfast to my wife."

"Derek."

Derek turned back to his cousin. "Yes?"

"Are you happy?" Not even to his cousin and closest friend would Derek confess his inner turmoil. To say it out loud would make it worse than it already was. "I've never been happier in my life."

"I'm so pleased to hear that. You surely deserve it."

"Does your father know that I've married?"

"I'm sure the word has reached him by now. I haven't had the pleasure of his company in days."

"I suppose we can expect a visit from him imminently."

"I suppose so."

"Let's get you married before that happens."

After he dispatched a footman to the village to alert the vicar about the midday wedding, Derek carried Catherine's tray upstairs. He was struck by the memory of delivering breakfast in bed to her in the cottage. Then he'd had no doubt she would be thrilled to see him, would welcome him with a warm smile and reach out to him for a kiss. How would he be received today, the day after she learned of his deception?

With a knot in his stomach, he opened the door and stepped into the still-dark room. He placed the tray on the bedside table and opened the heavy velvet curtains to allow in some light. She was on her back, her golden hair spread out on the pillow, her pink lips pursed in sleep. He watched her for a full minute, transfixed by her staggering beauty, before he tore his eyes off her to move forward with his plans.

Traversing the passageway to his own bedchamber, Derek found the clothing he'd asked Gregory to procure and brought it back to Catherine's room.

Perching on the edge of the bed, he took her hand, brought it to his lips and watched her slowly come awake. Her smile was warm, sweet, loving and welcoming. Then the memory of what had transpired the day before stole her smile. The loss was like a knife to his heart.

"Good morning, my love," he said as he had every morning since their wedding. "Did you sleep well?"

"Is Madeleine here? Did my sister arrive?"

"She did, but she is still abed." Derek poured Catherine's tea and stirred in the lemon and honey she preferred.

"I'd like to see her." Catherine sat up, and the sheet covering her fell to her waist, exposing her luscious breasts.

Derek swallowed hard, wishing he still had the right to reach out to caress them the way he would have only yesterday. "You will. Shortly."

Her face flaming with color, she tugged the sheet under her arms and took the teacup from him. "Is it true about her betrothal to your cousin?"

"It is. I've just come from seeing him, and I have to say I've never seen him in such a state. The vicar will be here shortly to marry them."

"And my father and Lord Lindsey?"

"We have no word of them, but we're under the assumption that they will arrive at some point today."

"We must make sure your cousin and Madeleine are married before then."

"And we will, my love. Don't worry."

At his words of love, she became very interested in her teacup.

"Since we have a couple of hours before the wedding, I have something I'd like to show you."

"The only thing I wish to see is my sister."

"You wouldn't want to wake her prematurely when she was up all night and is to be married today, would you?"

She rolled that delectable bottom lip between her teeth. "I suppose another hour or two won't matter after all these weeks."

He spread marmalade on the sweet bread Amelia had provided and handed the plate to his wife.

"Thank you," she murmured.

Once again, he mourned the loss of their easy rapport, the laughter, the harmony and the comfort. *Patience*, he told himself. *Be patient and give her time to come to know you in a new way*. Derek never before would've described himself as an impatient man, but he found now that he was extremely impatient to get back what had been lost between them.

He helped himself to the second piece of sweet bread and poured a cup of the coffee Amelia had brewed for him. They ate in silence, which was so unlike the spirited meals they'd shared since their wedding. Silence had never been so painful.

While they ate, Mrs. Langingham bustled in with clean towels for Catherine's toilet and left as silently as she had come, closing the door behind her.

When they were done, Derek took Catherine's teacup, set it on the tray and reached for the borrowed clothing. "Once you are dressed, I will take you to what I wish to show you."

"That is what you'd like me to wear?" she said of the breeches and linen shirt.

"I thought you might wish to resume your search for the key."

"But I assumed—"

"That the duke would no longer allow you to look for your grandmother's key?"

She nodded.

"You underestimate the duke's desire to please his wife."

She stared at him as if he'd spoken words she couldn't possibly understand.

"I'll leave you to dress and return for you shortly." Before he left the room, he went to the wardrobe and withdrew the boots she'd been using to work at the dig site and left them by the foot of the bed. When he glanced at her over his shoulder she continued to stare at him.

Good, he thought. If he could continue to surprise her, maybe he stood a chance of winning her back.

He had thoroughly surprised her. The duke himself had brought her breakfast. He who had a houseful of servants had poured the tea and spread the marmalade. Himself. He'd thought to provide the clothing she needed to continue her search for her grandmother's key.

As Catherine washed and dressed, she thought of the wall she'd built around her heart and was filled with foolish hope. Who was this man to whom she was married? Was he really so different from the boorish aristocrats she'd had the misfortune to know in the past? Was that possible?

She brushed her long hair until it shone and then twisted it up into a knot that she secured with several well-placed pins.

His soft knock on the door announced his return. Entering the room, he was every bit the dashing duke in the fine gray coat. Though he'd seen her in breeches before, standing before him now in men's clothing, Catherine felt inadequate and less than feminine for the first time.

However, the heated sweep of his eyes over her body disabused her of any doubt that he found her feminine.

"Are you ready?"

"Yes."

"Come with me then."

Even though she'd planned to keep her distance from him today, she couldn't resist curiosity about what he was so eager to show her. She followed him through a confounding maze of hallways and passageways. "I'll never be able to find my way back to my bedchamber."

"It will be familiar to you in no time at all."

"I wish I were so confident."

His smile was warm and loving. "Trust me."

She wanted to. Oh, how she wanted to somehow get back what had been lost, but the deception loomed large between them, reminding her to guard and protect herself from further hurt.

He led her down the grand staircase, past an open door. "That is my study. I spend most of my time there. You should feel free to enter that room whenever you have need of me."

She wanted to be immune to him and had planned to let him do the talking today, but she discovered she didn't possess the will to be intentionally rude to him. "I wouldn't want to interrupt your work."

"I will always want you to interrupt my work."

The wall she had built around her heart might just as well have been made of sand for the ease with which it crumbled when he unleashed that private, intimate smile on her.

They reached a small set of stairs, and he guided her up to the next landing with a hand to her elbow that heated the flesh beneath her thin linen shirt.

"This way," he said gruffly. "You'll want to pay attention to this route as I think you will wish to traverse it rather frequently."

"Is that so?"

"That is so," he said with an arrogant confidence that was so far removed from the demeanor of her Jack Bancroft that Catherine nearly didn't recognize him as the same man.

She was about to say so when he told her to close her eyes. Exasperated, she did as he requested and let him lead her a short distance with the hand he kept on her elbow.

"Okay," he said, sounding excited and animated as he released his hold on her arm. "You can look now."

Catherine opened her eyes and blinked several times to focus in the sunlight that streamed into the enormous room. She sucked in a sharp, deep breath when she realized they were in his library where the shelves were so high she had to tip her head to see all the way to the top. There had to be thousands of volumes! With her hand on her chest to contain her galloping heart, Catherine turned to take it all in.

"What do you think?" he asked, smiling at her stunned reaction.

"I've never seen so many books in one place! Even the library in Father's London home can't compare."

"I've spent many years cultivating our collection."

"Have you read them all?"

"Some but not even close to six hundred." He took a step closer but stopped short of touching her, which seemed to cost him. "I'm wondering how long it would take you to read them all."

"Decades," she said, continuing to marvel at the sheer magnitude.

"That would be fine with me," he said with an endearingly hopeful smile. "Come, look at this." He led her to a table where a huge leather-bound book lay open. "A few years back, I hired a man to catalog our collection. It took him two years to sort and organize everything, but it's all now listed here by title and author and location on the shelves."

Catherine took in the neat, precise penmanship, realizing she could spend months just flipping through the catalog to see what was available.

"You'll be interested in this," he said, taking her hand to tug her along. "All the travel volumes are shelved here."

Catherine gasped at the row after row of books about the places she most wished to visit—Paris, Rome, New York, Cairo, New Delhi. Seeing a book about the pyramids, she ventured a shy glance up at him and found him watching her with great interest. "May I?"

"My darling wife, my library is your library."

Warmed throughout by the love and affection she saw in his eyes, Catherine forced her gaze off him and withdrew the volume from the shelf to flip through a series of intricate drawings of ancient Egypt.

"I thought you might wish to take on the role of overseeing the expansion of our collection," he said casually, as if he weren't offering her the stars, the moon and the sun in one statement.

She again looked up at him to gauge his intent. "You can't be serious."

"Why not? You certainly know more about books than I ever will, having already read so many."

"You've probably read more than I have," she said, for the first time feeling that her extensive reading was inadequate next to someone else's.

"Doubtful." Something about the way he said that single word made her think he might be downplaying his own accomplishment so as not to take away from hers. "At any rate, it's something I think you'd enjoy, so why wouldn't I turn that role over to you?"

Stunned and amazed, Catherine glanced up at him again. The raw yearning she saw on his face quite simply stole her breath.

"I aim to show you, my love," he said, running a finger over her cheek as if he couldn't wait any longer to touch her, "that as my duchess you will want for nothing."

His use of the word "duchess" shattered their fragile accord, reminding her once again of his deception.

Apparently, he realized his error because he winced. "Catherine, darling, *please*." Taking the book from her, he placed it on a table and drew her into his embrace. "Please don't hate me. I couldn't bear it."

"I don't hate you," she said softly. For how could she? If nothing else, he'd saved her from the cruel fate of a forced marriage with Lord Lindsey, and for that she would be eternally grateful.

"You are angry, and you have every right to be."

"I am numb," she said, finding it hard to breathe when pressed against his muscular chest.

"Perhaps once the shock wears off and you have time to consider everything, you might come to see that I acted out of love." His lips were soft against her forehead, and

Catherine had to resist the yearning to tilt her head back to offer him her mouth. "Perhaps you will see that despite everything that's happened, none of the things that truly matter have changed between us."

"I very much wish to believe that."

"You *can* believe that." With both hands on her face, he compelled her to look up at him. "For the rest of my life, I'll never forget the moment your cap fell off and your glorious golden hair came streaming down your back." To emphasize his point, he tugged on the pins holding her hair up, and it cascaded free.

"Your Grace!" What had taken a quarter hour to secure, he'd undone in a heartbeat. He combed his fingers through the strands reverently and touched his lips to her face, leaving a damp trail of soft kisses in his wake. "Derek," he whispered. "My name is *Derek*. Say it, Catherine. Say my name. I've so longed to hear my real name uttered from your sweet lips."

Somehow Catherine knew that if she gave him that, she'd be granting her approval of what he'd done when she most assuredly did not approve. Though it cost her something dear, she stepped back from him and held out her hand for the pins he'd removed from her hair.

His mouth set in an expression of displeasure she hadn't seen before as he dropped the pins into her hand.

Her hands trembled as she attempted to restore order to her hair without a mirror. All sorts of emotions jumbled around inside her, competing for attention: sadness, desire, hope, fear, love, despair. He seemed genuinely devoted to fixing the damage his lies had done to their fledgling marriage, and while Catherine was as confused as she'd ever been, she found she could not be deliberately unkind to him.

"Thank you for showing me your library."

"*Our* library," he said testily. "It's *ours*. Everything I have is yours. While you may not wish to be married to an unsavory aristocrat, you are, in fact, married to a duke."

"Thank you for the reminder," she said in an equally testy tone. "I might've forgotten otherwise."

Clearly unused to being challenged by anyone, he stared at her, agog. The charged silence extended a full minute as neither of them blinked. He was the first to look away, and once again his pain was palpable. His pain, she discovered in that moment, was her pain, too.

Catherine wanted to go to him, to the man who'd shared the agony of his early losses with her, who'd talked of the parents taken from him in an instant and the twin he'd missed his entire life. She wanted to put her arms around him and assure him that somehow they'd get through this and find their way back to each other. But how could she make such assurances when she was no more certain of their future than he was? So she stayed still and waited to see what he would do.

"We have a few hours before your sister marries my cousin," he said. "If you're amenable, we can look for the key until it's time to clean up for the wedding."

Catherine weighed spending more time alone with her husband against the overwhelming desire to see her sister. Since they were apparently joined for life, she decided she'd have plenty of time with him. Right now, seeing her sister took precedence over everything else, if for no other reason than she needed to tell someone she trusted about everything that had happened since she left home.

"I very much appreciate your accommodation of my efforts to find my grandmother's key. The clothes, the tools, your assistance. But at the moment, my need to see my sister is my top priority."

"Very well. I will take you to her at once."

"Thank you, Your Grace."

"Derek," he said once again. "My name is *Derek*."

As he ushered her out of the library, the name was on the tip of her tongue, where it remained stuck for the time being.

Chapter Nineteen

The duke led her to the west wing of the vast house. On the way, he drew her attention to a portrait of his parents. Catherine took a fleeting glance at the handsome couple and made a note of its location, so she could return for a deeper study at a later date.

Outside the bedchamber assigned to Madeleine, her devoted maid Evangeline hovered. When she saw Catherine coming toward her, she let out a most unladylike squeal and rushed toward her. The young woman had been a dear friend of the McCabe sisters back in their village, and they'd brought her with them when their father became the earl.

Catherine embraced the maid, who seemed embarrassed when she pulled back. "My apologies, Your Grace," she said, curtsying before the duke. "I am just so very happy to see Her Grace."

"No apologies needed," he said. "Her Grace would like to see her sister. Is Lady Madeleine awake?"

"Not yet, but I know she'd want you to wake her, Your Grace," Evangeline said to Catherine. "She has missed you so terribly. We all have."

"Thank you, Evangeline. I've missed you, too." Turning to the duke, Catherine looked up at him. "Thank you for your assistance."

Nodding, he said, "I will fetch you for the wedding."

As he walked away, Catherine noticed the way his tailored clothing hugged his muscular frame.

"You found yourself a handsome one, *Your Grace*," Evangeline whispered with a giggle.

Catherine couldn't deny that her husband was indeed a handsome man. "Yes."

"Is he a good man? A kind man?"

"He's . . ."

"I'm sorry," the maid said. "It's certainly none of my business."

Catherine couldn't leave her old friend with the wrong impression, for other than some rather significant untruths, he had been both good and kind to her. "He is a good and kind man."

"I am happy for you then. You certainly deserve nothing less after the way you lost Ian."

"Thank you. I'm going in to see Madeleine now."

"I'll wait out here to give you some privacy. If you need me, just call."

"We will." Leaving Evangeline with another quick hug, Catherine eased the door open and snuck inside, closing the door behind her. She opened the drapes to let in some light and went to her sister's bed. With a hand to Madeleine's shoulder, Catherine nudged her awake. "Maddie," she whispered.

Madeleine let out an unholy shriek when she saw her sister and launched into Catherine's arms. In tears, they hugged for a long time.

"Oh, thank God," Madeleine said. "I was so very worried

about you, Katie. We all were. Even if Father and Mother never said so, they were, too."

Catherine was saddened to hear that her parents had never expressed concern about her absence, at least not to her sister anyway. "I'm sorry I worried you, but I couldn't stay there and be forced into a marriage with that boor."

"I knew exactly why you ran off, but how in the world did you end up *married to a duke*? Aren't you the one who always said you'd rather be trampled by horses than be married to an aristocrat—and one who every single miss in London aspired to marry, no less? And what in heaven's name are you *wearing?*"

Catherine winced at the reminder of her disdain for the *ton,* of which she was now apparently a high-ranking member. She experienced an odd feeling of jealousy at realizing her husband had been the toast of the Season. Naturally, all the marriage-minded young women had wanted to marry the handsome, fabulously wealthy duke who was now her husband. "You won't believe how it happened. *I* still don't believe how it happened."

Madeleine held out her hand to encourage her sister to sit next to her on the bed. "I want to hear all about it."

"*I* want to hear all about how you ended up engaged to his cousin."

"And I shall tell you. After you tell me your story first."

Snuggled up to her sister, Catherine told her everything that had happened since the day she ran away from home and how she'd come to be wearing men's clothing.

"So he led you to believe he was the *estate manager* when he was actually the *duke?*" Madeleine asked, incredulous.

"Yes, and I fell for his story because I was so besotted I would've believed him if he told me the sky was yellow."

"How did you find out he'd lied?"

"Lord Lindsey showed up and referred to him as Westwood, and he had no choice but to tell me. He swears he was going to tell me today, but I no longer know what to believe. I'm all jumbled up inside. He tells me the same heart that loved me as Jack Bancroft still loves me as the Duke of Westwood."

"Do you believe that? Do you believe he loves you?"

"Yes," Catherine said softly. "I believe he does."

"And do you love him?"

"I loved the man with whom I spent ten of the loveliest days of my life, living a dream that was shattered when I found out that he'd lied to me from the very beginning. I loved *that* man more than I've ever loved anyone."

"Even Ian?"

"Yes," Catherine said, pained to admit the truth. "Even Ian."

"That is saying something after the way you mourned him." Seeming lost in thought, Madeleine rolled her bottom lip between her teeth. "Is it possible that you could come to love him just as much as the duke?"

"I don't know," Catherine said, expressing her deepest fear. "I have no idea who he really is." Although he'd worn down her defenses by showing her his library, how was she to know whether he was merely trying to win her over by using the things she'd told him to his advantage? What if she gave him her heart a second time and he lied to her again? "I have to relearn him as if I've just met him. I have to find a way to trust a man who has lied to me every day of our acquaintance."

"It seems to me, from what you've said, that he went to extraordinary lengths to protect you from a fate worse than death. Can you deny that?"

"No, I can't."

"He is very well regarded in town, known as much for his intellect and financial prowess as he is for his handsomeness and title. I would think you at least owe him the chance to show you who he really is before you decide anything for certain."

"You are right. Of course, that is what I must do, but I'm so very angry to have been tricked. I'm having a hard time getting past that."

"I can understand why you're angry. You've always been the smart one in our family, so naturally it would gall you to be deceived this way."

"Yes," Catherine said, "I am truly galled."

"You are also truly married to the man, so you may have to put aside your gall to promote harmony in your life and your home."

Catherine's deep, pained sigh answered for her.

"If he is anything at all like his cousin, you should consider yourself a lucky woman." Madeleine turned on her side and propped her head on her hand. "Is he handsome?"

"Extremely."

"Is he charming?"

"Very much so."

"Is he kind?"

"Yes," Catherine said, thinking of the tender way he'd cared for her when she was ill, the reverence with which he'd loved her and the indulgence he'd shown for her need to find her grandmother's missing key. "He is kind."

"And the rest." Madeleine's face burned with a heated blush. "Is it bearable?"

"It is far, *far* more than bearable. It is pleasure unlike anything I ever could've imagined possible between a man

and a woman. Even last night, when I was as angry with
him as I've ever been with anyone, it was still miraculous."

"Oh, Catherine, you do love him! How could you not
love a man like the one you've just described?"

Catherine moaned. "I am so *humiliated* by the ease with
which he deceived me that I don't *want* to love him anymore."

"In light of his deception, I do believe it is fair for you
to be angry and to perhaps make him suffer for a while, so
he knows you won't abide such behavior in the future. But
if you truly love him, don't take it too far and let your anger
drive him away."

Catherine thought about what her sister had said. "You
are quite right. I shouldn't let him off too easily, but I don't
wish to completely ruin what we shared before his lies
came to light. There was something positively magical
about those days and nights."

Madeleine reached for Catherine's hand and squeezed.
"You may be able to recapture that magic. In time."

"That would be nice." She turned to her sister. "Now,
tell me how you came to be affianced to Mr. Eagan."

Madeleine blushed fiercely again. "He is, without a
doubt, the most utterly charming and handsome man I've
ever met, even if he is a rakehell of the highest order."

"Father must've had an apoplexy when you took an
interest in him."

"You don't know the half! I had a ferocious row with
Father *and* Mother that Mr. Eagan overheard." Madeleine
shuddered with distaste. "It was so unsavory."

"I take it as a good sign that he overheard but didn't
run away."

"Quite to the contrary," Madeleine said with a satisfied
smirk. "He declared his intentions to court me and promised Father he would be respectful at all times."

"And has he been?"

"*Yes*," Madeleine said with exasperation. "He has yet to even kiss me! I fear if I had to wait any longer than today for his kiss I might go absolutely *mad*."

Catherine laughed at her sister's dismay. "You love him then?"

"Terribly. The very sight of him makes my heart pound and my mouth go dry. I get all fluttery and achy." Her face flushed from chin to forehead. "Down there."

"I know that feeling."

"Catherine, you must tell me what to expect on my wedding night. I honestly have no idea what I should do or say or *anything*."

"Oh, my darling, you mustn't be afraid. If Simon truly loves you, and I suspect he does if he has reformed his rakish ways to be the man you need him to be, then he will take all due care to ensure your pleasure."

"How will he do that? You have to tell me."

Catherine thought about what she should say and how she should say it. "He will remove your clothing and his."

"*All* of it?"

"Yes, all of it," Catherine said, laughing. "It is really quite exquisite." Catherine thought of the first time she'd lain with Jack—or rather Derek. It was nearly impossible to think of him as anyone other than her Jack. "The feel of his skin against yours is a most thrilling sensation. I promise you will enjoy it. He will touch you and kiss you—all over."

"Everywhere?" Madeleine asked, her voice a startled squeak.

"*Everywhere*," Catherine said, tingling at the memories of such intimacies with her own husband.

"Oh, my Lord." Madeleine put her hands over her ears. "I am utterly unprepared to hear such things."

Catherine pulled on her sister's arms to remove her hands from her ears. "That's not even the best of it."

"There's *more*?"

"Oh, yes, much more."

"I may expire on the spot from hearing about this. How will I ever endure *doing* it?"

"You will more than endure it, my dear. You will come to crave it."

"I can't imagine that." Madeleine set her jaw in the mulish expression Catherine knew so well. "You may as well tell me the rest."

Smiling indulgently at her sister, Catherine said, "Are you aware of what a man has . . . down there."

"It's a phallus," Madeleine said proudly.

Catherine bit back a laugh at Madeleine's use of such a scientific word. "Yes. When a man is aroused, his phallus becomes hard. It throbs and pulses."

Madeleine shuddered. "It sounds dreadful."

"I assure you," Catherine said, laughing now, "it is *not* dreadful." She smiled thinking of the first time she saw Jack's—*Derek's*—phallus and how she'd feared it wouldn't fit inside her. "When you first see it, you may worry it won't fit."

"*Fit?* Fit *where?*"

"He will put it inside of you, love."

Madeleine's mouth fell open in utter shock. "Inside of me."

"Your body will ease his entry by producing moisture. After the first time, which does hurt a small bit, it will be highly pleasurable."

"It sounds like complete torture. Maybe I have been hasty in agreeing to this marriage—"

Catherine stopped her sister by placing two fingers on her lips. "With whom would you rather experience this 'torture'? Your lovely Mr. Eagan or Lord Lindsey?"

At the reminder of the vile lord, Madeleine seemed to rally. "You will stand up for me, won't you?"

"Of course, I will."

With the help of one of the housemaids, Catherine found her way back to her bedchamber where another maid loaded gowns of every imaginable color into the wardrobe.

"Ah, excuse me," Catherine said.

Startled, the young maid spun around, her eyes widening. "Oh, Your Grace, it is true what they said!"

"What who said?"

"The other maids. They said Her Grace is as lovely as a fairy princess, and it's true. You are!"

Embarrassed by the girl's effusiveness, Catherine said, "That is very kind of you to say. What is your name?"

"I'm so sorry, Your Grace!" She dropped into a curtsy. "I am Julia, your lady's maid. His Grace instructed me to take good care of his lady wife."

"It is very nice to meet you, Julia, but I do not require a lady's maid. I am quite capable of dressing myself."

"His Grace mentioned you might say that very thing, and he asked me to remind you it is nearly impossible for a lady to tie her own corset."

"*His Grace* knows I rarely wear a corset," Catherine said, and then realized she'd embarrassed the young woman with her candor.

Julia cleared her throat. "All your lovely new gowns require a corset if they are to fit properly." She took a careful and close look at Catherine's figure. "At least you won't need the bust cream that is all the fashion in town."

"Bust cream?" Catherine asked in disbelief.

"Oh, yes, Your Grace," Julia said, her expression deadly serious. "Lady's maids are using the cream to enhance the assets that you were fortunate to come by naturally."

Catherine had never heard anything more ridiculous and was thankful for her natural assets.

"His Grace said that I am to dress you for your sister's wedding." As she spoke, Julia moved about the room, laying a chemise made of finest linen, drawers, silk stockings and garters on the bed. "It's so exciting, is it not? Two weddings in one week! What a happy place Westwood Hall has become all of a sudden."

"Yes," Catherine said. How was she to send this dear, sweet girl away without hurting her feelings? Of course, *His Grace* had known she never would. "A happy place indeed."

"Might I suggest this for an afternoon wedding?" Julia withdrew a satin gown in the palest shade of blue. "It will look so lovely with your eyes."

"That would be fine. Thank you."

"You don't have to thank me, Your Grace. It is my pleasure to serve you."

"I do have to thank you. I will always thank you. And you must call me Catherine when we are alone."

Scandalized, Julia struck a hand to her heart. "I could never!" The young girl swallowed convulsively. "Your Grace."

Resigned to never again hearing her given name from people who were of the same station she'd been before her father ascended to the earldom, Catherine turned herself over to the eager maid. Julia worked with single-minded determination over the next hour to transform her into a duchess. Hot tongs were applied to her hair, rouge to her cheeks and paint to her lips. Silk stockings were affixed to garters, and her corset tied so tightly she could barely breathe.

Throughout the entire ordeal, Catherine avoided looking at the mirror and allowed her mind to drift. This would be her life from now on. Constant fawning, dressing, primping—all useless fripperies to a woman more concerned with and accustomed to the more practical aspects of life.

He'd said she could be any kind of duchess she wished to be. Did that extend to teaching the village children how to read? Tending to the tenant families when they were struck by illness? Continuing the search for her grandmother's key until it was found and not until the duke ran out of patience with her folly? On this first day, he'd been trying to impress her and earn back her favor by providing the clothing she needed to work at the dig site. While she'd been pleased by the gesture, she would reserve judgment to see how long he kept up the pretense of allowing his duchess to dig in the dirt.

It wouldn't take long to determine if he'd meant what he said. As a plan to test his fortitude took root in her mind, a smile tugged at her lips. She would test him at every turn and decide for herself if his intentions were truly honorable.

"Your Grace," Julia said. "You can look now." The hint of humor in her maid's tone wasn't lost on Catherine.

For some reason Catherine was exceptionally nervous as she raised her eyes to study her reflection. A gasp escaped from her lips. She had been completely transformed. A once provincial woman was now a regal duchess from head to toe. Rising from her vanity, she went to stand in front of the full-length mirror, gaping at the sight before her.

"Are you not pleased, Your Grace?" Julia asked timidly.

Catherine cleared her throat and tried to get her brain working again. "I am very pleased," she said, though she barely recognized the woman staring back at her. "Thank you."

A knock on the door had Julia scurrying to answer it. In the mirror, Catherine watched Julia curtsy to the duke.

"Her Grace is all ready, Your Grace."

"Thank you, Julia. That'll be all." As he dismissed the maid with three little words, he was every bit the imperial duke and nothing at all like the man she'd spent ten glorious days loving with her whole heart. In the mirror she could see he was also every bit the duke in his attire— black velvet coat, striped trousers, creamy white shirt with the new fashionable collar and tie, and black shoes polished to a brilliant shine.

Because she could no longer delay the inevitable, she turned to him and watched his eyes heat with desire and satisfaction. Naturally, he was satisfied. He'd gotten his way. He now had a duchess who looked every bit the part. She was certain he was quite satisfied indeed.

"You are divinely beautiful," he said in a hoarse whisper.

Though the word "divine" made for a better-than-average compliment, she said, "Anyone can be divinely beautiful with the proper resources." The moment the words were out of her mouth she felt like an ungrateful, catty shrew.

"All the resources on God's green earth could not create that which is naturally yours alone."

That, she thought, *was a much better-than-average*

compliment. "Thank you, Your Grace," she said because anything else would've been rude.

"Derek," he said tightly. "My name is *Derek.*"

Catherine met his gaze but refused to budge. If he expected her to give him what he seemed to most want, he would have to earn it.

The battle of wills lasted until he finally blinked, looked away and extended his arm to her. "Shall we?"

Catherine closed the distance between them and slipped her hand into the crook of his arm to let him lead her downstairs to her sister's wedding.

Chapter Twenty

Derek stood by his cousin's side and Catherine next to her sister as the vicar performed the marriage ceremony for Madeleine and Simon in the parlor. Outside the door, Mrs. Langingham dabbed at her eyes with a lace handkerchief while the rest of the household staff gathered around her to watch the ceremony. Derek and his cousin had probably shocked the staff by marrying within days of each other, but they had each married for love, something he certainly wouldn't have expected for either of them as recently as two weeks ago.

As the vicar droned on about the sacred covenant of marriage, Derek took covert glances at his achingly beautiful duchess, still trying to believe she was real. Listening to Simon and Madeleine speak their vows and hearing the obvious joy in both their voices made Derek sad for what he'd denied himself and Catherine with his deception. Would they ever again know the kind of joy they'd experienced during the blissful week at his grandmother's home? Would she ever again laugh as freely as she had then or love him with the abandon that had changed his life forever? What if she couldn't get past what he had done? Were they destined to live in this state of purgatory, knowing what was possible between them but never again achieving that level of utter perfection?

Tortured by his thoughts, Derek forced a smile for his beloved cousin and Simon's new bride, saying and doing all the right things, going through the motions even though he felt dead inside because his own wife never once looked his way during the ceremony or the celebratory luncheon that followed. Derek forced himself to swallow the delicious food Amelia and her staff had made, but he might as well have been eating dirt, so consumed was he by despair and desperation. The last time he'd experienced such despair had been the day he'd awoken to learn of his parents' deaths. Needless to say, that wasn't something he cared to remember or relive, but his unrest over Catherine and the state of their marriage took him right back to that awful day.

"Derek?"

Simon's voice interrupted his painful musings. "I'm sorry. What did you say?" The four of them sat at a round table in the cozy breakfast room, which had been transformed for the celebratory luncheon.

"Madeleine and I think the four of us ought to take a wedding trip together, somewhere none of us has ever been."

"That would be nice." Derek wiped his mouth with a white cloth napkin. "Catherine desires the opportunity to travel. I promised to show her the world, so wherever she wishes to go would be fine with me."

"Where shall we go, Catherine?" Madeleine asked, her cheeks flushed with excitement. "You've always wanted to see the pyramids. Shall we go to Egypt?"

Derek watched her, hoping for some spark of excitement or interest or anything. But his wife merely shrugged, as if it didn't matter to her in the least when he knew otherwise.

"Wherever you wish to go," she said to her sister.

"But I thought—"

A loud crash from the front of the house had Derek and Simon rushing toward the front door. "Stay here," Derek called back to the women as he and Simon ran for the door to find two footmen fending off a livid Lord Lindsey, accompanied by Lord Brisbane. They must've left before first light to have gotten there so quickly.

The skirmish had resulted in one of the large stone planters being knocked over. It lay shattered in the driveway, dirt and flowers scattered about.

Derek reached for the pistol he'd tucked into the back of his dress pants in anticipation of this very moment and fired a shot into the air, which startled everyone involved, as he'd intended.

"State your business," he said to Lindsey.

"You have something that belongs to me, and I want it back," Lindsey said, his face red from the exertion of fending off the footmen, who were no less than fifteen years younger than him. He straightened his rumpled coat and used his fingers to return the greasy strands of his hair to the top of his otherwise-bald pate.

The thought of such a swine getting his hands on either Catherine or Madeleine made Derek thankful he hadn't eaten much. "We have nothing that belongs to you here, so be on your way."

"I was promised betrothal to the earl's daughter. I am here to collect her."

"I'm afraid you're too late, my lord," Derek said, his tone dripping with condescension. "Both the earl's daughters are legally wed to other men, which means you have no business here."

The viscount's face turned a startling shade of purple as he turned to the earl, who visibly cowered. "I will see you hanged."

Marie Force

Derek rolled his eyes. "Save the melodramatics."

"This man owes me a king's ransom," Lindsey said, "and I will collect it, or I *will* see him hanged."

"How much does he owe you?" Derek asked while Simon stood by his side, prepared to act if need be.

"Five thousand pounds."

Shocked to his core, Derek shifted his gaze to the man who was his father-in-law. "Is this true? Do you owe this man *five thousand* pounds and did you promise him one of your daughters in marriage to pay off this outrageous debt?"

"It is true, Your Grace," Brisbane said, casting his eyes down in shame.

It was all Derek could do to remain still when he wanted to pummel the man to within an inch of his miserable existence.

A gasp from behind him had Derek spinning in time to see Catherine and Madeleine's stricken expressions.

"Papa," Catherine said tearfully. "How could you?"

"Are you aware that Lindsey attacked Catherine and would have raped her, had she not known how to defend herself?" Derek asked the earl.

His face lost all color. "I . . ."

"Save it," Derek said. "We have no need of your excuses." To his footmen, he said, "Keep them out here. Don't let either of them out of your sight."

"Yes, Your Grace."

Derek turned to go back inside, fueled by fury and disbelief. "Please wait in the drawing room," he said to Catherine and Madeleine, pausing until they had followed his orders before continuing toward his study. The Brisbane earldom had been solid when the earl's brother and nephew had died. How had the new earl gone through the entire fortune in less than a year?

"Gambling," Simon said grimly, reading Derek's thoughts. "Word in London is the earl placed a series of bad bets. When Lindsey got a look at the daughters, he offered the earl a way out of his troubles."

"Disgusting," Derek said, storming into his study.

"Truly revolting. Thank goodness you happened upon Catherine digging on your land and saved them both in the process."

If only his wife could see it that way, Derek thought as he wrote out a note for the money his father-in-law needed to pay off Lindsey.

"Derek, you don't have to give him all of it."

"Yes, I do, or Lindsey will never leave any of us alone."

"It's a ridiculous amount of money."

"Thankfully, I have a ridiculous amount of money."

"I'll share the cost with you."

"No need, cousin." Derek signed his name with a flourish and brought the note with him when he returned to the portico where four footmen had the two men separated. Over his shoulder, he said to Simon, "Consider it a wedding gift."

Derek handed the note to Lindsey. "The earl's debt is paid in full. You will leave him and every member of his family in peace from this moment on, or you'll deal with me. Do I make myself clear?"

Lindsey took the note from Derek. "There's nothing special about the earl's daughters anyway," Lindsey said snidely. "The brief taste I had of Lady Catherine—"

Derek would never know how that sentence ended because he punched Lindsey square in the face and watched with great satisfaction as the other man toppled backward down the stone stairs, landing in a lump on the driveway. "Her Grace, the Duchess of Westwood, is *my* wife and under *my* protection," Derek said, containing the urge to murder the disgusting viscount. Descending the stairs, he added a kick to the man's genitals.

The wretched man howled in pain as he grasped his wounded privates.

"That was for Catherine. If you ever so much as dare to speak her name out loud again, I'll gut you." To his footmen, Derek said, "Please get this refuse off my property."

"Yes, Your Grace," the senior footman said as he tended to Derek's order.

"That," Simon said gleefully, "was exceedingly well done, Your Grace."

Maybe so, Derek thought, but he'd forgotten how painful it could be to smash one's fist into another's face. He hadn't been in a fight since Eton.

"Your Grace," the earl said tentatively, "I can't possibly thank you enough—"

"Save your thanks and remove yourself from my sight and my property. It's no wonder your daughter disdains the aristocracy after the example you have set. I would advise you to find some honor to go along with your new title."

Chastened, the earl spun on his heel and went down the stairs. A minute later, he and his horse left a cloud of dust as they departed.

"Positively brilliant," Simon said, clapping Derek on the back. "But I hate to be the one to tell you that you're bleeding."

Derek looked down to discover his knuckles had been laid open and were indeed bleeding somewhat profusely.

"Your Grace," Mrs. Langingham said, "we must tend to your injury at once." She steered him inside where he came face-to-face with his wife, who radiated tension as she twisted her hands in obvious distress.

"The viscount is gone," Derek said. "Neither you nor your sister will hear from him again."

"You are hurt," Catherine said, her gaze shifting to his bloodied hand.

"I'm fine."

"Take him into the drawing room," Mrs. Langingham said. "I will fetch some ice and clean cloths." She bustled off to see to the supplies.

Catherine took him by the arm and steered him into the drawing room. It was the first time she had touched him willingly since finding out about his title.

Madeleine stood by the window watching the goings-on outside. "Father is gone!"

"I sent him away," Derek said. "Any man who would gamble away his daughters isn't welcome here." He took a seat, his heart giving a happy lift when Catherine sat beside him, cradling his injured hand in her lap.

"You hit Lord Lindsey," she said.

"I did, and I promised to gut him if he ever so much as speaks your name out loud again."

"Thank you," she said with the first hint of the warmth that had once been his. "For that and for paying off my father's outrageous debt."

"It was a small price to pay to get them both out of our lives." And a small price to pay to have her look at him with admiration and new respect. "I assume you will want to see your mother and siblings. They will always be welcome here, but you'll have to forgive me if I'm not interested in seeing your father again for a while."

"I share your thoughts where he is concerned even as I mourn the loss of the man I used to think I knew so well," Catherine said.

"He changed when he became the earl," Madeleine said when she joined them, sitting with Simon on the smaller of the two sofas. "He's not the loving father who raised us."

"No," Catherine said. "He isn't."

Mrs. Langingham returned with the ice, clean cloth and a poultice for the swelling.

Derek took it as a positive sign when Catherine insisted on seeing to his wounds herself, gently cleaning his raw knuckles before applying the poultice in delicate dabs that caused him no additional discomfort. Then she wrapped his hand in a strip of cloth and placed the bag of ice on top of it. All the while, she held his hand in her lap, and he tried to contain the galloping pace of his heartbeat.

Her care, concern and affection brought him right back to the bliss they'd shared before it all went so terribly wrong. Would the incident with Lindsey and her father provide a path back to her? If so, he would need to send both men an engraved thank-you letter. Or would this be a temporary détente in the tensions between them?

Derek didn't know, and the not knowing hurt far worse than the wounds on his hand ever would.

Madeleine had watched the goings-on between Simon's cousin, the duke, Lord Lindsey and her father with a detached sense of the surreal. She'd gotten married today, so it was difficult to think past her wedding, her new husband and her looming wedding night, even with the arrival of the detested viscount and her father. He'd never even asked about either of his daughters or ensured their well-being before leaving with his tail tucked firmly between his legs.

No matter, Madeleine told herself. She now had a husband to see to her well-being. If his yawning theatrics were any indication, her well-being would be seen to sooner rather than later.

"Are we keeping you up, cousin?" the duke asked dryly.

Madeleine had watched the way the duke had looked at her sister throughout the morning, noting the yearning and desire that came through in every word he said to her. He clearly cared for Catherine, which brought comfort to Madeleine.

"I've had a series of late nights," Simon said, stretching.

The duke rolled his eyes.

"What? I'm not used to keeping such hours."

"Perhaps you should retire early then," the duke suggested.

Early? Madeleine knew a moment of pure panic. She thought she'd have until darkness fell before she'd be expected to perform her wifely duties. But if, as the duke suggested, they were to retire early—

"A capital idea." Simon stood and extended his hand to her. "Come, wife. Let us go rest."

"Rest," the duke muttered under his breath. "Is that what we are calling it?"

Catherine stood to hug her sister. "Everything will be fine," Catherine whispered in Madeleine's ear. "Trust your husband and his affection for you."

Madeleine nodded even as she feared she might faint.

"Breathe," Catherine whispered. "Just keep breathing."

Simon took hold of Madeleine's hand. "Let us be off, my love. I find I can barely stay awake after the late nights we've had."

When he spoke to her in that intimate tone reserved only for her and looked at her with such love and joy, she began to relax ever so slightly, enough anyway to get air to her lungs. She let him lead her up the stairs, through winding hallways to the west side of the large manor.

"My family has long occupied this side of the house while Derek is on the other." Simon pointed out portraits of his ancestors as they traversed the corridor. "This is the grandfather that Derek and I share. He was the duke before Derek's father."

"Derek looks like him," Madeleine said.

"Yes, he does. Derek's temperament is very much like our grandfather's as well. He was a kind and generous man."

"Are your parents in residence?" she asked. "I thought they might attend our wedding."

"My father is in London, where he spends most of his time, and my mother is unwell."

"Oh, I'm sorry."

"Thank you, but it has been so for quite some time now. In fact, I can't remember a time when she wasn't confined to her rooms cared for by nurses."

"Are you close with your father?"

Simon laughed. "Not at all. He's . . . How do I say it without being disrespectful to the man who fathered me?"

"I would hope you would feel free to speak your mind with me. We are married now, aren't we?"

His beautiful eyes heated with desire as he put his arms around her and kissed both her cheeks. "We are indeed married."

Madeleine licked lips that had gone dry. "Then you should be able to tell me anything." She watched his eyes follow the movement of her tongue and became truly aware of his desire for her.

"My father is a ruthless, bitter, jealous scoundrel, who has gone out of his way to make my life, my mother's life and Derek's as miserable as he possibly could. We are all happier when he is in London."

"You have been so alone," she said, gazing up at him with concern and empathy.

"Not so alone. Derek and I had each other and a wonderful grandmother who doted on us until she died about ten years ago. Mrs. Langingham is like another mother to us and keeps us out of trouble." Simon smiled and winked, looking every bit the rake of the first order. "Most of the time, anyway."

"You are not alone anymore." A fierce feeling of loyalty and need filled Madeleine's chest. She wanted to give him everything he'd lacked in his life before her, in the hope that he'd never be sorry for giving up his freedom to marry her.

"I'm not alone, and thank goodness for that," he said, stepping closer to her. "I promised your father I'd treat you with respect and honor until we were married."

"Do you plan to stop that now that we are married?" she asked, alarmed until he smiled.

"I will never treat you with anything but the utmost in respect and honor. However, I find that I desperately wish to properly kiss my wife, among other things."

Madeleine swallowed hard. "Your wife would very much like to be properly kissed by her handsome husband."

He tucked her hand into the crook of his elbow and escorted her to his suite of rooms, ushering her in ahead of him. Fresh air greeted them from windows left open to the warm afternoon. Candles had been lit and placed around the room, casting a romantic glow over the rich, masculine furniture and the huge four-poster bed. "This is your room through here," he said, leading her into a hallway that boasted the modern water closet and bathing room she'd used earlier and through the doorway to the more feminine room done in shades of lilac.

"All of your things have been put away, but you should feel free to redecorate and make this space your own in any way you see fit."

"Oh," she said, trying to hide her disappointment. "All right."

"What is it?" he asked. "Why do you seem unhappy?"

"I'd rather hoped . . ."

"What, love? If I don't know what you hope for, how can I make sure you get it?"

She took a deep breath and summoned the courage to look at him and speak the words that were in her heart. "I'd rather hoped we would share a room." She cleared her throat as she felt her face heat with embarrassment. "And a bed."

That rakish smile of his would be her undoing. "My silly, silly goose." He tweaked her nose affectionately. "You will keep your clothing in here and tend to any business and correspondence here. You will sleep, every night of our lives, with my arms wrapped around you to keep you where you belong."

Madeleine was forced to lick her dry lips again. "And where do I belong, Mr. Eagan?"

"Wherever I am." He cupped her face in his hands and studied her for the longest time, so long she began to wonder if something were amiss. But then he lowered his face toward hers while keeping his eyes wide open and fixed on hers. The first brush of his lips against hers was so faint and so tentative, she wasn't entirely sure it had happened. Then he came back for more, and there was no doubt in her mind that she was finally being kissed. Heat flooded her body and made her legs feel wobbly beneath her as she clung to him, trying to keep up with the relentless movements of his mouth over hers.

"I knew you would taste sweeter than the sweetest honey," he whispered, leaning his forehead against hers. "That first day, after the standoff with your parents, I wanted to kiss you so badly."

"I wish you had."

"I couldn't. I'd only just promised your father I wouldn't."

"From what I've heard about you, such a promise wouldn't have stopped you in the past."

"My past ceased to exist the moment I laid eyes on you, the most beautiful woman I've ever seen, who is now my most beloved wife."

"Simon?"

"Yes, love?"

"Would you kiss me again?"

"I would be delighted to kiss you again." He touched his lips to hers, softly, gently.

Chapter Twenty-One

Madeleine tried to get closer to him, seeking relief from the aching need that his kisses inspired in her. She wondered if this was it or was there more to kissing?

"Open your mouth, my sweet."

She did as he asked, wondering what he intended to do.

"Yes," he said, breathing heavily now, "like that. Just like that."

His open mouth came down on hers and his tongue . . . Oh, dear God, his *tongue* rubbed against hers, making her see stars. Nothing in her life could've prepared her for the riot of emotions that zipped through her with every new stroke of his tongue.

"I knew that day in the park that once I started to kiss you, I'd never want to stop."

"Please don't stop." He made her feel wanton and brazen, two things she'd never been before him.

His low chuckle made her smile as he walked her backward the way they'd come until they had returned to his room. After closing the door, he turned her to face away from him and dropped hot kisses on her neck as he unbuttoned the pale yellow gown she'd worn for her wedding.

Madeleine had expected to feel shy and modest about disrobing in front of him, but after his kisses, her clothing felt extra tight and restrictive.

Simon made fast work of removing her gown and corset, leaving her only in a linen shift, stockings and garters. "So very, very lovely," he whispered as he kissed a heated path from her wrist to her elbow. Then he removed his coat and tore at the buttons and fasteners on his own clothing until he stood before her wearing only his drawers.

A nervous titter of laughter had her pinching her lips together.

"Do you find something amusing, wife?"

"*You* are amusing. I thought you were very tired, but you don't seem tired at all."

"I'm not the slightest bit tired. I wanted to be alone with my wife."

"*Oh*," she said on a long exhale.

"What do you know about the act of love?"

Madeleine's face felt hot. "Nothing. I had no idea that people used their tongues . . ." She gasped when he ran his tongue up her neck.

"Wait until you see the many ways a tongue can be used in the act of love."

Her legs trembled violently beneath her.

He swept her up into his arms and walked her to the bed, tucking her in under the covers. Leaning over her, he kissed her. "Don't go anywhere. I'll be right back."

Where did he think she would go? Her legs were still trembling, which would make it difficult to walk even if she had somewhere to go. Was it always like this, she wondered? Would her legs and hands shake every time her husband kissed or touched her? She would have to ask Catherine. While she waited, she grasped handfuls of the bedding and tried to calm herself.

She'd always prided herself on being a practical sort of person, and any practical person would know that people had been doing whatever was about to happen here since the beginning of time. Acting as if she were the first to ever lie with a man was silly, and she was never silly if she could avoid it.

Simon emerged from the water closet and came toward her, resembling the Greek gods she'd seen in the books Catherine was always bringing home from the village library. Although her husband could put those gods to shame with his golden good looks and muscular body.

As he came closer, the trembling began anew.

Then he got into the bed with her and drew her into his warm embrace. "You're shaking, my sweet."

"I can't seem to make it stop."

"Are you so nervous to be alone with me?"

"I don't want to be."

"I want you to be entirely comfortable with me. We will only do what feels good to both of us. I promise."

"I-I may not be ready to . . ." Her face burned with embarrassment, and she wished she could take back the words. A man like him wasn't used to simpering virgins. He was far more accustomed to doxies who fell on their backs with their legs spread, ready to give him whatever he wanted.

"Shhh. Don't fret. I only want to make you feel good. Will you let me?"

She nodded because she found that words escaped her when he looked at her with such tenderness and desire. And the last thing she wanted to do in that moment was think of him with other women.

"Could we remove this?" he asked, his fingers sliding over the shift that covered her.

Every part of her felt overly warm at the thought of being entirely naked before him, but she mustered her courage and managed a slight nod. Since she'd become a woman, only Evangeline had seen her unclothed. She hoped her new husband would be pleased by her.

As he raised the shift over her hips, his hazel eyes darkened and his lips parted.

"You are so incredibly lovely," he whispered. "I still can't believe you agreed to marry me."

She ran her fingers through his blond hair, because she could now that they were legally wed, and learned the silky, soft texture as the strands slid between her fingers. "You saved me from a fate worse than death by marrying me."

"And in return, you saved me from myself."

"Did I?"

"You certainly did. My life had no meaning or purpose until I strolled into Lady Crenshaw's ballroom and found my purpose."

The shift slid up over her belly, and he pressed a warm kiss to her fevered skin.

"She was surrounded by fools dazzled by her exceptional beauty, but I saw *her*, the woman who would fidget if her mother allowed it, a woman who was unimpressed by the ritual taking place around her."

Madeleine sucked in a sharp, deep breath, moved by his words as much as the slide of his lips over her skin. "I saw you across the room and wanted to know you."

He looked up at her. "Did you?"

She nodded. "I hoped that you would find your way to me."

"I was drawn to you by a power bigger than myself and stronger than anything I've ever experienced before."

He captured her lips in another of those kisses that made her feel weak and strong at the same time. When their lips finally parted, her shift cleared her head and he reached for her, bringing her bare chest into intimate contact with his. "Ah," he gasped. "Sweet Jesus."

Catherine had been right when she said that the feel of his skin against hers would be like heaven.

For the longest time he only held her close to him while she worked up the nerve to touch him, to run her hand over his lanky, muscular back. Every inch of him was tight with tension. Between them, a hard column of flesh throbbed against her belly.

"Touch me, Madeleine. Anywhere you wish to. I am all yours."

Emboldened by his gruffly spoken words, her hand traveled down to his waist.

"Don't stop there. Touch me everywhere."

She slid her hand over the rounded globe of his buttock, drawing a deep, tortured groan from him. And when she squeezed it, he gazed down at her with an expression gone fierce.

"Did I do something wrong?"

A dimpled smile transformed his fierceness into tenderness. "You did it too right. You're making me forget that you haven't done this before."

"Teach me, Simon. Show me what to do. I feel so . . ."

"What do you feel? Tell me."

"Inept, inexperienced, foolish, unworthy—"

His kiss stopped her tirade and made her forget what else she'd been prepared to say. "Nothing about you is inept or foolish or unworthy. You are beautiful and sweet, and you will not speak poorly of my wife, do you understand me?"

"Yes, sir," she said with a small smile.

"That's better. Now close your eyes, and don't worry about anything other than pleasure."

Madeleine did as he requested, giving herself over to him and the sweet kisses that moved from her lips to throat to shoulder and below. With her eyes closed, she was utterly unprepared for him to take her tight nipple into his mouth and suck. Her hips lifted off the bed, seeking something.

"Easy, sweet love. Nice and easy." He switched sides and did it again and again and again, until she was half out of her mind with need.

And then he moved lower, with kisses to her ribs and belly and . . .

"Simon." She covered her most private area with her hands. He couldn't possibly mean to—

Taking hold of her hands, he moved them to her sides and settled between her obscenely spread legs and blew a light stream of air against the hair that covered her.

Mortification spread through her in a fiery fever that converged in a tight throb between her legs. And then . . . *Oh dear God*, was that his *tongue? There?* That couldn't be something people did in their marriage bed. Could it?

"Relax, sweetheart. Let me make you feel good."

He expected her to relax when he had his tongue there and his fingers . . . oh, oh God, inside her . . .

Madeleine let out an inelegant squeak that was quickly followed by a moan when he sucked on the tight ball of nerves between her legs as he slid his fingers in and out of her. A quickening sensation had her breathing faster and gripping the sheets into tight fists as she held on for dear life.

"Let it happen, sweet," he whispered before sucking on

her flesh again and igniting a firestorm that blazed through her. "Yes, *yes*, like that. Just like that."

Before she could process the shock of what had happened, an impossible feeling of pressure quickly usurped the pleasure. She twisted her hips, trying to get away.

Simon's hands on her hips held her still as he pushed into her. "It'll only hurt this one time, my love, and then after that it will feel divine. I promise." With that, he pushed hard and drew a sharp cry from her.

He gathered her in close to him, holding her tight while his manhood throbbed inside her.

The longer he held her, the more difficult it became for her to remain still.

She squirmed, needing him to move or do something, anything to relieve the ache that seemed to intensify with every second he remained lodged inside her.

"What do you need, love?"

"I don't know," she said, feeling inept and foolish again.

"Do you trust me?"

She looked up at the face that had become so familiar and so dear to her and nodded. "I trust you, Simon."

"Hold on to me."

Madeleine wrapped her arms around him, and gasped when he pushed even farther into her before retreating and doing it again. It didn't feel good, per se, but it didn't hurt anymore. Rather, it burned as she struggled to accommodate the length and width of him.

"You feel so good," he whispered, "so hot and tight and sweet. I've never felt anything better than this."

Buoyed by his words and the intense expression on his face, Madeleine relaxed as much as she was able to and tried to move along with him.

Simon threw his head back and bit his lip. "*Yes*, like

that." Raising himself up so his arms bore most of his weight, he picked up the pace, seeming to lose himself in her before surging into her one last time and crying out. "*Madeleine*." He came down on top of her, breathing hard and fast.

She caressed his back, hoping to bring him comfort.

"Sweet Madeleine." After a long period of quiet, he raised his head and met her gaze. "Did I hurt you terribly?"

She shook her head.

"I never want to cause you another second of pain." He kissed her sweetly before withdrawing from her.

Madeleine was horrified to see blood on his manhood.

He followed her gaze. "It's perfectly normal for women to bleed the first time." Rising from the bed, he went into the water closet.

She heard water running before he returned with a warm cloth that he held against her tender flesh. The heat felt divine, and Madeleine marveled at how quickly he'd brought her around to feeling comfortable with him in their unclothed state. Now that she had the chance, she took a closer look at his chest and noticed the light sprinkling of golden blond hair that arrowed into a darker shade around his manhood.

When her visual tour made its way back to his face, she found him watching her with amusement dancing in his eyes. "Do you see something you like?"

She nodded.

"As do I." He leaned in to kiss her again, and she realized her lips were actually sore from their intense kisses. "I like everything about you."

"Can we . . ." She swallowed the nervous lump that settled in her throat and forced herself to look him in the eyes. "Can we do that again?"

"You will be too sore."

"No, I won't."

"Trust me, you will. For the rest of the day, we will take it easy, but tomorrow . . ." He placed a kiss between her breasts. "Tomorrow we will do it again."

Madeleine couldn't wait for tomorrow.

Chapter Twenty-Two

Long after Simon and Madeleine retired upstairs, Catherine and Derek remained in the drawing room, where they were served a light tea per his request. After the day they'd had, neither of them was particularly hungry.

Mrs. Langingham came in with a fresh cloth and more ice for Derek's bruised hand.

"Does it feel any better?" Catherine asked when they were alone again.

"It's fine."

"I want to thank you. For what you did for my father."

"I didn't do it for him," he said, giving her a pointed look that let her know he'd done it for *her*.

"I'm sorry about the money. It was an obscene amount."

"I don't care about the money. I care about your safety—and Madeleine's. And I am thankful that we have seen the last of Lindsey, if he knows what's good for him."

"I am thankful for that as well, but I'm sorry you were hurt in the process."

"He was hurt worse," Derek said with the small grin that had made her dizzy with desire before it had all gone so wrong between them.

Catherine returned his smile. "Yes, he was." She glanced shyly at him. "The kick at the end was my favorite part."

"You were watching?" he asked, astonished.

"Of course, we were watching. Our faces were pressed to the window."

Derek winced. "I didn't intend for you to see my baser instincts on full display."

"I found your baser instincts rather *stimulating*."

Shocked and thrilled, he said, "Is that right?"

She nodded and looked down at the floor, feeling embarrassed and oddly vulnerable.

He took her hand and brought it to his lips.

Catherine gasped with surprise at the tender gesture.

"This has been a long and emotional day. I would like to retire early with my wife, if my wife is amenable."

"That would be nice, Your Grace."

"Derek," he said, tightly. "My name is *Derek*."

The word he wanted so badly to hear sat on the tip of her tongue, but something kept her from saying it. She wanted to be certain that he would fulfill the promises he had made to her before she surrendered entirely to his wishes. What he'd done for her and her sister today had gone a long way toward softening her heart toward him once again, but she'd learned to be wary where he was concerned, knowing how badly he could hurt her.

He tucked her hand into his arm and escorted her upstairs, the path becoming somewhat familiar to her. But it would take far longer to acclimate to the opulence of his home with its priceless furnishings and gilded details. Even the modern water closets were a new but most welcome marvel.

"Would it be possible to have a bath, Your Grace?"

"You may have anything you want, Catherine," he said,

his jaw set with displeasure at her use of his title. "You need only to ask, and it shall be done."

"I would like to meet the tenants and their families."

"I will take you myself tomorrow."

"Do you have the time for that?"

"I will make the time for you."

"Would you be opposed to my working with the children to teach them to read? I very much enjoyed my work with the children in my former home and would like to continue it."

"I would not be opposed as long as it doesn't take you away from home too often as I would miss having you here with me."

They went into her room where Julia flitted about, laying out nightclothes.

"That'll be all, Julia," Derek said in that regal tone Catherine was still getting used to hearing from him.

Julia curtsied. "Good evening, Your Graces."

"Allow me to assist you," Derek said when they were alone. He went into the bathing room and turned on the water to the tub, the pipes clanging loudly. Then he returned to unbutton her gown and untie her corset.

Catherine felt shy and undone by his attention. She'd fully expected him to become like other aristocratic husbands and leave the details of life to his staff. That he wanted to tend to her personally touched her and further thawed the wall of ice that had formed around her heart. She turned to him, holding her dress over her bosom.

"I want you to know . . ."

He caressed her cheek. "What do you want me to know?"

"I see the effort you are putting forth to make things right between us, and I am trying to come to terms with everything that has happened." She looked up at him, feeling madly vulnerable. "I would just ask that you try to be patient with me."

"I will give you all the time you need to come to terms with your new situation. I understand that what I did hurt you deeply, which was not my intention."

"I know that, and I understand why you did it." She shuddered at the thought of being shackled to Lindsey.

"And I understand that my deception cracked the foundation under us. It will take time to fix the damage. But you should know that I will give you all the time you need. There is nothing I wouldn't do to fix it, to win back your love, to have you look at me the way you did during the blissful days we spent at the cottage."

His heartfelt words brought tears to her eyes.

He kissed her forehead. "Enjoy your bath and join me in my room when you're finished. I'll be waiting for you."

Catherine watched him walk away, standing in the middle of the opulent bedroom that had once belonged to his mother, thinking about the things he'd said and done to convince her of his sincerity. So far, he was nothing at all like the boorish aristocrats she'd known before him, and it was becoming clear to her that she couldn't judge the man she'd married on the same scale as she judged the vile Lord Lindsey, her uncle or even her own father.

She finished undressing and went into the bathing room to sink into the delightfully warm water in the lavender-scented bath her husband had drawn for her.

Her *husband*.

The Duke of Westwood, a man who was well regarded according to her sister, and not at all like the upper-class men she'd known before him. No question, his deception had hurt her deeply, but his rationale couldn't be faulted. She did believe that Derek loved her as much as Jack had.

And until she had reason to believe otherwise, she would commit herself to making their marriage work.

It would take time for her to adjust to her new position and to fully absorb the expectations her husband—and the society she'd disdained—would have for her. But she would try her best to live up to those expectations, beginning with a visit tomorrow to the tenants and their families.

If she could teach the children how to read and continue to cultivate the duke's literary collection while helping him to care for the estate and his many obligations, she might be able to carve out a happy life for herself as a duchess, even if it was not a life she would've wanted for herself had she been given the choice.

As the water began to cool, she heard his voice telling her he'd be waiting for her, and her body tingled in anticipation of another night in his arms. She was still as attracted to him as she'd ever been, and after his actions that day to defend her and her sister, she wanted nothing more than to show him how indebted she was to him.

While he waited for Catherine, Derek sat in front of the fire in his room, drink in hand as he stared at the flickering flames and thought about the eventful day. His injured hand throbbed and ached, but he'd gladly put up with the pain if it meant that Lindsey was permanently removed from their lives. Derek was under no illusions that he'd seen the last of the earl, for he was, after all, Catherine and Madeleine's father. At some point in the future, perhaps the sisters would find a way to make peace with their father, but Derek hoped it wouldn't be any time soon. Men like him, who treated women as a commodity, disgusted Derek.

When the earl should've been protecting his precious daughters, he had been using them as pawns in a high-stakes game he was woefully unprepared to play. No wonder Catherine was so repulsed by the nobility. Men in his social strata could be a boorish, pampered, overly indulged bunch of slugs at times. Determined to prove to her that he was different, he would take her to the village tomorrow to meet the tenants. He would encourage her to pursue the things that interested her. He would show her the world and give her anything she desired.

All she had to do in return was love him. Memories from their first days together, the best days of his life, filled his heart and soul. They could have that again. He knew it without a doubt. If only he could convince her to give him another chance. In all his thirty years, he'd never known desperation like that which he'd experienced when she froze him out of her affections after his lies were revealed.

He could only hope that he would never again feel the way he had then. Today had been a good day. He'd been given the opportunity to show her how he intended to behave as her husband, from procuring the clothing she would need to continue the dig, to showing her the library, to paying off and disposing of the evil viscount. Would it be enough to win back her love?

He didn't know, and the not knowing was driving him toward insanity. Sighing, he took another sip of whiskey and let the amber liquid burn its way through him, warming the parts of him that'd gone cold in the face of her rejection.

A rustling sound outside the door that joined their rooms had him looking up in time to see her step through the door, seeming tentative and uncertain of her welcome.

That would never do. He put down his glass and stood to draw her into the room, closing the door behind her.

Derek took a moment to simply look at the glorious creature who was his wife. Her blond hair, like spun gold after being brushed, fell down her back, while her big navy-blue eyes looked at him with something new and different in them that was at once familiar, too.

His heart lurched from the surge of hope he experienced at realizing the chill between them had thawed at some point. While she retained an aura of reserve in his presence, he no longer sensed disdain.

"How was your bath, my love?"

"It was very nice. Thank you. What a luxury to have a bathing room."

"People said I was crazy to spend the money on such a newfangled invention, but I haven't regretted the investment."

"You are ahead of your peers on such things, are you not?"

"My uncle would tell you I'm a frivolous risk taker."

"Have those risks not paid off handsomely?"

"They have," he said, smiling warmly.

"Then it sounds to me as if your uncle is envious of your successes."

"My uncle is infused with many of the seven deadly sins—envy, greed, lust."

Catherine cringed. "And this man is now my sister's father-in-law."

"Don't worry. Simon will keep her far away from Anthony and his many vices. We go out of our way to avoid him whenever possible." Derek stepped closer to Catherine and looped a finger through the belt of her silk robe. From what he could tell, she'd worn nothing under it. "My uncle is the very last thing I wish to discuss tonight when there are so many other things I'd rather talk to you about."

"Such as?" she asked, looking up at him with the eyes that had owned him from the start.

"We can talk about anything you'd like to."

"I would like to know more about what you expect of me as your duchess."

He slid his arms around her and brought her body in snug against his. "As I have said, my only desire is your happiness."

"That is overly simple, Your Grace. Surely, you expect me to run your household—"

"Only if you wish to. Mrs. Langingham has done a capable job of seeing to my needs for many years now. If you would like for her to continue in that role, all you have to do is say so. If you wish to be involved, that is fine, too."

She gazed up at him, her expression unreadable.

"What are you thinking?"

"That I keep expecting you to be a certain way, and then you surprise me."

"I shall endeavor to continue to surprise you for the rest of our lives. If you are waiting for me to be typical and boorish and overbearing, I fear I will disappoint you."

She shook her head.

"No?" he asked.

"I am not disappointed. I am relieved."

Derek's chest eased as it became clear that she believed him. "I swear to you, Catherine," he said fiercely. "I am exactly the same man you fell in love with in the cottage."

"You are far more than my Jack Bancroft ever dreamed of being."

"I cannot help the fate I was born into, nor can I turn my back on the obligations that were foisted upon me by my father's untimely death. Not even for you."

"I wouldn't ask you to."

"Does that mean you are willing to accept me for who and what I am?"

"It means I want to try."

He hugged her as close to him as he could get her. "You

have made me so happy, Catherine, happier than I've ever been in my life. The thought of losing you after what we shared has been unbearable to me. I hope you will accept my sincere apology for the deception."

"Seeing Lindsey again today reminded me of the fate that awaited me had I not been under your protection. I would like for us to start fresh."

"I want nothing more than another chance to prove my love to you."

She curled her hand around the back of his neck and brought him down for a kiss, her mouth opening under his and her tongue sliding along his bottom lip.

Her show of passion made Derek feel light-headed with relief and love and desire so fierce it took his breath away. Without breaking the kiss, he walked her backward to the bed and encouraged her to lie back. When she was settled, he raised his head and gazed down at her, dazzled by the sight of her lips swollen from their kisses. He wanted to worship her and show her how much she meant to him. Tugging on the belt to her robe, he untied it and pushed the two sides apart to reveal his beautiful wife.

"I always knew that I would have to marry," he whispered as he placed a kiss between her breasts. "But I never imagined I'd find the perfect wife for me."

Her fingers slid through his hair in a loving gesture reminiscent of their first days together.

He left a path of kisses from her breasts to her mid-section and below.

Catherine gasped as he opened her to his tongue, squirming under him until he laid an arm across her hips to keep her still.

Derek did everything he could think of to please her—touching, caressing, stroking, kissing and loving. As he made love to her, his every thought was on her pleasure.

He would never stop trying to please her or hoping to hear his name—his real name—uttered from her lips in the throes of passion.

But though she actively participated and experienced fulfillment that he felt and heard in her gasps and sighs, she didn't give him the one thing he wanted most.

Not yet, anyway.

Chapter Twenty-Three

In the morning, Derek kept his promise to Catherine by taking her to meet the tenant families, many of whom were hard at work tending to the land entrusted to their care. They were shocked speechless to be visited in the middle of a workday by the duke and his new duchess.

Catherine charmed everyone she met with her down-to-earth warmth and graciousness, making her husband proud with each stop they made.

The Flanagan family invited them inside their home for refreshments, and Derek nodded to Catherine to go on ahead. Though he had many tasks awaiting his attention at home, nothing was more important than furthering the bond with his wife. This was what she wanted, and as such, he wanted it, too.

With a baby tied to the front of her, Mrs. Flanagan bustled around the tiny kitchen, preparing tea while three other little ones, paralyzed with shyness, clung to their father.

"Might I hold the baby for you, Mrs. Flanagan?" Catherine asked.

"Oh, I wouldn't want her to dirty your pretty dress."

"I don't mind at all." Catherine held out her arms,

smiling warmly at the other woman while Derek watched, overcome with pride and love for his wife.

Mrs. Flanagan handed over baby Rosie, who stared up at Catherine with a look of befuddlement.

"Hello there, little one," Catherine said, charming the baby the same way she did everyone else. "Aren't you a sweet thing?"

The baby gurgled and blew spit bubbles that made Catherine laugh with delight.

"She likes to spit," one of the little girls said.

"She can do whatever she likes before she knows better," Catherine said. "Wouldn't it be nice if we could remember a time before we were supposed to have manners?"

The little girl giggled and moved closer to Catherine, who drew her in with an arm around her waist. "Do you help to care for your baby sister?" she asked the girl, who couldn't have been more than five.

She nodded gravely. "I watch her and play with her."

"And what's your name?"

"I'm Dalia, and that's Tommy and Lizzie," she said of the younger siblings who were still on their father's lap.

"I'm sure you're a big help to your mama."

"She is," Mrs. Flanagan said, pouring tea for the adults. She placed a tin of shortbread cookies on the table, which the children eyed with obvious interest.

To Mrs. Flanagan, Catherine said, "May I offer the children a cookie?"

"One each, Your Grace," their mother said. "Or they will spoil their dinner."

Neither Catherine nor Derek took any so there would be more for the family.

"Do you like books?" Catherine asked Dalia, who nodded enthusiastically.

"We have a small library in the village," Mrs. Flanagan said, her hand on Dalia's shoulder. "We're frequent visitors, but this one would go every day if she could. I read to her every night before bed."

"Would you like to learn how to read them yourself?" Catherine asked.

Dalia glanced at her mother before nodding, in awe of the duchess who took such an interest in her.

"In the village where I used to live, I taught the children how to read and write. I would love nothing more than to do the same here."

"Your Grace," Mrs. Flanagan said, flabbergasted by the offer that would open a world of opportunity to the children that many of them wouldn't have had otherwise. She looked to her husband. "I don't know what to say!"

"I believe we should say thank you to Her Grace," Mr. Flanagan said, smiling warmly at his wife.

"Yes," his wife said, tears filling her eyes. "Thank you so much."

"It'll be my pleasure to work with the children. If there's ever anything I can do for you, please ask."

"You have already done so much, and we've only just met," Mrs. Flanagan said.

The baby had fallen asleep in Catherine's arms.

When Catherine looked over at Derek, he saw joy and satisfaction in her bright smile.

On the walk home, Catherine held his hand as she talked to him about her plans to teach the village children.

"Why don't they have shoes?" she asked him.

"Who?"

"The children."

"They didn't have shoes?" He was ashamed that he hadn't noticed.

"No, they didn't. I'll want to order shoes for every child. I can use my household allowance."

He stopped walking and turned to her. "Catherine, if you want to buy shoes for the children, buy shoes for the children. You're their duchess now. If you see a need that must be addressed, address it."

"I don't have to ask you first?"

"Not unless you are planning to buy an island or a small nation."

She let loose with a genuine laugh that made him realize that he hadn't heard her laugh since the night of his birthday, before Lindsey had come and ruined everything.

"I've missed your laugh, my love."

"It feels good to laugh with you again."

"May I ask you something?" he said as they began to walk again.

"I suppose."

"You may not believe me, but the morning after my birthday, I was going to tell you the truth over breakfast. Would it have made a difference in how you reacted if you'd heard it from me rather than Lindsey?"

She appeared to give that significant thought. "I'm not sure it would've mattered. It's the deception that upset me more than how it was uncovered."

Derek took a deep breath and let it out slowly, trying to be patient as they fumbled their way back to each other. If only it could be as simple outside the bedchamber as it was inside where everything between them still made perfect sense. "I hope that someday, the deception will be a distant memory, perhaps something that makes us laugh when we remember it."

"Perhaps, but not yet."

He took heart in the fact that she held his hand all the way home, where they encountered the real Jack Bancroft outside the stable. He had only now returned from the visit with his mother.

"Mr. Bancroft," Derek said as they approached the other man.

He looked from Derek to Catherine and then back to Derek, seeming uncertain of what he should say.

"Her Grace has been made aware of my true identity."

"Ah," Jack said, smiling as he nodded to Catherine. "It is an honor to meet you, Your Grace."

"You as well, Mr. Bancroft," Catherine said.

"I trust you had a good visit with your mother and family?" Derek asked the younger man.

"A very good visit indeed. But it's nice to be home."

"We won't keep you. Welcome back."

"Thank you, Your Grace."

Derek tucked Catherine's hand into the crook of his arm as they strolled toward the kitchen entrance.

"He is very handsome," Catherine said when they were out of earshot.

Derek had always liked Jack Bancroft and relied heavily upon his expertise in the areas of farming, logging and animal husbandry. But hearing his wife call the man *handsome*, Derek wanted to run him through with the sharpest sword he could find. "I suppose," he said, uncertain of how he should reply.

"You are more so," she said softly.

Four little words. That was all it took to make what was wrong right again. "Am I?"

She glanced up at him and nodded.

That small nod moved him more than almost anything ever had. He wanted to be the only man she ever noticed, the only one she ever wanted or needed. They weren't quite back to where they'd been before it all went wrong, but they were closer than they'd been in days. He would take the small victories where he could find them. "Would you like to work at the dig site this afternoon?"

"I'm sure you have other things to attend to."

"I cleared my schedule to spend the day with my wife."

"In that case, I'd much rather swim than dig. It's so warm."

"Then we shall have a picnic and a swim."

Stretched out on a blanket beside the lake, with the warm sunshine beaming down upon her naked limbs, Catherine felt more settled than she had since discovering the secrets her husband had kept from her.

Derek.

He wanted her to call him Derek.

Like he had on the day of his birthday, he'd made love to her in the water, with her face down on the warm rock.

In that one way, it was as if nothing had changed between them, even as everything else had changed, but when she thought of that night at the cottage when Lindsey had given her the truth that her husband had withheld from her, the memory still had the power to make her heart ache.

Despite the heartache, she couldn't deny the efforts he made to make her happy—taking her to meet the tenants, encouraging her desire to teach the children, allowing her free rein in any areas in which she showed interest and making himself available to spend time with her when he had many other things that required his attention.

"What would you be doing today if I had never come here?"

"I'd be sad because I didn't have you."

"You wouldn't have known me in this scenario."

He took her hand and brought it to his lips. "I'd been looking for you all my life. I just didn't know it."

"You're sweet to say so, but I still want to know how you spent your time before you met me."

"I worked a lot. Probably too much, because I didn't have anything better to do."

"There's more to life than work."

"I know that now," he said with a meaningful smile. Keeping his hold on her hand, he said, "It's always been important to me to make my parents proud and to protect what was left to me by my father."

"They would be proud of you. How could they not be?"

"I hope they would be. It's not possible to know for sure. I lost them when I was so young I barely remember them."

"I'm sorry that you lost them."

"I'm sorry, too. I miss them every day as well as the brother I never knew. He was born first. If he'd lived, he would've been the duke. I'd be a second son, free to do whatever I wanted. Sometimes I try to imagine that life with my brother here overseeing the duchy and me off to pursue my own interests."

"Where would you go?"

"I'd be on my way to Africa with Sir Walter Green."

Her eyes widened with surprise and delight. "The archaeologist?"

"You know of him?"

"Oh, yes! I've read every word that's been printed about his plans to uncover the ancient civilization."

"You'll get the chance to meet him in person when he comes for a visit before his trip. He'll be arriving any day."

She gasped. "You *know* him?"

"I do," he said, laughing at her reaction. "I'm one of the sponsors of his trip. Since I'm not able to go myself,

I do what I can to support him and others who are doing exciting things."

"I can't believe he's actually coming here."

"Marriage to a duke does have its advantages, my love." She smiled. "As I'm beginning to see."

Catherine's days were full of exciting activity. She spent each morning working with the village children on their reading and writing skills while assisting Mrs. Langingham with the running of the household as needed. She deferred to the other woman on most things, ceding to her experience and wisdom while learning from her. In between commitments, Catherine spent time in the duke's library, making long lists of titles that she'd like to add to their collection while devouring at least one new book every day or two. Having experienced her excitement over the evening they'd spent with Sir Walter Green, Derek began consulting with Catherine on his investment decisions. They spent hours poring over the various prospectuses that were sent to him on a daily basis.

She found the work being done by the brothers in America the most exciting of all and dreamed of crossing the ocean to see their flying machine for herself.

A few days later, Derek received word that his friends Lord Enderly and Mr. Nelson were coming soon for a visit.

"They won't believe what's become of us," Simon said bluntly over dinner. He and Madeleine had finally emerged from their rooms, the two of them glowing and obviously besotted with each other after days alone together.

"I'm wondering what's become of your father," Derek said.

"He'll crawl out from under his rock one of these

days. I'm sure he's licking his wounds and filled with disappointment to hear that you met the deadline and held on to your title."

"What deadline?" Catherine asked, noting the stricken expression on her husband's face.

"Oh, bollocks," Simon said, tuning into Derek's distress. "She doesn't know about the deadline?"

"No," Derek said, his jaw tight with tension.

"What is it that I don't know about?" Catherine asked her husband while her sister seemed to hold her breath.

"We will discuss it later," Derek said. "When we are alone."

She returned his pointed glare. "We will discuss it now, Your Grace."

Simon stood and urged his wife to do the same. "We will give you some privacy," he said. "My profound apologies, Derek." Simon ushered the footmen out of the dining room and closed the doors behind them.

"What just happened?" Madeleine asked her husband.

"I put my foot in it," Simon said, swearing softly under his breath. "Derek was required to marry by his thirtieth birthday to retain his title."

"Oh! I remember hearing something about that in town. When was his birthday?"

"The same week they married."

"And Catherine doesn't know that?"

"I think she knew about his birthday, but not the deadline attached to it."

"Oh no."

Simon went into the drawing room and poured himself

a stiff drink. "It never occurred to me that he hadn't told her that when he told her the rest."

"Just when things between them seemed to be getting better."

"I'm a bloody idiot."

Madeleine went to her husband and put her arms around him. "It's not your fault. He should've told her everything when he had the chance."

Downing the rest of his drink, Simon put down his glass and returned her embrace, his gaze fixed on the closed doors to the dining room as he wondered if Derek would ever forgive him for making things worse.

Chapter Twenty-Four

For a long time after everyone else left the room, Derek stared at the far wall and tried to think of something he could say to ward off this latest catastrophe.

"What deadline was Simon referring to?" Catherine asked, her backbone rigid as she seemed to steel herself for yet another blow.

Fear filled every corner of his being. She'd been on her way to forgiving him for the deception about his title, but this . . . This would undo everything once again. He should have told her everything when she found out about his title. If he had, he wouldn't be faced with having to share yet another deception with his precious wife. His only excuse was his complete lack of experience in dealing with women for anything other than sex, but of course that was no excuse.

"I was required to marry by my thirtieth birthday to retain my title," he said in a dull, flat tone that perfectly mirrored the way he felt as he said the words. Any hope he had of returning to the bliss of their first days together disappeared like smoke up a chimney when his words registered with her.

"You must've been very happy to find a desperate, dirty

female digging on your property at such a fortuitous time, Your Grace."

Her words cut him deeply, but he deserved every one of them. "It wasn't like that."

"Wasn't it?"

He shook his head. "Ours was a love match from the beginning."

She stood and threw her cloth napkin onto the table. "Ours was a *deception* from the beginning! What else do I not know?"

What did it say about his level of adoration for her that her rage only made her more magnificent in his eyes? "Nothing. There's nothing else."

"And I'm expected to take you at your word on that?"

"It is the truth."

"Do you even know what that word means?"

"I do, and I apologize to you again for not telling you something you should've heard from me."

"I appreciate so many things about you—your kindness, your generosity, your commitment to your title and the people who rely upon you. I appreciate that you saved my sister and me from a terrible fate with Lindsey by settling my father's debts. But I have no idea how to reconcile that man with one who finds it so easy to lie to the woman he claims to love. I'm not one of those simpering debutantes who circled around you in London ballrooms, so desperate to make a match with a duke that I will tolerate deceit."

"I know you're not, and that's one of many reasons why I love you so much."

"You say you love me, but I don't think you know the meaning of the word."

"That is not true! I look at you, and I see love. I see everything I've ever longed for, since the day I was orphaned and left with no one."

Tears filled her eyes and spilled down her cheeks. "I would like some time alone. Please do not come to me tonight." She left the room, the door closing with a slam that echoed through the large room like a gunshot.

Derek felt more alone than he ever had in his life.

Catherine fell onto her bed, sobs wracking her body. She had only just begun to believe in him again when another crack was revealed in the foundation beneath them.

He'd *had* to marry her to hold on to his title.

No wonder he'd been in such an all-fired rush to get to Scotland that night.

Lindsey was only part of the reason.

Today is my birthday, he'd said that first day they went swimming. When she'd asked how old he was, he'd said *thirty*. How relieved he must've been that day to no longer have to worry about turning over his kingdom to the uncle he despised.

Her heart ached as the tears continued unabated.

A knock on the door had her sitting up and wiping her face. "Go away."

"It's me, Madeleine."

Catherine got up and went to admit her sister, closing the door behind her.

Madeleine hugged her. "I'm so sorry you're upset. Simon feels terrible about what he said."

"It's not his fault." Catherine wiped her tears and went to sit on the edge of the bed. "He's not the one who should've told me."

"I understand why you're upset. Derek should've been honest with you about everything from the beginning." Madeleine sat next to her on the bed and rested folded hands on her lap. "It's just that I've seen the way he looks at you, and it's very obvious that he adores you. Perhaps he felt that if he told you the truth about his birthday after you found out about his title, that you'd never believe his intentions were pure."

"How will I ever know what his intentions truly were?"

"Does it matter so much? You are married to a man who clearly loves you. Has he done everything the way he should have? Absolutely not. But perhaps you could find it in your heart to forgive him."

"How many times am I going to have to forgive him?"

"In the course of a lifetime, perhaps many times. Just as he will have to forgive you at times."

Catherine glanced at her younger sister, offering a small smile. "When did you become so wise about marriage? You have only been married a few days."

"And in that time, I have decided the good times will far outweigh the bad with my dear Simon. Surely you must feel the same about Derek."

"Every time I begin to trust my feelings for him, something happens to make me question everything. Maybe we're destined for one of those aristocratic marriages in which the couple lives in separate residences." The thought of such a lonely existence, after the bliss she had found in that first perfect week with her new husband, gutted her.

She wished she could go back to the days in his grandmother's cozy cottage, before reality intruded to ruin everything.

"You should get some rest," Madeleine said.

"Would you mind helping with my dress and then telling Julia to take the evening off?"

"I can do that."

After helping Catherine undress and hugging her, Madeleine left the room.

Catherine got into bed and turned on her side to look out

at the stars twinkling in the evening sky through the curtains she'd left open to allow in the warm breeze. She fully expected her husband to defy her request and come to her anyway. And when he didn't, she ached with loneliness.

In the morning, she bathed and then asked Julia for a breakfast tray in her room, hoping to avoid her husband for as long as she could. She dressed in the clothing he'd given her to wear at the dig site and headed out to put in a few hours looking for her grandmother's key. The shovels they'd been using were right where they'd left them, tucked behind one of the big oak trees. Seeing the second shovel, her heart gave a lurch as she began the lonely task of digging in a new area.

The sun beat down upon her, making the task even more arduous than it already was. She'd become accustomed to Derek breaking the ground for her. Doing it herself made her sad.

Her sister's words from the night before were heavy on her mind as she worked, stopping only when the sound of something on the path that led to the dig site had her looking up. One of the newfangled motorcars she'd read about, driven by Jack Bancroft, came around the last bend before the glade. This motorcar had an open back and was full of men she recognized from the estate.

Baffled and curious about the car as much as the appearance of the men, Catherine leaned against her shovel.

Bancroft nodded to her. "Your Grace." He didn't seem at all surprised to find her dressed in men's clothing and digging on the duke's property.

"Mr. Bancroft, what are you doing here?"

"We're here to help." He barked orders at the other men, who nodded to her as they fanned out along the circle she and Derek had dug around the perimeter, twenty paces from the large oak in the middle of the field.

"I'm afraid I don't understand."

"His Grace informed us that you are out here looking for a key that your grandmother once buried on the property. We were told to help you find it."

Catherine was too stunned to move for several minutes after the men arrived. Despite her harsh words the night before, the duke had sent eight men, who surely had more important things to do, to help her.

A short time after they arrived, she heard horse hooves on the path and looked up to see Derek riding Hercules. He took in the sight of the men attending to his orders, nodded to her and then took off.

Derek rode Hercules hard, taking his frustrations and fear out on the horse, who was more than happy for the chance to expend some energy. Having Catherine close by but out of reach to him had made for a sleepless night for Derek. This morning, he'd been told by Mrs. Langingham that Catherine had headed out early to the dig site. That's when he'd had the idea to send her some help.

The stunned expression on her face brought him satisfaction.

Maybe if he kept showing her how important she was to him, how much he wanted her to be happy, she would forgive him once again.

Or perhaps that was wishful thinking.

All he knew was that one night without her had been torture. What if that was the first of many nights they would spend apart? How would he stand to be away from her after the bliss he'd found in her arms?

More than ever, he wished his parents were there to tell

him what he should do to win back her love. Of course, if his parents had been there, none of this would've happened because his father would still be the duke and Derek free to wander the world. If his father had lived, Derek never would've met Catherine or found her digging on his property. Lindsey would've found her and forced her to marry him.

The thought of his lovely Catherine with that beast of a man was almost enough to make him sick.

Even if she never spoke to him again, she was safe, and that was what mattered most to Derek.

Or so he told himself.

Over the next few days, Catherine worked with the children in the village in the morning and at the dig site in the afternoons, along with the men from the estate, who continued to show up each day to give the dig a few hours before leaving to tend to their other duties.

Her husband had made himself scarce. She hadn't seen him in days.

Simon and Madeleine had gone back to town to attend some of the Season's final balls and events, leaving Catherine with far too much time alone to think about how much she missed her husband.

And oh, how she missed him. Enough to ask Mrs. Langingham where he was at the end of the third day without him.

"He had meetings in town, but we expect him back later tonight. He didn't tell you he was leaving?"

Catherine shook her head.

"That doesn't sound like him."

Catherine felt the need to defend him. "He thought I wouldn't want to know."

"Why would he think such a thing?"

"We had a disagreement."

"Oh," the older woman said, nodding with understanding. "Well, these things happen. I'm sure whatever it is will work itself out when he returns."

"I hope so."

Later that night, Catherine lay awake waiting and listening, hoping to hear signs from the adjoining room that her husband had returned home. By the time she heard the low murmur of male voices, it was all she could do to stay in her bed when she wanted to run to him.

Three days without him had been endless.

Drawn by something bigger than herself, Catherine got up and put on her robe. She went through the bathing room, stopping at the closed door to his room. Would he be happy to see her? Or was he still angry after their disagreement? Had he missed her, too, or did he regret shackling himself to a woman who didn't want the life he'd been born into? She rested a hand on the door, wishing for answers she didn't have.

Then the door opened, startling her and sending her flying into her husband's arms.

Thankfully, he reacted quickly, catching her as he took two steps backward, seeking balance.

"Hello to you, too, wife," he said, pleasure dancing in his eyes as he looked down at her.

"H-hello."

His valet, Gregory, looked on in amusement as he unpacked the duke's bag.

"If you wouldn't mind excusing us, Gregory," Derek said. "I haven't seen my new wife in three very long days."

"Of course, Your Grace. Good night to you both." The door closed quietly behind him, leaving them alone.

When Catherine would've pulled back from him, he

tightened his hold on her. "Don't go," he said. "I missed you terribly."

"You didn't tell me you were leaving."

"I didn't think you'd care."

"I did." She cleared her throat and forced herself to look up and meet his intense gaze. "I *do* care. And I didn't appreciate hearing of your departure from our housekeeper."

"Won't happen again." He continued to look down at her, appearing to drink her in. "I'm glad to hear you cared that I was gone."

"It was very quiet around here without you, Simon and Madeleine."

"Were you lonely?"

"I kept busy."

"But were you lonely?"

She forced herself to look up and meet his intense gaze. "Yes, I was."

"I'm sorry you were. I never want you to be lonely again. The next time, you will come with me when I have to go to town."

"Why did you go?"

"I was hoping for the opportunity to meet with my uncle, but no one has seen him in quite some time. I even hunted down his mistress, who hasn't seen him either."

"He keeps a mistress?" she asked, filled with distaste for the man who'd sired Simon.

"He has for years. His wife has been unwell."

"Would you take a mistress if your wife were unwell?"

"If my wife were unwell, I'd be so distraught that the thought of lying with another woman would be the very last thing on my mind."

She smoothed her hand over his broad chest. "That is a very good answer."

Derek laughed, which made her smile. She enjoyed the

sound of his laughter, especially when she was the cause of it.

"Are you worried about your uncle?"

"Not particularly. He always shows up eventually. The longer he stays away, the happier Simon and I usually are. But I don't wish to discuss him. I'd much rather talk about you."

"What about me?"

"I didn't care for sleeping alone the last few nights."

"No?"

He shook his head and held her gaze as he brought his lips down on hers.

In the instant his lips connected with hers, Catherine discovered that she didn't care about the issues that stood between them. She cared only about being closer to the man who had brought her such extraordinary pleasure, who had protected and cared for her while indulging her every interest from the day they met. She loved that man, and for tonight, she would keep her focus on him and not think about the one who had deceived her more than once.

"Were you planning to bathe when I interrupted you?"

"No," he said, his lips warm and persuasive on her neck. "I was on my way to look in on you. I was hungry for the sight of you."

She looped her arms around his neck and ran her fingers through his hair. "I was equally hungry for the sight of you."

"That's the best news I've had in many very long days."

After that, there were no more words, only deep, drugging kisses that reminded her of the days following their wedding when they hadn't been able to fully sate their desire for each other. She couldn't deny that some of the magic between them had returned with him, and the time apart had apparently been good for them both.

He removed her robe and night rail, his eyes filled with love and desire as he looked at her and ran his hands reverently over her body.

Her skin felt tight, especially the tips of her breasts and the place between her legs.

Derek moved quickly to remove his clothing and urged her into his bed. His haste only made her more desperate to feel the way she did only when he touched her this way. When he joined her, he put his arms around her and resumed the kisses that made her head spin in the best possible way.

Keeping his arms around her, he moved onto his back, settling her on top of him.

Catherine remembered how scandalized she'd been the first time they'd done this, but now she knew what he wanted and how to do it. Just because she knew how, though, didn't make the task any easier. Her muscles fought the intrusion at first. And then, when she sank down on top of him, he let out a low growl of pleasure. His hands on her hips guided her as she moved, gasping every time she took him in.

"You are so incredibly beautiful," he whispered, watching her intently. "I want to memorize the way you look right now so I'll never forget it."

Her heart contracted in her chest. He was everything she'd never dared dream of for herself, and in that moment of perfect harmony, of utter magic, his deceptions ceased to matter.

Chapter Twenty-Five

After their late night, Derek requested that their breakfast be served in their room, and he delivered hers in bed. "Wake up, sweet Catherine," he said, kissing her creamy white shoulder. He'd awakened with a new feeling of optimism. The time apart had done them good, and her warm welcome the night before had been a balm on the wound that had threatened to fester between them.

"I have coffee for you."

"I don't like it," she muttered.

"Excuse me?"

"I don't like coffee."

"I thought you did."

She shook her head. "I didn't want to be rude when you were so excited about it."

Laughing, he said, "So I wasn't the only one telling untruths."

"Your untruths were far more significant than mine, Your Grace." A glimmer of humor in her expression took the sting out of her comment.

Smiling, he said, "I'll fix your tea."

"Yes, please." She turned over and sat up, pushing golden hair back from her face. Drawing the sheet up to cover her breasts, she accepted the steaming cup of tea fixed just the way she liked it. "Mmm."

"Mrs. Langingham brought word from the village that several of the children are ill with fever. She thought you might wish to stay home this morning."

"Has the doctor been summoned?"

"I told her that would be your first question, and yes, he has, for all the good he will do. I'm actively trying to hire a younger, more sophisticated doctor to tend to us."

"It's not influenza, is it? We had an awful outbreak of that at home a few years ago, and several children and adults died."

"She didn't call it that, but I will ask for an update."

"I also hope it's not the pneumonia that killed the king's eldest son."

"Let us hope it's not either of those things. That was such an awful tragedy."

"I want to go see what is happening in the village for myself."

"You don't have to do that."

"I know I don't have to. I want to."

"You could spend the morning in bed with your husband."

"There will be other days for that." She got up from the bed, magnificent in her determination. "Today we have more important things to do."

"*We* do?" he asked, his lips curving into an adoring smile.

"Well, I do. I wouldn't presume to tell you what you have to do."

"But I should like to be bossed about by you."

"In that case, get dressed. We're going to the village."

* * *

The Flanagan family had been the hardest hit by the outbreak. Little Tommy and Lizzie were very sick, and baby Rosie was also lethargic with fever, the sight of which struck fear in Catherine's heart, as she had seen the ravages of influenza before. Poor Mrs. Flanagan was a wreck as she tended to her sick babies.

"Your Graces," she said, looking frazzled when Catherine and Derek appeared at her door, "I'm afraid we aren't up for guests today."

"Of course, you aren't," Catherine said. "We've come to help you with the children."

Mrs. Flanagan seemed truly shocked by that.

"Tell us what we can do to help."

Thus began a two-day siege of backbreaking work on behalf of the Flanagans and other families in the village. Catherine organized a huge fire pit in the center of town where bedding and other linens were burned. Hot water was brought in to sanitize the homes and bathe the stricken children.

Derek lost track of time as he helped out where needed, hauled pots of hot water along with the other men and watched his magnificent wife take command of the situation. She did everything from rocking feverish babies to bathing toddlers to cooking for weary parents to tending to siblings who hadn't been stricken by the fever, determined to keep them clean, fed and well.

Mrs. Langingham and Amelia sent loads of food and warm soups to the stricken families.

During the second night, he feared they were going to lose baby Rosie Flanagan as her fever spiked even higher than it had been during the day.

Mrs. Flanagan walked the baby until she was too exhausted to go on, which was when Catherine took over.

She was still walking the child when Derek fell into a rocking chair, too tired to remain awake for another minute. He felt like a coward in the face of his wife's extraordinary efforts.

He awoke with a crick in his neck to the good news that Rosie had survived the night and that most of the children who'd been stricken had improved ever so slightly overnight.

Mr. Flanagan, who had slept in the bedroom with Dalia, emerged from the room and seemed shocked to find the duke and duchess still there.

"Your Grace," he said, "we owe you and Her Grace an enormous debt of gratitude that we can never repay, but you must take your wife home to sleep now. I should hate to see her become ill as well."

"As would I, sir," Derek said. To Catherine, he added, "Mr. Flanagan is correct, my dear. You need your rest." He could see that she wanted to argue the point, but rather she handed baby Rosie over to her father.

"You are an extraordinary woman," Mr. Flanagan said, his throat tight with emotion. "We will never have the words to properly thank you."

Dalia threw her arms around Catherine, who hugged her tightly. "Practice your spelling, and we will get back to lessons as soon as everyone returns to good health."

"I practice every day," Dalia said.

"That's what makes you my very best student." Catherine kissed the top of the child's head and allowed Derek to usher her out the door where other villagers continued to tend to the fire she had ordered. People called out their thanks to Derek and Catherine as they headed for home.

"Mr. Flanagan is correct that you are an extraordinary woman, my love."

"I didn't do anything special. I just helped where I was needed."

"You did far more than help. You brought love, compassion and practicality to people who badly needed it. I have never been prouder of anyone in my life than I am of my wife today."

"That is very kind of you to say. I don't intend to allow my lofty new title to change who I am as a person."

"I believe that is quite apparent to everyone after your exceptional efforts."

"We must never forget that we will someday be judged by the way we cared for the people who depend upon us."

"That is very true, and with you by my side, I shall be judged most favorably."

"I am beginning to understand, Your Grace, that your title and resources allow me to help people in a way I never could before."

"My name is Derek, and you should use *your* title and *our* resources any way you see fit to help make this world a better place. I would actually pity the fool who got in the way of the Duchess of Westwood when she has her mind set on something."

Catherine smiled at him, and even though he could plainly see the fatigue in the dark circles under her eyes, he felt the magic between them as plainly as he had at the beginning. One small step at a time, they were returning to the place where they began, and he couldn't wait to get there.

After returning home, they bathed and slept for several hours, rising in time to dress for dinner with Derek's friends, Lord Enderly and Mr. Nelson, who had come from town for a visit with the newlyweds.

"I had to see this with my own eyes," Enderly said as Derek strolled into the drawing room with his wife on his arm. Enderly bowed dramatically before them. "Your Grace," he said to Catherine, "I bow down to the woman who brought our friend up to scratch. You cost me a small fortune in lost wagers, but judging by the happy smile on my dear friend's face, I would say the loss was worth it."

"Catherine, may I present the fool known as Justin, Lord Enderly," Derek said, embracing his friend with a slap on the back, proud to show off his beautiful wife. "And this is our dear friend from America, Aubrey Nelson."

Catherine greeted the handsome men with a warm and welcoming smile. "Lovely to meet you both. I've heard much about you." Enderly had light brown hair and twinkling blue eyes, while Nelson had dark hair and eyes. Both seemed exceptionally fond of her husband as they accepted drinks and caught up on the latest news from town.

"You and Simon both," Enderly said in amazement. "You are the talk of the town."

"I know," Derek said. "I heard an earful when I was there, which is one of many reasons I'm very glad to be here."

"Simon is bearing up well on behalf of you both," Aubrey said. "I've never seen anything quite like the way the two of you went from confirmed bachelors to happy matrimony in the blink of an eye."

Derek took hold of Catherine's hand, smiling at his wife. "When the right one comes along, you do whatever it takes to keep her from getting away." He brought her hand to his lips and brushed a gentle kiss over her knuckles.

"Simon told us that Lindsey showed up making demands, that you paid off the earl's debt and sent the viscount away with a limp," Enderly said.

"I did," Derek said, holding up the hand that was still bruised and scabbed from the fight.

"I would've liked to have seen that," Nelson said.

"It was quite a show," Catherine said. "His Grace ensured that we will never see Lindsey here again, which is fine by me."

Enderly's expression indicated his surprise at her use of Derek's title, but he was too polite to mention it.

Derek kept hoping he might one day hear his given name from Catherine, but it hadn't happened yet. He was trying to be patient and thankful for the progress they had made, but until he heard her say his real name, he wouldn't be fully convinced that they had survived their troubles.

As the evening with his friends progressed to after-dinner drinks in the billiards room, Derek began to feel strange. His throat hurt, his head felt fuzzy and his body overly warm. He threw open the windows to let out the stink of Enderly's cigar that made him unusually queasy. Under normal circumstances, he'd want one for himself.

Over dinner, Catherine had expressed an interest in learning to play the game, and he'd promised to teach her, which was why she had joined them in the typically male domain. He'd much rather have her with him than be separated the way they would be in town.

"Westy," Enderly said. "You're sweating profusely. Are you unwell?"

Catherine looked up at him and gasped. "Your Grace! What is the matter?"

"I'm not sure exactly. But I don't feel well at all." In fact, he felt worse by the minute.

"Let's get you to bed," Catherine said, taking him by the arm to lead him.

"My apologies, gentlemen," he said to his friends.

"No apology needed," Aubrey said. "We shall check on you in the morning."

Catherine guided Derek up the stairs and through the winding corridors that led to his bedchamber, where she steered him to the bed. "Sit while I remove your boots."

"Call for Gregory." The room seemed to tilt, making him feel nauseated. "He can do it."

"I will take care of you myself."

"You shouldn't be anywhere near me. Clearly whatever the children had is contagious."

"If I am going to get it, I have already been exposed." She helped him out of his jacket, waistcoat, shirt and pants with the aplomb of the most seasoned valet.

Without his clothing, Derek began to shiver uncontrollably.

"Into bed with you," she said, pulling the covers up and over him.

"S-so cold," he said, his teeth chattering as his throat began to seriously hurt. "Didn't think adults could get what the children had."

"Some of the adults came down with it when it hit our village at home," she said, running a cool cloth over his forehead.

"Did they survive it?" he asked, gritting his teeth against the out-of-control shivering.

"They were fine." Leaning in to kiss his cheek, she said, "Close your eyes and rest. I will be here."

The moment she felt confident he was asleep, Catherine summoned Mrs. Langingham. "We need the doctor for His Grace," she said, frantic. "He has the fever, and when it struck the adults in my village, every one of them perished. We must do something immediately." She had lied to him when she told him they recovered, the first lie she'd ever told him.

Mrs. Langingham went pale. "I will send for the doctor at once." She grasped Catherine's arm. "His Grace is young and strong."

Catherine nodded in agreement but didn't tell her that men and women in her village had been young and strong and had succumbed nonetheless. Later they'd heard that the fever had virulent strains that attacked the seemingly healthy and killed them within days.

That couldn't happen to him, to *Derek*.

Tears filled her eyes, which were still tired from the sleepless nights tending to the village children. He had to be all right. Any other outcome was simply unacceptable.

The doctor came and thoroughly examined the duke. "I'm sorry there is nothing to be done but to see to his comfort," the doctor said, grimly. "And pray."

"There has to be something we can do!" Catherine said frantically. "He was fine a short time ago."

"It is indeed unusual for someone of his age and good health to be so stricken. It's possible the duke was infected some time ago, but is only now experiencing the symptoms."

Panic-stricken, Catherine thought back to the first time he'd taken her to the village to meet the families. Had he been infected then?

"Has he been under any unusual strain?" the doctor asked, his thick eyebrows knitted with concern that only added to Catherine's panic.

"We have had some, ah, *adjustments* since we married," she said, thinking of every time she had rebuffed his efforts to repair their fragile union, every time he had asked her to call him by his real name and she had refused. Had the strain she'd caused by refusing to forgive him led to his illness? One thing she knew for certain: she would never forgive *herself* if he died.

"I will check on him in the morning," the doctor said as he prepared to depart. "In the meantime, apply cool compresses to his face and regularly change the bedding so he is kept warm and dry."

Catherine took note of the doctor's instructions and had to bite back the urge to beg him to stay. Surely there had to be *something* he could do to make Derek well again.

The doctor left, and Mrs. Langingham came in with clean sheets, towels and blankets piled high in her arms. "What did he say, Your Grace?" she asked, her concern coming through in every word she said.

"That we have to wait and see and pray."

"We will do all of that and more. I read in one of my journals that cool baths can benefit fever patients. If he worsens during the night, we can try that."

"How would we ever get him to the bathing room?"

"We will enlist the help of his friends, who would do anything for him."

Catherine bit her lip as she studied her husband's handsome, sweaty face and hoped it wouldn't come to that.

Chapter Twenty-Six

At six the next morning, desperation set in. Mrs. Langingham sent footmen to roust the duke's friends from their beds to assist in moving him to the bathing room.

Catherine had removed wet, sweaty clothing and covered his private area with a thick towel. She'd been up all night, bathing his face as the doctor had directed and holding him close when the fever made him shiver with cold even though the room was overly warm.

With her head pressed to his chest, she was aware of the moment that his heart rate seemed to slow, which had her up and running for the door to summon help.

Justin and Aubrey were big men, but Derek was bigger, and they struggled to move his unconscious body. Jack Bancroft and one of the burlier footmen came in to help. They lowered Derek into the cool bath Catherine had drawn for him, and he immediately began to shiver uncontrollably while moaning in agony.

Seeing him in such obvious distress broke something in her, and she began to cry.

Aubrey put his arms around her and patted her back. "There now. He's young and strong, and he'll get through this. I know he will."

Catherine barely knew the man, but she clung to him and his assurances as Mrs. Langingham bathed Derek's face with cool cloths. She seemed to have an endless source of them, thankfully.

Her husband needed her, so Catherine pulled herself together and relieved Mrs. Langingham. "Go get some rest while you can," she said to the older woman.

"I don't think I could, Your Grace," she said tearfully. "If you don't mind my staying close by."

"I don't mind." After hugging Mrs. Langingham, Catherine took her place by Derek's side at the tub, leaning over to bathe his face and chest with the cool water, keeping at it until her knees and back ached.

Derek's teeth chattered so hard that she worried he would break them.

Placing her hand over his heart, she felt it beating faster and stronger than it had been earlier. A check of his forehead indicated his fever had maybe come down a little.

"Let's move him back to bed."

The men came in to get him, and Catherine efficiently dried him and changed the wet towel covering him for a dry one. They settled him back in bed, and she bundled him with heavy quilts. Exhaustion tugged at her, but she bustled around the room, cleaning up soiled towels and clothing.

"I will take those, Your Grace," Mrs. Langingham said.

"He seems slightly more comfortable, so we should get some rest while we can," Catherine said.

"Yes, Your Grace. Please call for me if you need anything at all."

"I will. Thank you for your help."

Mrs. Langingham glanced at the duke. "I love him like my own. From the time he was a very little boy, he has been like a son to me."

"He loves you just as much."

"If anything were to happen to him . . ." She shook her head as her eyes welled with tears. "I'm sorry. Don't mind me. Of course, he will recover."

"Yes, he will," Catherine said, wanting to comfort the other woman even if Mrs. Langingham's despair added to her own. "I'm sure he'll be much better very soon."

"Let us pray it is so." Mrs. Langingham took the soiled laundry and left Catherine alone with her desperately ill husband.

As she crawled into bed next to him and felt the heat radiating from him, she had reason to wonder if all the prayers in the world would be enough to save him.

"A fever, you say." Anthony took a sip of his first morning tea and absorbed the news that had arrived through villagers traveling to town from Westwood Hall.

"Mr. and Mrs. Eagan have left to return to Essex to help tend to him," James reported. "From what we were told by the messenger, His Grace is gravely ill."

"Is he now? Well, isn't that unfortunate."

"I thought you might think so, my lord."

"We should probably leave for Essex today to see if we might be of assistance to the duke and duchess."

"As I expected you might wish to do so, my lord, I have begun to pack."

"Excellent, James. If the worst were to happen, it would be wise for me to be nearby when I am needed," Anthony said, filled with a gleeful feeling of destiny. "Order the carriage. We will set out within the hour."

* * *

After another long day in the sick room, Catherine was ready to fall over from exhaustion, and Derek was no better.

Simon and Madeleine arrived at six o'clock that evening.

"We came as soon as we heard," Simon said, walking right up to Derek's bed and smoothing his hand over his cousin's blazing forehead. "Dear God. He's burning up."

"He has been for almost a day now," Catherine replied.

"What can we do?" Madeleine asked.

"The doctor was here again earlier and said there is nothing we can do but keep him dry and comfortable."

"Surely there has to be something else we can do," Simon said with desperation that matched Catherine's.

"There isn't." She'd had all day to think about how she would spend the rest of her life if her husband were to die, which was a very real possibility that she'd had no choice but to entertain during the course of that endless day. Whether he lived or died, she would forever regret the way she'd behaved since finding out about his title.

She had been an awful shrew to a man who'd done nothing but try to help her from the moment they first met.

His deception had hurt her, but his love had saved her.

When she should've shown him gratitude, she had given him nothing but enmity.

"I am so ashamed," she whispered.

Madeleine came instantly to her side, wrapping her arms around her sister. "Whatever for?"

"For the way I have treated a man who has given me nothing but love and care since the day we met."

"Please don't do this to yourself." Madeleine smoothed ratty strands of hair back from Catherine's forehead. "You had every right to be upset about the things he kept from you."

"All he asked of me was that I call him by his true name,"

Catherine said as tears slid down her cheeks. "I couldn't even give him that."

"You will. When he wakes up and returns to himself, you will call him by his name every day for the rest of your lives."

"What if he doesn't wake up?"

"He will," Simon said, continuing to stroke Derek's damp hair. "He's far too stubborn to die."

He said what she needed to hear, but she heard the uncertainty in the way his voice wavered.

"When was the last time you ate or slept?" Madeleine asked.

"I don't know. The staff has brought me food, but I haven't been able to bring myself to eat."

Madeleine sprang into action, drawing a bath for Catherine and tending to her as if she were her maid, washing and rinsing her hair, and then drying her before helping her into a night rail, Madeleine's every movement matter-of-fact and filled with love and affection. While Catherine sat staring into the flames of the fire they had built to warm the shivering duke, Madeleine dried and brushed her hair. They were no sooner finished when Mrs. Langingham appeared with a tray that contained tea and toast and scrambled eggs.

Catherine ate without tasting anything, more to appease the others than for herself. When she'd eaten as much as she could keep down, she thanked them and crawled back into bed with Derek, holding him and trying to offer comfort through periods of shivering followed by thrashing bouts of sweats.

"Easy, my love." She ran yet another cool cloth over his face. "I am here, and I love you. I love you, *Derek*. Please don't leave me. I need you so much. We have to find the key and see the pyramids and venture to America. We need to see if the Wright brothers succeed in building a flying machine and whether Sir Green is successful in Africa. I don't want to do any of those things without you."

As she spoke, she noticed that he seemed to settle somewhat, so she kept it up. She spent hours reading to him from the books the staff brought from the library, telling him of the places she wanted to experience with him, the children they would have and how beautiful they would be.

"They will be the most beautiful children ever born, and we will love them and protect them always. We will teach our firstborn son to be a forward-thinking duke in the tradition of his father. He will need you to show him the way. If he's even half the man you are, he will be a son we can be proud of."

Derek whimpered as a tear slid down his cheek.

Heartbroken, Catherine wiped it away and pressed her lips to his, which were dry and cracked from the fever. Caressing his face, she said, "I love you, Derek. Please come back to me. You have ruined me for anyone else but my beautiful duke."

She talked to him until she was hoarse and parched, but she never stopped telling him how much she loved him or how desperately she needed him, *Derek*, the love of her life. Leaning her head against his chest, she accepted that if he died she would never get over losing him.

While Simon handled estate business in Derek's stead, Madeleine wandered the winding hallways of the massive manor house, wishing to familiarize herself with her new home. She was restless and out of sorts as the household held its collective breath, hoping the duke would recover. Earlier, she'd looked in on Catherine. She'd been sleeping next to Derek, who seemed less agitated than he'd been the night before.

Clinging to that small bit of hope, Madeleine walked through the portrait gallery as well as the conservatory where the outdoors had been brought inside with lush greenery and intricate rock gardens.

She went up a small flight of stairs and down a long hallway toward a set of open double doors where the raised voices of two men drew her attention. Ducking into an alcove, she held her breath and listened to what they were saying about the duke.

"The doctor said that when the fever lasts this long, people rarely survive."

"That is very good news indeed," the other man said. His voice was more refined than the first one. "It'll save us from having to take matters into our own hands—again. If only he'd been with his parents the way he was supposed to have been, we wouldn't be having this conversation. I would've been the duke twenty-four years ago, the way I should've been."

Madeleine suppressed a gasp as she realized she was hearing Simon's father confess to having killed Derek's parents. Filled with horror, she couldn't move or breathe or do anything other than stand there and listen as the two men reminisced about the details of what they'd done more than two decades ago.

"Hopefully, nature will take care of things for us this time," Simon's father said, sounding elated. "Our patience will be rewarded."

"Indeed, Your Grace," the other man said.

"I like how that sounds, James."

"You've waited long enough for the respect you deserve, Your Grace."

"Yes, I have." Two glasses clinked together. "This might

also be a good time for my poor, sick wife to come down with the same fatal fever that will kill our dear nephew."

"Is a double dose in order for Lady Eagan today?"

"Make it a triple. Let's not leave anything to chance when we're this close to having it all, my friend. Perhaps by the day's end everything will be sorted to our satisfaction."

Feeling sick, Madeleine couldn't bear to hear another word. She darted from the safety of her alcove and ran as fast as she could with skirts hampering her progress, the whole time fearing that someone was going to grab her from behind. Her heart beat so fast she feared it would explode before she reached the landing below.

Desperate to find Simon, she took several wrong turns before she found the stairs that led to Derek's first-floor office. She opened four doors before she burst into the office where Simon was meeting with Jack Bancroft.

Simon stood and came around the desk. "What is it, my dear? What has you so agitated?"

"I . . . I heard something."

Simon took her by the hand and led her to a love seat, putting his arm around her. "Tell me what has you so upset."

"I heard a man."

"What man?"

"Your father."

"How do you know it was him? You haven't met him yet."

"I know because of what he was saying about Derek and his parents."

Simon went perfectly still. "What about his parents?"

She choked on a sob. "He . . . He said Derek was supposed to be with them when he killed them."

In a tone she had never before heard from her husband, Simon said, "And you are certain you heard him say that?"

She nodded. "The other man was calling him Your

Grace because Derek is going to die, and he will finally be the duke."

"Dear God," Jack said, his voice barely more than a whisper.

"There's more," Madeleine said, wiping tears from her face. "Your mother . . ."

"What about her?"

"He told the other man to give her triple the usual dose, so she would appear to succumb to the same fever as the duke."

"Triple dose of what?"

"He didn't say."

Simon sat very still for a long moment during which Madeleine couldn't imagine what he must be thinking. Then he glanced at Bancroft. "Please notify my father that I'd like to see him in the duke's office immediately, and after he is with me, take his valet, James, into custody."

"Yes, sir," Bancroft said.

"Don't tell him why. Just say it's urgent."

"As you wish, sir." Bancroft left the room.

"I need you to go upstairs to our rooms and stay there until I come for you, do you understand?" he asked, more serious than she had ever seen him.

"What is going to happen, Simon?" she asked, fearing for his safety.

"I'm going to do something that should've been done years ago."

"Let's call the magistrate or someone who can help us. I fear he will kill you."

"He wouldn't dare."

"He's killed before! What would stop him from doing it again?"

"I will kill him before he ever has the chance to kill me.

Now, please go, my love. If there's to be trouble, I don't want you anywhere near it."

"Simon—"

He silenced her with a kiss. "Go, please."

"I love you."

"I love you, too. I'll come find you as soon as I can."

It took every ounce of fortitude that Madeleine could summon to force herself to stand and leave the room. Glancing back over her shoulder, she met Simon's gaze before leaving the room and rushing up the stairs to wait for him.

As she went, she prayed that wouldn't be the last time she ever saw her sweet husband.

Chapter Twenty-Seven

At first, Simon couldn't believe what he heard, but as his wife's words had permeated the shock, he found that he wasn't as surprised as he should've been to learn that his father had been involved in the deaths of the duke and the duchess.

He took a series of deep breaths to calm himself before he squared off with the father who had caused him nothing but pain and suffering his entire life. Nothing Simon had ever done was good enough for his father, so he'd long ago stopped trying to please the man who couldn't be pleased by the son he disdained.

Simon asked himself—what would Derek do? His cousin had suffered so terribly over the tragic loss of his beloved parents, so Simon figured Derek would've probably taken Anthony outside, shot him in the driveway and then buried him somewhere he'd never be found. Perhaps it was fortuitous that Simon was forced to stand in his cousin's stead at this critical moment in the history of their troubled family.

When his father appeared in the doorway to the office ten minutes later, Simon was ready for him.

"Come in, Father."

"You beckoned," Anthony said in the disgusted tone he often used to speak to his only child. Simon was so accustomed to the tone that it barely registered with him anymore.

"I did."

"What do you want? And who do you think you are using this office while the duke is indisposed?"

"I am the duke's closest friend and confidant. I am acting in his stead the way he would want me to."

"Such a sad, little nobody jumping into the duke's grave before he's even cold. You know what the worst part of inheriting his title will be? That one day it'll go to you, a weak, pitiful excuse for a man."

"That may be so, but at least I don't resort to murdering innocent people in a failed attempt to take things that don't belong to me the way you do."

Anthony sneered at him. "What're you talking about?"

"You know exactly what I'm talking about. Too bad Derek wasn't with his parents that night the way he was supposed to be. Then you might've gotten rid of all of them at the same time. That's how you meant it to happen, right, Father?"

The tendon in Anthony's neck throbbed the way it did before he snapped. What used to frighten Simon senseless no longer had any effect on him. "*Who* told you that?"

"What does it matter? It's the truth, is it not? You killed Derek's parents, and you've been drugging Mother for years to keep her out of your way."

"You can't prove any of this."

"Yes, I can. You were overheard saying as much. As we speak, Mr. Bancroft is taking James into custody. If it's a choice between his neck or yours, which neck do you think he will choose to protect?"

Anthony was apoplectic. "He wouldn't dare speak a word! He knows I'd cut the tongue out of his mouth!"

"You can't very well do that if you're not here."

"What does that mean?"

"You have one hour to pack your clothing and depart from this house. You are permanently banned from *ever* stepping foot onto this or any other property owned by the duke. You will leave England and stay gone. *Forever*."

"You and what army will get me out of here?"

Bancroft appeared at the doorway to the office with every man who worked on the estate standing behind him.

Simon looked his father in the eye, hoping his hatred came through in every word he said. "The people who faithfully serve the duke will see you removed bodily if it should come to that."

"You do not have the authority to make such decisions."

"I am doing it anyway. There is nothing I wouldn't do to protect my cousin and what's rightfully his."

"And when he dies?"

"He's not going to die."

Anthony snorted. "Wishful thinking."

"*Get out*, Father." Simon had never felt rage so powerful in all his life. "Go far, *far* away so none of us ever has to see your wretched face again. If I ever hear of you returning, I will hunt you down and kill you with my own hands. Is there any part of that you don't understand?"

Anthony engaged in a staring standoff with his son that ended when Anthony looked away. "You will not get away with this."

"You have fifty-eight minutes. I suggest you use them wisely."

With a filthy look for his son, Anthony spun around and headed for the door.

Bancroft and the other men parted to let him through.

"Go with him," Simon said to Bancroft. "Make sure he doesn't take anything else that doesn't belong to him. Send someone to fetch the doctor again." Was it too late to save his mother or was she lost, too?

Left alone in the office, Simon sank into a chair, his legs like water under him as he absorbed the magnitude of what had transpired. His father had *killed* Derek's parents, and nearly killed his own wife. Simon had long known that his father had a ruthless ambition that drove him to say and do things far outside the pale, but to kill his own brother and sister-in-law, to poison his own wife.

Simon's stomach turned, and it took everything he had to keep from casting up his accounts.

Madeleine. She would be frantic by now.

He left the office and took the stairs two at a time, looking to the left where Derek lay on his sickbed, but taking a right to go to his own rooms. After he saw to his wife, he would check on his cousin, who would have to be told the dreadful news when he recovered. *If* he recovered.

Simon couldn't imagine having that conversation with the man who had been like a brother to him.

When he stepped into the bedchamber he shared with Madeleine, she flew across the room and into his arms, sobbing with relief.

"Thank God you're here. I was so worried that he would hurt you."

"I am fine, my love, and he is packing his bags as we speak."

"Did I do the right thing, Simon? All I could think about while I waited was what I would do if I had told you something that got you killed."

"You did the right thing, sweetheart. You helped to rid us of unspeakable evil. I'm so very sorry you had to hear the things you did, and I swear to you I am nothing like the man who sired me."

"I already know that."

He held her close to him for as long as he could. "I have to go make sure he leaves. Stay here and wait for me. I'll be back as soon as I can."

"Please be careful. I couldn't bear to lose you."

Simon smiled and kissed her. "I'm afraid you're stuck with me."

Days and nights blended together. Mrs. Langingham brought word of Lord Anthony's banishment, but Catherine didn't care enough to ask her, Simon or Madeleine for the details during their frequent visits. She also heard from Rutledge that Mr. Flanagan and two other men in the village were ill with the same fever that ravaged Derek.

She kept her full attention on her husband and the fever that raged on into a fourth day.

Exhaustion dogged her every waking moment as she continued to tend to him. She never left the room except to bathe and change her clothing. Sitting beside his bed, she held his hand and talked to him about the life they would have if only he would come back to her. She told him over and over again how much she loved him, using his name in every sentence she uttered.

He never stirred.

Catherine began to lose hope that he would recover. People kept saying he was young and strong. If that were true, why didn't he wake up and look at her the way no one else ever had? She would give anything to feel his love for her, to hear him call her Cat, to have his strong arms around her.

"It's my fault," she said to Madeleine when she brought a tea tray and tried to get Catherine to eat something.

"How can you say that?"

"I withheld my love from him, and now he's dying from a broken heart."

"Don't be silly. He knows you love him."

Catherine shook her head as she cradled Derek's hand between both of hers. "All he wanted was for me to call him by his name, but I wouldn't give him that." She dropped her head into her hands. "Why didn't I give him that when he'd given me *everything?*"

Madeleine stroked her hair. "You need some rest, Catherine."

"I need *him!*" She broke down into helpless sobs. "I need *Derek.*"

Catherine was so upset she almost didn't feel the light pressure of his hand squeezing hers. Until he did it again, causing her to let out a gasp. "Derek!" She climbed onto the bed and caressed his face. "Derek! Please wake up and come back to me. *Please*. I need you. I love you, Derek. Please wake up."

Derek was underwater fighting to break through the surface.

Cat. *Catherine*. He needed to get back to her. His throat hurt so badly he could barely swallow, and his eyelids were made of stone. They refused to open.

"Derek! Wake up. *Please* wake up."

His body refused to cooperate with his desire to see her sweet face. He concentrated on opening his eyes and blinking her into focus.

"Oh, God, Derek!" Her tears landed on his face as she kissed him. "I love you, Derek. I love you so much, and

I'm so sorry for everything. I don't care that you're a duke. I just need you to come back to me."

He couldn't keep his eyes open. "Cat."

"I'm here. I'm right here, Derek, and I always will be."

His lips curved into a small smile. "You called me Derek," he said, his voice gravelly and rough. Someone had surely stuck a hot poker down his throat.

"I called you Derek." Her body rocked with sobs. "You are my Derek, my love. My only love."

He gave her hand a gentle tug that brought her into his arms.

"Madeleine," she said between sobs. "Tell Simon and Mrs. Langingham that His Grace is awake."

"I will!" Madeleine said joyfully. "It's so good to hear your voice, Your Grace."

"Why is she so excited?" Derek asked when they were alone.

Catherine continued to sob uncontrollably.

"Cat." He licked dry lips. "Why are you crying?"

"You've been so very, very ill for *days* now. I thought for sure I was going to lose you."

"My throat hurts like the devil."

"Tea! I'll get you tea with lemon and honey." She started to get up, but he tightened his hold on her and wondered why he felt weaker than a newborn lamb.

"Don't go. Stay with me."

"But your throat . . ."

"Mrs. Langingham will be here in a matter of moments with tea and everything else I could want or need. But the only thing I really need is you. I just need you."

"I am here, and I'm not going anywhere. You scared me so badly. All I could think about was that you were going to die thinking that I didn't love you anymore when that couldn't be further from the truth. I don't care that you're the duke. You could be the *king,* and I wouldn't care."

A low chuckle rumbled through his chest before he began to cough.

"Rest, my love," she said, caressing his face as she gazed at him the way she had during those blissful days at his grandmother's cottage.

"I'm sorry to have frightened you, but I'm thankful to have you back."

"You never lost me."

"Felt like I did," he said, closing his eyes when he couldn't keep them open anymore. "Worst loss of my life."

As he predicted, Mrs. Langingham brought tea and food and tender care for both of them as they recovered from his illness.

Catherine slept for twelve hours, waking up as the sun streamed in the next morning and immediately checking on Derek, who slept peacefully beside her.

She snuggled up to him and smiled with gratitude when he turned and put his arm around her.

"Good morning."

"Mmm, morning," he said, sounding better than he had the day before.

She rested her hand on his cool forehead and smoothed it down over his face. "How're you feeling?"

"Like I got run over by a horse." A vicious bout of coughing seized him. "You should get far away from me before you get sick."

"She's been thoroughly exposed," Mrs. Langingham said as she came bustling into the room, opening the curtains to let in the warm sunshine. "She hasn't left this room in days except to bathe and change her clothing."

They sat up in bed to receive the breakfast trays that two of the maids carried in.

"Is that so, wife?"

"That is quite so. I was afraid you'd die if I left for any longer."

"I'm too stubborn to die."

"I didn't know that at the time, so I refused to leave anything to chance."

After they had broken their fast, a soft knock on the door preceded Simon poking his head in. "Are you awake?" he asked.

"Come in, cousin," Derek said.

"It certainly is good to hear your voice, even if you sound like hell," Simon said, taking a seat next to the bed. He looked dreadful, as if he'd been up all night.

"I'm sorry to have given you all a scare."

"It was far more than a scare, Your Grace," Simon said.

"Never fear, dear cousin. You're still not in line to inherit the title."

"Thank God for that." Simon looked down at the floor and then back up at Derek. "There're some things I need to tell you, and I've been struggling to find the words I need. I fear shocking you so soon after your illness."

"I've never seen you so troubled," Derek said as another bout of coughing seized him.

Catherine patted his back until he settled into the pillows.

"I am deeply troubled," Simon said. "The other day, Madeleine was getting to know her new home and overheard my father speaking bluntly to James."

Derek sat up straighter. "What did she hear him say?"

"I'm ashamed and appalled to have to tell you that my father and James were behind the deaths of your parents."

Derek gasped as Catherine let out a cry of dismay,

grasping her husband's hand. He held on tight to her, absorbing the blow.

"I'm so sorry, Derek," Simon said tearfully.

"You are certain?" Derek asked in a hushed tone.

Simon nodded, his face grim. "I confronted him, and he didn't deny it. Since you were indisposed, I acted in your stead to banish him from the property and the country. I told him if we ever hear he has come back to England, I will kill him." Simon's tortured gaze met Derek's. "I hope you approve of the actions I took."

"I do. Of course, I do."

"There's more." Simon ran his hands through his hair, leaving it standing on end. "Madeleine heard the two of them discuss how they have been drugging Mother for years. The doctor is weaning her off the laudanum they've been giving her in double and triple doses."

"Dear God," Derek said. "So, she isn't ill?"

"We don't believe so."

"He's the devil," Derek whispered. "I always thought he was overly ambitious, but I had no idea he'd stoop to such depravity. My father was his *brother*. How could he do this to him, to me, to all of us?"

"Because he wanted something that was permanently out of his reach," Simon said.

"It was hard enough to think of how they died when I thought it was an accident, but this . . . And he *comforted* me after." Derek took a deep breath. "I fear I'm going to be sick."

Simon acted quickly to bring him a bucket.

Derek leaned over it and tossed up the meager contents of his stomach while Catherine rubbed his back.

"Sorry," Derek said after Simon returned from washing out the bucket in the bathing room.

"Please don't apologize to me. *I* should be the one

apologizing to you. What my father did to you . . . I'm so disgusted and revolted. I've hardly slept a wink as I tried to make sense of how he could've done such a thing."

"I was supposed to have been with them that night," Derek said, his face pale. "He would've killed me, too, and taken control of the duchy. How terribly disappointed he must've been to find out I'd been left in my nursery due to illness."

"Thank God you were left behind," Catherine said, drawing him into her embrace.

Derek clung to her as he tried to make sense of what Simon had told him.

"Madeleine said they were making plans for when you passed away, and that James was calling Father 'Your Grace.'"

"That's outrageous!" Catherine said.

"I agree," Simon said.

"The good news is that he is gone," Derek said. "If he knows what's good for him, he won't be back."

"I had hoped you would approve of banishment over prosecution that would drag the family name through the mud of a trial," Simon said, shuddering at the thought of the scandal that would've ensued. "We've also ensured that James and the so-called nurses Father had working for him will be punished for the roles they played."

"Of course, I approve. As much as I'd like to see him hanged for what he's done, he would prefer death to losing his privileged life of luxury and status."

"Indeed," Simon said. "The only bright spot in this otherwise horrific episode is that I will never again have to see his smug, arrogant face or hear about the many ways I've been a disappointment to him."

"You are a thousand times the man he will ever be," Derek said.

"That is kind of you to say, but often he was right about me. I've been a bit of a wastrel. But those days are behind me now. Going forward I will endeavor to be an asset to you rather than a liability."

"You have never been a liability."

"Yes, I have, but now I shall do whatever I can to support you the way I should have for all this time."

"The past is the past, my dear friend," Derek said. "I would be honored to have you more involved in the day-to-day management of the estate, but only if it's what you truly want."

"It is. I'm a family man now, and my wife wants to be here with her sister. I may as well make myself useful."

"In that case, I am more than happy to have your assistance, and I appreciate you standing in for me when I was ill."

"It was an honor and a privilege, Your Grace," Simon said, his voice wavering with emotion. "And from the bottom of my heart, thank you for recovering and saving the duchy from a woefully underprepared stand-in for you."

Derek laughed. "You're not getting rid of me that easily."

"Thank goodness," Simon said.

Chapter Twenty-Eight

For some time after Simon left them, Derek was quiet and contemplative as Catherine helped him to bathe and dress at his insistence. He said he'd spent enough time abed and needed to get back to normal.

His body, however, wasn't quite ready for normal. The act of bathing and dressing depleted his reserves rather quickly, forcing him to settle for taking some sunshine and air on the veranda off their bedroom.

"Tell me what you are thinking," Catherine said, enjoying the warmth of the sun and the return of her husband's companionship. She'd never missed anyone more in her life than she had him during the long days he'd been so terribly ill.

"I'm going over it and over it in my mind," he said. "Every minute I've spent with Anthony since my parents died. I'm trying to make sense of the way he prepared me to assume responsibility for my holdings when all the while he was wishing me dead, so *he* could be the duke."

"It's beyond comprehension."

"I am recalling a time he took me into the forest to climb trees. I was going through a phase, my grandmother called it, when I wanted to climb everything. He kept urging me to go higher. Was he hoping I would fall and die in yet another tragic accident, so he could inherit my title? He taught me to drive a hack and said real men drive fast. I remember him saying those exact words."

"He is clearly a vile human being who cares more about money and power than he does about family and the things that truly matter in this life."

Derek glanced at her. "And what truly matters to you, my love?"

"You do. You matter to me more than anything else in this world, and I promise that you always will."

He took her hand and brought it to his lips. "If I have you and your love, I could never want for anything else."

"Maybe a few children?"

"As many as we are blessed to have." Giving her hand a gentle tug, he brought her close enough to kiss her lips. "Will you do something for me, my beautiful Cat?"

"I would do anything for you."

"Will you marry me all over again, this time as Derek Eagan, the Duke of Westwood?"

"It would be my honor to marry you all over again, Your Grace."

"Derek," he said, smiling. "My name is Derek."

Returning his smile, she said, "I love you, Derek, and I will happily marry you again."

It took two weeks for Derek to completely recover from his illness. In that time, they received word that Mr. Flanagan and the other men in the village who'd been similarly stricken had also recovered.

Catherine took advantage of the time at home to plan the wedding her husband had requested. She had invited her family and his friends to come from London for a house party without telling them the true reason for the gathering.

She had received two letters from her father, expressing genuine remorse for his actions and how they had endangered her. He'd promised to take better care of her younger sister Hillary than he had her or Madeleine and to never again wager something too valuable to lose.

After reading and rereading his letters, debating for several days and discussing it with Madeleine, Catherine decided to invite her father to join them, hoping to have the opportunity to repair their fractured relationship.

Everyone was due by dinnertime, so she was running around with Madeleine and Mrs. Langingham, seeing to final details, while Derek and Simon were enclosed in the office so Simon could catch his cousin up on what he'd missed while he'd been sick.

By the time she made her way upstairs to change for dinner, Catherine was so exhausted that she had to lie down for a few minutes. Derek kissed her awake, and Catherine was startled to realize the day had grown dark while she slept.

"Our guests!"

"Are happily settled and said they'd see you at dinner."

"My first time as an official hostess, and I'm a failure," she said, horrified as her eyes filled with tears.

"You are not a failure." He kissed away her tears. "Our home is filled with family and friends who love you and understood that you have exhausted yourself taking care of me and preparing for our gathering."

"I'm so tired all the time lately. I can't seem to catch up."

"You're also very leaky," he said teasingly, as he wiped more tears from her face. "Is it possible you might be with child, my love?"

Catherine opened her mouth to reply and just as quickly closed it as she tried to recall the last time her courses had arrived. It had been before she'd met him. "It's highly likely."

"Nothing would please me more. Tell me you feel the same way."

"I do. Of course, I do. I just thought we'd have more time alone together before we started a family."

"We have been very reckless about preventing conception."

She returned his warm smile. "Yes, we have."

He held out his arms to her. "Come here."

She sat up and made herself at home in his embrace.

"I'm very much looking forward to our second wedding night and resuming our reckless ways."

Catherine laughed at his lascivious tone. Much to her husband's dismay, she had insisted on waiting until he was fully back to good health before resuming their physical relationship. "Soon enough."

He cupped her breast and ran his thumb over the nipple that sprang to life under his finger. "Not soon enough."

Her breast was so exquisitely sensitive that she trembled under his touch.

"Are you certain we have to wait until tomorrow?" he asked.

"Mmm, I am quite certain."

His deep sigh told her what he thought of waiting. He helped her up and waited for her while she changed into a dress for dinner, acting as her lady's maid as he handled the buttons on her back, finishing with a kiss to her neck.

She did what she could with her hair, not wanting to bother Julia when she was having her dinner with the rest of the staff. "Do I look presentable?" she asked Derek.

"You are exquisite, as always." He put his arms around her and held her close to him. "Are you excited for tomorrow?"

"I am very excited. Are you?"

Dragging his fingertip over her cheek, he said, "I expect tomorrow to be the best day of my life because my dearest love will marry me, the man I really am, and not the man I pretended to be to win her heart. I can't imagine anything will ever make me happier than that."

She went up on her toes to press a kiss to his lips. "I want you to be as happy as you make me."

"The greatest gift you have ever given me is your love. Your forgiveness is a close second."

"I was wrong to withhold my forgiveness from you for so long."

"I deserved most of what I got. I was wrong to keep the truth from you. We must promise that truth and forgiveness will be the foundation of our marriage going forward."

"I am more than willing to make that promise."

"As am I, my love." He kissed her and leaned his forehead on hers. "I wish we could spend this evening entirely alone."

"We will have a lifetime of evenings to spend entirely alone."

"I look forward to every one of them. But tonight, we must see to our guests." He extended his arm to her and tucked her hand into his elbow. They walked downstairs to greet their guests, who were gathered in the drawing room enjoying before-dinner drinks.

Catherine's sister Hillary let out a happy shout and ran into her sister's outstretched arms. "I've missed you so much!" At sixteen, Hillary had Madeleine's fragile beauty and Catherine's studious nature.

"I've missed you, too." Catherine hugged her tightly.

"You must tell me everything that's happened since we last saw each other."

"Your story will be far more interesting than mine! You're married to a *duke!*"

Catherine glanced at her husband, who watched them with amusement dancing in his gorgeous eyes. "Yes, I am. Derek, this is my baby sister, Hillary. Hillary, may I introduce you to my husband, Derek Eagan, the Duke of Westwood."

Hillary curtsied. "It is a pleasure to meet you, Your Grace."

"Likewise. Please call me Derek, as we are family now."

"And this is my mother, Lady Mary, my brothers, Lord Stuart and Lord Daniel."

While Madeleine, Simon, Justin and Aubrey looked on, Derek shook hands with each of Catherine's family members and had them under his charming spell in no time at all.

Her father hung back, seeming unsure of his welcome until Catherine said, "Hello, Papa."

He took hold of her hands and kissed her cheek. "Hello, my dearest. You are looking very well indeed."

Derek extended his hand to him. "It is nice to see you under better circumstances, sir."

"Likewise, Your Grace. I thank you both for including me."

"We included you because you are Catherine's father, and thus you are family to us. You are the only grandfather our children will ever know. I hope that you will be up to the task."

"I will, Your Grace. You have my word on that."

"Please call me Derek."

"I would be honored, and you should call me William."

Catherine beamed as she watched her father and husband make peace.

She tucked her hand into Derek's arm. "I suppose this is the right time to inform you all that you're here for our official wedding, which will take place tomorrow," Catherine said.

They accepted the joyful congratulations before heading into dinner. Having everyone she loved in the same room filled Catherine with elation that continued throughout an evening full of laughs and memories and stories shared by her family that had Derek laughing and smiling at her.

"Don't believe everything they say," Catherine said to her husband.

"Did you not chase the rooster through the village after it stole your cookie?" Stuart asked.

"I did do that," Catherine said, flushing with embarrassment as the others laughed.

"And did you not nearly burn the house down the first time you tried to bake bread on your own?" Daniel asked.

"I did that, too," she said, smiling sheepishly.

"As you can see, Derek," Hillary said, "your wife is quite the handful."

"I already knew that," Derek said, taking her hand, "and I wouldn't have her any other way."

Rutledge appeared at the door to the dining room. "Your Grace, if I may interrupt for a moment, Mr. Bancroft has a gift for Her Grace."

"Does he?" Derek said, casting a perplexed glance at Catherine, who was equally confounded. "Send him in."

Jack Bancroft appeared in the doorway a moment later, seeming bashful to be interrupting a family dinner. "My apologies for the disruption, Your Grace."

"Don't think a thing of it, Jack," Derek said. "Come in. Rutledge said you have a gift for Her Grace?"

"I do." Jack beamed with pleasure as he extended his hand and revealed the brass key that sat square in the middle of his palm.

Catherine let out a cry of happiness as she jumped up to go around the table for a closer look at the key. "Is that what I think it is, Mr. Bancroft?"

"It is, Your Grace. My men and I have continued the dig in your absence during His Grace's illness and recovery. We are pleased to have been able to help you find your missing item."

Catherine took the key he handed to her and promptly launched herself at the stunned man to hug him. "Thank you so very, *very* much, Mr. Bancroft. And please pass along my thanks to the other men as well."

"I will, Your Grace," he said, his face bright red after her effusive treatment. "I bid you all good evening."

Catherine hugged the key to her chest as she turned to Derek. "Thank you, too, for asking the men to help me. It would've taken the rest of my life to find it without their assistance."

"What is it, Catherine?" her mother asked.

"Before she died, Grandmother Anne told me if I ever found myself in a difficult situation, I should come to Essex to the home of the Duke of Westwood where she had buried a key when she worked on the estate as a young woman. She gave me very specific directions to find the large oak on the southeastern corner of the duke's property and said the key was buried twenty paces from the large oak that stood in the center of an open glade. The only remaining question was twenty paces in which direction. On the day we met, His Grace found me digging in the glade, looking for the key."

"What does it open?" Stuart asked.

"I believe it is the missing key to the Hepplewhite chest my grandfather kept in his bedchamber," Derek said.

"Our grandmother knew your grandfather?" Madeleine asked.

Catherine glanced at Derek. "We're quite certain they had tender feelings for each other."

"*No*," Catherine's mother said, scandalized. "She worked as a maid here!"

"Yes," Catherine said, "before she was married and before the duke married. We believe they might have been in love. She intimated that she was forced to depart quickly, leaving behind something valuable the duke had given her, something that could be of great use to me should I ever find myself without resources."

"When can we find out what it is?" Daniel asked eagerly.

"Catherine and I will investigate further and let you know," Derek said.

"I can't wait to hear," Hillary said. "It's so romantic!"

Hours later, after a spirited game of charades, Derek escorted Catherine upstairs to bed. "What a delightful evening," he said. "It's nice to hear laughter in this house that has been far too quiet."

"It'll never be quiet when the McCabes are in residence."

"I hope the McCabes will frequently be in residence." He opened the door to their bedchamber and ushered her in ahead of him. "Have you brought your key?"

"It's right here," she said of the key she withdrew from her bodice.

"I have never been so envious of a key."

Catherine laughed. "Can we look now? I've been burning with curiosity all evening."

"We can look." He led her into his large closet where the small chest held a place of honor on a shelf. Derek reached up to bring it down and set it on the table where his valet tended to his clothing. "Would you like to do the honors?"

"Yes, please." Catherine looked up at him. "Did you always know what the key I was looking for would open?"

"I suspected it would turn out to be the missing key to the chest that was passed from my grandfather to my father and then to me. I'm surprised my uncle didn't try to get his hands on it, but then again, he was far more interested in power than sentiment."

"Thank goodness. I'd be heartbroken if we found the key but couldn't find the things she left behind."

"I've debated over the years as to whether it would be worth destroying a priceless piece to get at what's inside. I'm glad now that I didn't."

"As am I." She looked up at him. "I'm strangely nervous."

"I'm excited to finally find out what's in there."

When she inserted the key and turned it, the lid popped open. Inside the chest, which was lined with rich burgundy velvet, they found a stack of letters, a pile of pound notes bound together and a velvet pouch, all of which they took with them into the bedchamber.

"Let's get comfortable before we dive in," Derek said, helping her to unbutton her dress before shedding his own clothing.

Naked, they got into bed, bringing their bounty with them.

Inside the velvet pouch, Catherine found several large diamonds, as well as emeralds and rubies. "It's a king's ransom," she whispered.

"Indeed." Derek untied the string that held the letters together, removed the first from the pile and read it aloud as he held Catherine close to him.

"My darling Anne, I find myself in a most unexpected situation, desperately in love with a woman I cannot have.

I'm unused to being told I can't have something that I want, and I want you, my dearest. I want you more than I want my next breath. I want you more than I've ever wanted anything in my life. In the blissful days and nights since you came into my life, I have thought more about the concept of 'destiny' than ever before. What meaning will my life have if I can't have you by my side? Never have I felt so confined by the title that has been at the center of my life until you appeared and became my life. I promise we will find a way, but you must be patient until I am able to contend with the formidable obstacles that stand between us. Until then, you have all my love and devotion. Michael."

"I'm heartbroken for them," Catherine said, dabbing at tears.

"As am I. This one is from her to him. Do you want to read it?"

Catherine took it from him. "*My darling Michael, I still can't believe I am to call you* Michael *and not Your Grace. But you are my darling, wonderful Michael. I find myself thinking of you almost every minute of every day as I try to make sense of the emotions that have me in your thrall. I had no idea that being in love would feel this way—all consuming, overwhelming and most of all, exciting. Our evenings together have changed my life, and even though society dictates there be no future for us, I remain hopeful that we will somehow find a way. When you touch and kiss me, I can't believe there are any obstacles, worries or concerns. There is only you, and you are all I need. With all my love, Anne.*" Catherine wiped away a tear. "I'm so sad for them."

"I know. I am, too. They were caught up in an impossible dilemma."

Catherine handed him another letter from Michael to

Anne. "*Dearest*," Derek read, "*I've been recalled to London to attend to urgent business. I'll be gone at least a fortnight, if not longer. I will miss you dearly every minute of every day and especially every night. Wait for me? Yours, Michael.*"

Catherine read the next letter from Anne to Michael. "*My love, it has been a month since I last saw your dear face or kissed your sweet lips. I yearn for you. If I had the means, I would come to London to have even one minute with you. I hope you are soon able to conclude your business and come home to me. All my love, Anne.*"

Derek picked up the last letter, from Michael. "*My sweet, beautiful girl, you have changed my life in ways you will never fully understand. But alas, my life of duty and obligation was predestined long before I was born. As I am required by family canon to make a suitable marriage by my thirtieth birthday to retain my title, I am forced to take a wife. I only wish that wife could be you, the heart of my hearts. I'm sorry to have to end us this way, but it is for the best. Inside the Hepplewhite chest in my bedroom you will find a gift that will provide you with everything you will ever need in this life. I am only sorry it couldn't be more, that it couldn't be me. The key to the chest is buried in our secret place in the glade, there for you to find when you are ready. With every beat of my heart, I will miss you and love you. Yours, Michael.*"

Heartbroken, Catherine said, "So he went to London knowing he wouldn't be back."

"It seems so."

"I can't bear it. She must've been devastated."

"She also must've had to leave quickly if she went without the gift he left for her and locked their letters inside."

"Or maybe she didn't want his gifts after he broke her heart."

"Maybe so. I think his heart was broken, too."

"I'm sure it was."

Derek gathered up the priceless letters, put them carefully on the bedside table and then turned to face his wife. "I'd like to think they brought us together to finish what they couldn't."

She rested her hand over his heart. "That's a lovely thought."

"Did your grandparents have a happy marriage?" he asked.

"I always thought so, but now that I know she yearned for another man, I'm not really sure. What about yours?"

"My grandmother loved my grandfather very deeply. He died when I was four, so I don't remember him well enough to know if he returned the sentiment. I can only hope he loved her a fraction as much as she loved him."

"Life can be so very complicated," Catherine said, sighing.

"And other times it's so very, very simple." He cupped her face and kissed her. "With every beat of my heart, I will be thankful for the key that brought you to me."

"And with every beat of my heart, I will be thankful to the vile viscount who gave me reason to run to you."

Epilogue

The following morning, Derek stood at the altar of the tiny village church that had witnessed generations of Eagan family milestones and watched his beloved Catherine come toward him, once again wearing his grandmother's wedding dress. She walked alone, an independent woman who needed no one to give her away in marriage. Madeleine served as her only attendant.

Simon, the brother of his heart, stood by Derek's side, supporting him the same way he had all their lives.

The church was full to overflowing with their household staff as well as the villagers and tenants, who were overjoyed to have been invited to the wedding of their duke and his duchess. After the ceremony, they would host a breakfast on the lawn of Westwood Hall that had been opened to all, at Catherine's insistence.

His duchess had a deft touch with people that would serve him well in the years to come. After searching far and wide for the perfect wife, he had found her right in his own backyard. For the rest of his days, he would marvel at the many strokes of fate that had brought them together— and the abiding love that had *kept* them together when their fragile bond had been sorely tested.

Carrying a bouquet of fragrant white flowers that she had insisted on picking herself from their garden, Catherine's wide-eyed gaze never wavered from his as she closed the distance between them to join him by his side where he planned to keep her forever.

More than anything, he loved to see her smiling and happy. Though she wouldn't have chosen to be a duchess, she had chosen *him*, and in so doing, had completed him in a way that no one else ever could. He would be thankful for her and her love for the rest of his life. And when she said the words, "I, Catherine, take you, Derek, to be my husband," tears stung his eyes, and his heart . . . His heart had never been fuller than it was as she looked him in the eye and took *him* to be *hers*.

Forever.

The festive atmosphere of the wedding breakfast extended well into the afternoon. Derek's elated staff kept the food and drink flowing as local musicians entertained the partygoers.

"You were right to invite everyone," Derek said. Arm in arm, they stood off to the side, watching the festivities.

"They will always remember the day their dear duke took a wife."

"As much as this day has meant to me, I will also always remember the thrill of our first wedding ceremony."

"I will, too. Stealing away into the night to marry. What a story we will have to tell our grandchildren."

Aubrey Nelson approached them, extending his hand to Derek and kissing Catherine's cheek. "My sincere congratulations, Your Graces."

"Thank you, dear friend," Derek said.

"For a while there, we wondered if we'd ever see this day," Aubrey said with a teasing grin.

"As did I," Derek said, drawing Catherine in closer to him. "But then I found Catherine digging a hole on my property and was saved from the particular hell known as the marriage mart."

"I sent a cable to my mother in New York to let her know there was hope for me because you had married," Aubrey said. "She replied that I should invite you all to spend next summer at our home in Newport."

Catherine gasped. "Oh, Derek, can we?"

"We would love to," Derek said to his friend. "Please tell your mother we gratefully accept her kind invitation and would love to host her and the rest of the Nelson family here at some point."

"I will pass that along. She will be thrilled to have a duke and duchess coming to visit. You will make her the toast of Newport society with your mere presence."

"Aubrey's mother is the daughter of an earl," Derek said to Catherine.

"She and I have that in common."

"Indeed," Aubrey said.

"And for you, Mr. Nelson," Catherine said, "was the Season a success?"

"If by success you mean I am still unshackled by marriage, then yes, it was a swimming success."

Justin joined them in time to overhear Aubrey's comment and laughed. "It was equally successful for me."

"Someday, my friends," Derek said, smiling at Catherine, "you will meet someone who makes you wonder what was so grand about being single."

"I hope that day is a *long* way off," Aubrey said.

"Will we see you back for the Season next year?" Derek asked.

"God, I hope not. As much as I enjoy spending time with all of you, I hope I've seen the inside of my last ballroom."

"Your mother may have something to say to that," Justin said.

"She may have to retire her dream of me marrying into the English nobility."

"Do you plan to stay for the coronation?" Derek asked.

"You didn't hear?" Justin said. "The coronation has been postponed. King Edward was stricken with appendicitis of all things."

"Isn't that often fatal?" Catherine asked, alarmed.

After standing in wait for most of his life, Edward VII had finally succeeded his mother, Queen Victoria, as the monarch only last year. The thought of the popular king dying so soon after ascending to the throne was horrifying.

"Sir Treves and Lord Lister performed a radical operation that drained the infection from the organ. Our dear king is not out of the woods yet, but he is expected to recover."

"That is such a relief," Catherine said. "Sometimes I feel like our society is advancing so quickly I can barely keep up."

"Fortunately, there was something that could be done to save the king, when only a few years ago he surely would've died," Enderly said.

"Very fortunate indeed," Catherine said. "Will you be able to join us in Newport next summer, my lord?"

"You are family now, Your Grace. You must call me Justin."

"Only if you call me Catherine."

"It would be my pleasure, and I would love to join the

house party in Newport. From what I hear, the industrial debutantes are far less *desperate* than what we are used to here."

"Did someone say house party?" Simon asked as he joined them with Madeleine on his arm. Throughout the festivities, they had remained close to Simon's mother, who'd been wheeled out of the house in a special chair so she could attend the party. She was expected to make a full recovery, but it would be some time before she recovered her full strength.

"Mr. Nelson has invited us to his family's home in Newport next summer," Catherine said.

"Oh," Madeleine said, her eyes glittering with excitement. "Would it be terribly rude for me to invite myself and Simon to join you?"

Aubrey laughed. "Not at all. Of course, you are all invited."

"Perhaps while we're in America," Catherine said, "we'll have the chance to meet with the brothers who are intent on building the flying machine!"

"We will do it all, love," Derek said, snuggling her in close to him. "But for now, I wish to take my wife off to celebrate."

"Only you could find a way to score *two* wedding nights with the same wife," Simon said.

"I am inordinately lucky that the extraordinary Catherine McCabe Eagan, Duchess of Westwood, agreed to marry me not once but twice."

"I am the lucky one, my love," she said, gazing up at him with her heart in her navy-blue eyes.

"All this talk of love," Aubrey said, shuddering, to Justin. "It's making me itchy."

"I agree. Whatever it is that's captivated our friends, I hope we don't catch it."

"You should be so lucky, Enderly," Simon said, smiling at his wife.

Derek nodded in agreement. "I predict that before long, you'll both be eating your words with a fork and a spoon."

"With all due respect, Your Grace," Justin said, "bugger off with your predictions."

Derek and Catherine left their friends laughing and went to say their good-byes to the family and friends who had come to share in their special day.

After they'd made their escape, Catherine was surprised when he led her to the stables rather than the manor house.

Jack Bancroft stood waiting to help Catherine into the motorcar the men had arrived in that day at the dig site. This time the car had been festooned with streamers.

"My felicitations, Your Graces," Bancroft said, bowing to them.

"Thank you, Mr. Bancroft," Catherine said, allowing him to help her into the car.

Derek shook the other man's hand and said something that made him smile before getting in behind the wheel.

"Where are we going, husband?" she asked.

"You shall see shortly, wife."

"What did you say to Mr. Bancroft that made him smile?"

"I thanked him once again for the critical role he played in helping me get to the best day of my life."

"He did play a rather critical role. Perhaps we should make him a godfather to our children."

"That is a capital idea. He would be thrilled."

"Do you have other motorcars?" she asked.

"This is the first one I've owned, but I hope to acquire more before much longer."

"Why did we not take the motorcar when we went to Scotland?"

"Because it would require more petrol than we could carry with us to safely arrive."

"Oh, I see. I hadn't thought of the petrol that would be required."

"Someday, I imagine we will be able to buy petrol at roadside stop-offs."

"Perhaps that is a concept we ought to invest in if everyone will soon need it."

Derek looked over at her. "That is a brilliant idea, my darling, and further proof that you are the absolute perfect wife for me."

"I want to be the perfect wife to you."

"You already are. You don't have to be one single thing other than everything you already are to be perfect for me."

She took hold of his hand. "Likewise, my dear."

They drove a short distance before she realized where they were going.

"Oh! Derek! The cottage! Are we going to the cottage?"

"We are."

She clapped her hands in glee. "There's nowhere else I'd rather go tonight."

"I hoped you would feel that way. I would very much like to change the memories of the final moments we spent in a place where we'd been so happy."

"I would, too. Thank you for bringing me here."

"Mrs. Langingham has filled the icebox with enough to hold us over for several days if we decide to stay."

"A few days at the cottage sounds like heaven to me."

He pulled up to the cottage that had been lovingly prepared by Mrs. Langingham and turned off the engine.

"My heart beats with excitement at the sight of our little cottage," she said.

"We can use it as a getaway spot any time we need some time alone. My grandmother would thoroughly approve." He helped Catherine out of the car and allowed her to lead the way inside, where everything was just as they had left it.

Catherine turned and put her arms around him. "Thank you for thinking of this and for bringing me to our first home."

"Thank you for marrying me, not once but twice."

"I would marry you thrice if that's what it took to make you mine."

"All you had to do was look at me with those incredible navy eyes to make me yours. I am your servant and your slave. I will do anything within my power to make you happy all the days of your life."

"All you have to do to make me happy is love me."

"Done." He kissed her then, content in the knowledge that they had hours and days to spend completely alone, which meant he could take his time to worship every inch of her sweetness. His fingers glided over the back of her dress, encountering the same row of buttons that had confounded him the first time around. "Damnable buttons," he muttered.

She laughed at his distress, the same way she had before. Then she turned to present her back to him, and he began the arduous job of unbuttoning the dress. "I will be a grandmother before you complete your task," she said many minutes later.

"I once again promise you that a woman is responsible

for the design of this dress. No man in his right mind would agree to putting so many buttons on a wedding gown."

Catherine dissolved into helpless giggles that became moans when his lips skimmed the back of her neck.

"I love that moan. I want to hear it every day for the rest of my life." He pushed the dress down over her arms, and it fell into a pool around her feet.

"Let me get the dress. It's too precious to leave on the floor."

"I've got it." He held her hand while she stepped out of the dress and then picked it up and laid it over the back of a chair.

She turned to face him. "Remember when we found the dress in the dowager duchess's closet, and you said you were certain the duke wouldn't mind if we borrowed his grandmother's dress?"

"Mmm," he said, his lips now on her neck. "I remember everything."

"I like knowing I was married—*twice*—in your grandmother's dress."

"I like that, too, and she would as well. All she ever wanted for me was for me to find someone who made me happy. I had despaired of that ever happening until I found you."

"I too had expected to spend the rest of my life alone after I lost Ian, and then there you were on your great big horse, looking for all the world like a conquering hero come to save the day."

Derek laughed at her description. "I don't know about that."

"You saved me, Derek. I was sick and desperate and about to be found by the vilest human being I'd ever met who had a claim on me." She shuddered thinking about the desperate days and nights before she met Derek.

"It pains me to think about you alone and afraid and ill. I never want you to be alone or afraid again."

"I never want you to be ill again. *Ever*."

"I'll do my best to stay robustly healthy for you."

She curled her arms around his neck. "Now I want you to take me to bed and make me yours in every possible way."

With one arm around her waist, Derek lifted her, walked them into the bedroom, quickly divested them of their remaining clothing and followed her into bed and snuggled into her outstretched arms.

"Right here in your arms is the home of my heart," she said.

He kissed her softly. "All the riches in the world could never have bought what you alone have given me."

After that, there were no more words. Only soft sighs and deep groans as he kissed and caressed every inch of her, driving her to ecstasy again and again before he finally entered her.

Derek let his head fall back as he absorbed the intense pleasure. "I love you, Catherine, my perfect duchess."

"And I love you, Derek, my duke, my everything."

Thank you for reading *Duchess by Deception*, my first historical romance, which I started in 2010, sold to the team at Kensington Publishing in 2017, finished in 2018 and now it's on sale to readers in 2019! What a journey! A special thanks to my editor, Martin Biro, for his excitement for this book, as well as the amazing, dynamic Kensington team. I enjoy working with each one of you.

Thank you to my team: Julie Cupp, CMP, Lisa Cafferty, CPA, Holly Sullivan, Isabel Sullivan, Nikki Colquhoun, Jules Barnard and Jessica Estep, who make it all happen behind the scenes, and to my marvelous beta readers, Anne Woodall and Kara Conrad. I appreciate each of you so much!

To my fabulous readers, thank you for following me into yet another genre. I hope you enjoyed Derek and Catherine's story. Coming later this year, find out what happens when the group travels to Newport, Rhode Island, for the summer house party at the Nelson family home.

Join the Gilded Reader Group at
www.facebook.com/groups/GildedSeries
for news about upcoming books
and the *Duchess by Deception* Reader Group
at www.facebook.com/groups/DuchessByDeception
to discuss Derek and Catherine's story
with spoilers allowed.

Join my newsletter mailing list at marieforce.com.
Follow me on Facebook at
facebook.com/MarieForceAuthor,
on Twitter @marieforce and on Instagram @marieforceauthor.
I love to hear from readers!
You can e-mail me at marie@marieforce.com.

Thanks again for reading!

xoxo,
Marie

Travel to Gansett Island and fall in love with
Marie Force's bestselling and beloved series of
contemporary romance novels—available in
mass-market paperback for the very first time!

FALLING FOR LOVE

Ever since he won an Academy Award for best original
screenplay, Grant McCarthy's personal and professional
lives have fallen apart. Worst of all, Abby, the woman
he was supposed to marry, is engaged to someone else.
And with his father recovering from a serious injury,
Grant is back at home on Gansett Island helping run
the family marina. He should be focused on
winning back the love of his life, but he's got a
new distraction to deal with . . .

Exasperating, annoyingly sexy Stephanie, who runs
the marina restaurant, is working her way under
Grant's skin—and into his bed. And as a major
tropical storm cuts off Gansett Island—and the two of
them—from the mainland, Grant begins to suspect
Stephanie is hiding something big from her past.
When he finds out what it is, what will be more
important to him? Winning Abby back or helping
Stephanie to right a terrible wrong—and maybe even
getting his own life back on track in the process?

Read ahead for a special look.
A Zebra mass-market paperback on sale in May 2019!

This whole thing was Janey's fault. If she hadn't gotten married, Grant wouldn't have had to watch *his* woman, wearing a slinky, sexy bridesmaid gown, prance around at the wedding with her new *fiancé* hanging all over her. If it hadn't been for Janey and her stupid wedding, Grant wouldn't have felt the need to make Abby jealous by dancing with Stephanie from the marina.

Too bad it hadn't ended there. No, he'd had to make sure Abby was *truly* jealous by leaving with Stephanie. And now, as the hammer in his head reminded him of how much alcohol it had taken to get through the nuptials, the warm body sleeping next to him was an even bigger reminder of what a disaster last night had been.

Damn Janey and her damned wedding.

Grant was trying frantically to remember just how far things had gone with Stephanie. He was pretty sure there'd been some kissing in the cab on the way to his now-married sister's place. Janey had traded him the use of her house in exchange for pet-sitting duties while she and Joe were on their honeymoon. Since their mother had been driving him crazy with questions about the mess he'd made of his life, it had seemed like a good deal at the time because it would get him out of his parents' house. But now he was mad with his sister for getting married in the first place, and the sweet deal didn't seem so sweet anymore.

He wished he could escape, but he couldn't exactly leave his one-night stand in his sister's bed. What to do?

Then the warm body stirred.

Grant stayed perfectly still, hoping she wouldn't look at him or, God forbid, try to talk to him. He'd been with Abby so long he'd never had the chance to indulge in one-night stands. He had no idea what the etiquette was, and with a thousand hammers at work in his head, he had no desire to figure it out.

Out of the corner of his eye, he watched Stephanie—oh *Jesus*, she was totally naked—slide from the bed and get busy rounding up her clothes. Still pretending to be asleep, he caught glimpses of small breasts and pretty pink nipples that quickly had the attention of a part of him that didn't know enough to fake sleep. As his cock rubbed against the sheet, he realized he was naked, too.

He was desperately trying to remember how he'd ended up naked in bed with Stephanie, but he couldn't recall a single thing after being in the cab. Not that being naked with Stephanie hadn't crossed his mind far too often in the last few weeks . . . He'd even bought condoms, just in case his horny body won the war with his better judgment. But he'd never expected to actually go *through* with it. Maybe he hadn't. Maybe nothing had actually happened. That was possible, right? Naked didn't automatically mean sex, did it?

Shit, shit, *shit!* If Abby heard about this, he'd never get her back, not to mention what his father, who'd taken a special interest in Stephanie since she came to work for them, would have to say about it.

Stephanie turned her back to the bed to put on the formfitting black dress she'd worn to the wedding. Her pale skin was creamy white, and his eyes traveled from her shoulders to the two dimples at the bottom of her spine, above her firmly rounded ass. When he first met her, he'd thought she lacked curves. *Boyish* was the word he'd used to describe her. But now that he'd seen her naked, it was clear that her clothes had hidden small but rather interesting curves.

Not that he was interested in her curves. No, the only curves he craved were Abby's, and somehow he had to figure out a way to get her back. First and foremost, he had to stop drinking. Booze—and Janey's damned wedding—had landed him in bed with the wrong woman, and he couldn't let that happen again. If he had any prayer of winning back Abby, he couldn't get caught with another woman. Making Abby jealous was one thing, but his plan had clearly gone awry in a big way.

Stephanie never so much as glanced at the bed as she hooked her high-heeled sandals around her fingers and tiptoed from the room, closing the door behind her.

Grant let out a sigh of relief that he'd been spared the morning-after awkwardness. But then he remembered he was in charge of the family's marina while his father recovered from a recent head injury and his brother tended to his pregnant wife. With Grant stuck running the docks and Stephanie managing the restaurant, he'd have to face her in a few short hours.

Groaning, he turned facedown on the bed and buried his face in the pillow. Something poked his belly, and he fumbled through the rumpled sheet to see what it was. When his hand landed on a torn condom wrapper, Grant's heart nearly stopped beating.

"Shit, shit, *shit!*"

* * *

He'd rocked her world, and Stephanie would bet he didn't even remember it. As she shivered in driving wind and cold rain on her way to McCarthy's Gansett Island Marina, she relived the night with Grant McCarthy. Of course she'd figured out what he'd been up to at the wedding. He'd been using her to make Abby jealous. She'd also known he was drunk when they left and that he probably wouldn't remember much of what happened between them.

Still, that didn't stop her from taking full advantage of the opportunity for one night with the first guy she'd been attracted to in years. She was under no illusions that this was the start of something with him. He was in love with Abby and still hoping to reconcile with her, although Abby and her fiancé Cal had looked pretty darned cozy at the wedding.

If Stephanie were one to gamble, she'd bet on Abby being done with Grant, and him being the last one to realize it. But even knowing that, there was no way Stephanie was going to get all stupid over a guy who clearly wanted someone else. So they'd had sex. Big deal. Just because she hadn't been with anyone in ages didn't mean she was going to turn this into something it wasn't and would never be.

A tooting horn caught her attention, and she stopped to find Mr. McCarthy's best friend Ned Saunders pulling up to the curb in the beat-up woody station wagon that served as his cab.

"Jump in, gal. I'll give ya a ride."

Since she was soaked to the skin, Stephanie was thrilled to see the older man who hung around the marina every day. "Thanks, Ned," she said as she slid into the front seat. The floor was littered with coffee cups and old newspapers.

"Sorry 'bout the mess," he muttered.

"No problem. I'm happy to get out of the storm."

"'Tis a doozy of a nor'easter. Not seeing the newlyweds makin' it off-island today."

"That's too bad. They'll miss their flight, won't they?"

"Looks that way."

Stephanie appreciated that Ned didn't mention anything about her obvious walk of shame. "How long is the storm supposed to last?"

"Coupla days at least."

"The marina will be slow today," Stephanie said, dreading a quiet day to spend alone with Grant.

Ned took the final turn that led to North Harbor. As they passed the McCarthy home, called the "White House" by locals, Stephanie looked away as memories of the night she'd spent with their son resurfaced. Mr. McCarthy had been so nice to her. She'd hate to do anything to mess that up.

"The boy's confused," Ned said, breaking the silence.

"Excuse me?"

"Smartest kid I ever knew," Ned continued as if she hadn't spoken. "From the time he was first able to talk, he's been asking questions, studying people, filing stuff away to use later in his stories. When it comes to people in his own life, though . . . well, sometimes he ain't the sharpest tool in the shed."

Stephanie's entire body was on fire with mortification as she continued to stare out the window. *How does he know? And what will he tell his best buddy, Grant's dad?*

"Don't think he gets yet that it's really over with Abby. When he finally catches a clue, I suspect it's gonna hurt."

Her mind raced as she hummed with tension. It was like he could see inside her or something!

"A nice girl like you would wanna watch herself in the midst of all that hurtin'."

Her mouth fell open, but damn if she could find the words. Luckily, their arrival at McCarthy's saved her from having to reply.

"Thanks for the ride," Stephanie muttered, reaching for her wallet.

Ned's hand on her arm stopped her from withdrawing money. "My pleasure, honey."

Stephanie was mortified all over again when tears burned her eyes. She made her escape from the car, but the almost paternal way Ned had treated her stayed with her long after his car disappeared from view. It'd been a long time since anyone had showed her that kind of care or concern, and it had felt good.

A ringing cell phone woke Capt. Joe Cantrell the morning after his wedding. He wanted to grab the phone and toss it across the suite where he and Janey had spent their wedding night, but more than that, he wanted his lovely *wife* to sleep a while longer.

After so many years of loving her from afar, thinking of her as his wife made him smile. He took the phone into the bathroom and closed the door. Seeing the office number on the caller ID further irritated him.

"This had better be good," he grumbled into the phone.

"So sorry to bother you, Cap," said Seamus O'Grady. Joe had hired Seamus to run the Gansett Island Ferry Company when he and Janey moved to Ohio so she could attend vet school. "Especially this morning."

"What do you need?" Joe asked with unusual brusqueness.

"I wasn't sure if you'd surfaced yet to take a look at the weather. Tropical Storm Hailey arrived overnight, and we've got a heck of a blow going on. I'm leaning toward stopping service for the rest of the day, but I know you and the wife are planning to take the ten-thirty boat off the island. Didn't want to screw you up."

As Seamus spoke, Joe went to the window and looked out over South Harbor. The wind and rain had whipped Gansett Sound into a froth of whitecaps, and the rain beat hard against the window. It was the kind of day they referred to as a barf-o-rama in the ferry business because they'd have to hose the vomit from the boats after each trip. "Go ahead and make the call," Joe said.

"You sure about that, Cap?"

"Such is the chance we take making travel plans from an island, right?"

"Right you are. Don't worry about a thing here. I gotcha covered. We'll get you and the wife outta here as soon as we can. By the way, it was a great wedding."

"Thanks, Seamus." Joe ended the call and crept out of the bathroom.

"What's wrong?" Janey asked. Her voice was husky and sleepy—and sexy as hell. She reached out a hand to him.

Joe tossed the phone into his suitcase and went to her.

She gave his hand a tug to draw him back into bed.

Feeling like the luckiest son of a bitch on the face of the earth to finally be married to the woman he'd loved for more than half his life, Joe snuggled into her warm embrace.

"Now tell me what's wrong," she said.

"There's good news and bad news." He kissed lips that were puffy and swollen from a night of passion. "The bad news is they're shutting the ferries down because of the storm."

Janey gasped. She'd been so looking forward to their honeymoon in Aruba, which they'd chosen because it was outside the hurricane belt. So much for that logic.

"How can there be good news after that?" she asked

with her lip curling into the same pout she'd sported as a
ten-year-old.

Joe maneuvered her so she was under him and brushed
tangled blond hair off her face. "The very good news is we
don't have to leave this bed today."

Janey smiled up at him and ran her hands from his
shoulders down his back and curved them over his ass, a
move that always drove him crazy, as she well knew.
"That's very good news indeed."

"I'll get you there, baby," he said as he dipped his head
for a kiss. "Might take a day or two, but I'll get you there."

"Doesn't matter where we are. As long as it's just the
two of us, that's what matters."

"Have I told you yet today that I love you love you?"
he asked.

"Not yet," she said, smiling at the reminder of how he'd
once told her he wanted her to *love him* love him.

"Well, I do."

"I think you need to prove it." Flashing a coy grin, she
lifted her hips against his erection, letting him know what
she wanted.

"Again?" he asked, quirking an eyebrow in amusement.
"No one told me I was marrying an insatiable wench."

Janey laughed and guided him to exactly where she
wanted him. "Better get used to it, buddy. You're stuck with
me now."

He entered her in one smooth thrust. "Thank God for
that."

Driving wind and rain woke Mac McCarthy early on
the morning after his sister's wedding. His chest tightened
with anxiety when it occurred to him that the storm had
probably shut down the ferries for the day.

He glanced over at his wife, Maddie, sleeping on her

side the way Dr. Cal had instructed to minimize stress on the baby. The thought of being unable to get her help if she needed it made him crazy. A high-risk pregnancy on an island was a fool's errand, but he'd had no luck convincing her to move their family to the mainland until the baby was born.

Hoping the weather wasn't as bad as it sounded, Mac got up to look out the window. Sure enough, it was every bit as bad as it sounded. In the distance, he could see the ocean whipped into a frenzy. Rain was coming down sideways in the blustery wind. Running a hand over his chest, Mac wondered if he was having a heart attack. The tightness had been ever-present since the accident at the marina that left his father injured.

The accident had briefly put Mac in the hospital, too, which had stressed out Maddie. After she went into premature labor and was put on bed rest for the remainder of her pregnancy, she'd refused to leave their island home. Mac had no choice but to cede to her wishes.

Mac went to his dresser to retrieve his phone. A text message from the Gansett Island Ferry Company made it official: service was temporarily suspended. With the wind gusting to what sounded like at least fifty miles per hour, the airport would be closed, too. No way out, Mac thought as the pain in his chest intensified.

Nightmare scenarios such as this had driven him crazy for weeks now. Even when the ferries were running, it was a long hour to the mainland and then more time to get to a hospital. In the meantime, what if something happened that Cal couldn't handle? What if Maddie needed something Mac couldn't get for her? What if something happened to her—

"Mac?"

He turned away from the window and went to her. "I thought you'd sleep a while yet," he said, smoothing a hand over her caramel-colored hair. "It's early."

"Why are you up?"

"The wind woke me." His chest began to ache again as he wondered how long they'd be without ferry service. He turned on the bedside light so he could see her in the early morning gloom. "How do you feel?"

"Fat. Horrible." Tears filled her golden eyes. "Hideous."

"Aww, baby." He crawled back into bed and drew her—as best he could—into his arms. They hadn't been able to make love in weeks, which wasn't doing much to help his overwhelming anxiety. "Don't say that. You're gorgeous, glowing, and radiant." How would they get through two more months of her being stuck in bed all day, every day?

"You have to say that. You did this to me."

She was so petulant and cute that Mac laughed, even though he knew she wouldn't appreciate it.

Fat tears spilled from her eyes and wet her cheeks. "It's not funny."

"I know," he said, kissing away her tears. She'd been so happy and content yesterday at the wedding, surrounded by family and friends. The thought gave him an idea of how he could lift her spirits a bit before everyone scattered again after the storm let up.

Just as he was about to share his idea with her, the bedside light flickered and died.